THIS DAY'S BUSINESS

W.J. O'Brien

PublishAmerica
Baltimore

© 2005 by W.J. O'Brien.
All rights reserved. No part of this book may be reproduced, stored in a retrieval system or transmitted in any form or by any means without the prior written permission of the publishers, except by a reviewer who may quote brief passages in a review to be printed in a newspaper, magazine or journal.

First printing

ISBN: 1-4137-7666-3
PUBLISHED BY PUBLISHAMERICA, LLLP
www.publishamerica.com
Baltimore

Printed in the United States of America

To Annette, who supported me throughout this project.
How can I ever thank you enough?

"Whether we shall meet again I know not
Therefore our everlasting farewell take.
If we do meet again why, we shall smile.
If not, 'tis true this parting was well made
Why then lead on. Oh that a man might know
The end of this day's business ere it come."

Shakespeare's *Julius Caesar*
Act 5, Scene 1

CHAPTER 1

Worthy Oriental Gentlemen

The empire of Queen Victoria had conquered India, and for two centuries the aristocracy administered the government in its typical, arrogant fashion. The new rulers regarded their subjects with seldom-hidden contempt. After all, the sons and daughters of the crown were "civilized," and these natives were just "bloody wogs," something one scraped off one's shoe before entering the house. There were fortunes to be made there. The land and its people could be bled white with a clear conscience, all in the service of queen and country.

This prevailing attitude did little to promote a sense of well being within the population. Occasionally, there were bloody uprisings and open rebellion against the crown, but, as expected, they were put down with little regard for mercy. Mildly put, the British were hated. There were, however, signs of the slowly emerging middle class of Indians; the teachers, the doctors, and the engineers were looking forward to a time when the Union Jack no longer flew over India.

All thoughts of independence were placed on the back burner

when the calendar turned to December 13th, 1937, the day the empire of Japan invaded China in what has become known as the Rape of Nanking.

The Japanese Imperial hierarchy was feeling the pinch of a population explosion brought on by the prosperity of the 1920's. They witnessed the wonders of electricity, air travel, and automobiles, and had a growing awareness of their national identity. The 1930's ushered in an economic collapse that spared neither the world nor Japan; however, the growing clamor for goods and services was unrelenting. The ruling elite knew that the present state could only be maintained if the population remained manageably stable or if imports were dramatically increased. The former scenario seemed unlikely and the latter would wreck their ailing economy.

Unfortunately for the Japanese, the genie was already out of the bottle. Theirs was an island nation of few natural resources. They lacked the steel, rubber, petroleum and timber, the products of which fueled the great economies of the world and the egos of its leaders. The xenophobia brought on by centuries of isolation only complicated the picture. They viewed the British and the Dutch as the grand designers of the Gordian Knot that hung around their necks. The Dutch controlled most of the petroleum in the far east from the exploration to the refining while the British and French owned the tea and rubber plantations. Trucks and cars don't run on tea, but they do run on tires. They viewed these countries as coconspirators in a deliberate scheme to box them in, to keep them subservient. The Americans were willing to sell the empire all the scrap metal it could buy, but the Americans were the allies of the British, Dutch and French. It was seen as inevitable that they would, sooner or later, be forced to confront Uncle Sam. There seemed to be only one way to obtain these precious resources. They would have to take them.

Borrowing a page from their Axis brothers, the Japanese Air Force began a series of carpet bombing missions designed to break the back of the Chinese Army. Within six weeks Nanking Province was occupied and 150,000 people, mostly civilians, were killed. The Chinese military, still feudal in temperament and lacking modern weapons, had little choice: surrender or flee. They did both in large numbers. Round one went to the Japanese. The occasional headlines and sparse reports were generally overshadowed by the events of

THIS DAY'S BUSINESS

half a world away.

As the Japanese were holding dress rehearsals in China, the Germans were flexing their military muscle in the Spanish Civil War. Round two went to the Germans with their blitzkrieg invasion of Poland on September 1st, 1939. The world was looking west toward Europe, not east. The sucker punch was delivered at Pearl Harbor. As the world was reeling in disbelief, the Empire of the Rising Sun simultaneously attacked all over the Pacific. Round three went to the bad guys. Vast numbers of Americans, French, Dutch and British were taken prisoner. The world was truly at war, and in the east the tsunami of destruction and darkness was sweeping south and westward engulfing most of South Asia; the Chinese Army lay prostrate before the storm.

On April 29th, 1942, with the cutting of the Burma road, American General "Vinegar Joe" Stilwell was forced to retreat into India. Stilwell, who had been chief of staff to Generalissimo Chaing Kaishek and had commanded the Chinese 5th and 6th Army Group, fought a war of delay and attrition. If the Japanese were allowed to spill over into India then the war would be over. Precious time was needed to set a defense for the Indian sub-continent.

The port of Calcutta was the logical choice for a place to begin the buildup. It was one of the few deep water anchorages in the region, and it was the nearest to the action in the China Burma India theater of operations. There were three routes to Calcutta for the armadas of supply ships; all were very hazardous. The first, across the Pacific, was closed. The Japanese owned it. The second, from Britain and the Americas, forced the convoys to run a gauntlet of German submarines in the South Atlantic around the Cape of Good Hope on the southern tip of Africa and then up into the Indian Ocean. The third was considered the lesser of evils. The convoys would leave from New York, Reykjavik, Belfast and Liverpool, steaming in a zigzag fashion but always trending southward. The zigzag was thirty degrees left of baseline course for six minutes then thirty degrees right of course centerline for six minutes. The maneuver was used to foil the U-boats because it was determined that at least six minutes was needed to set up a firing solution for the torpedoes. If the target changed its course, the firing solution would be invalid...or so the theory went. What usually went was a lot of theory...to the bottom.

At a point roughly one hundred miles west of Lisbon, Portugal, a course change would be ordered south, southwestward past Cabo De Sao Vincente. One hundred and fifty miles later, helm control of seventy or eighty merchant ships and their escorts would answer full ahead for a mad dash toward the Strait of Gibraltar.

In a desperate scene, reminiscent of salmon breaching the current and fish ladders, the ships of the convoys would bunch up and attempt to thread the needle that is the Strait, long renowned for its unpredictable and treacherous currents. The U-boats knew this. Wolf packs lay in wait on the Atlantic side of the Strait, and Wolf packs lay in wait on the Mediterranean side. The merchant men were the fish in a barrel. The losses were often heavy in this area.

His mood was nearly as dark as the night that stretched beyond the wheelhouse toward infinity. At the age of twenty-eight years, Danny Hale was one of the younger men to enjoy the position of first officer in America's Merchant Marine fleet. The *S.S. Edward M. Hardy* at 21,000 tons, was his first assignment since receiving his new rating. He was expecting a lighter feeling in his heart, but the night swallowed that in one gulp.

The *Hardy* was not a new vessel like most in this convoy. Her keel had been laid on January 12th, 1931 at the Parthenon Shipyard in Mobile, Alabama. Twelve years was a long time for a cargo vessel to be at sea. Twelve years was a long time for many things. It had been at the height of the depression, and work for a seventeen-year-old barely out of high school had been practically nonexistent. Out of desperation, he had signed on as a deckhand aboard a tramp steamer bound for Antwerp. It was a journey that caused him never to look back.

Upon hearing of the news of the Japanese attack on Pearl Harbor, Danny Hale, like many of his fellow countrymen, had lined up at the recruiting office of the U.S. Navy. Much to his surprise, he had been rejected for military service. His status in the Merchant Marines dictated that his duties were aboard ship but not as a combatant. His duty had been to ensure the safe transportation of the tools of war for others to use.

THIS DAY'S BUSINESS

With his orders neatly folded in the inside breast pocket of his uniform and a shiny new stripe on his sleeve, Hale had reported to the Brooklyn Navy Yard where his next assignment, the *Hardy*, had been in dry dock for refitting.

His six weeks in New York City had been fast moving, not only for the repairs being made to the ship but also for his whirlwind courtship and marriage to Muriel Brock, who had left the poverty of Gainsboro, North Carolina, and headed north in search of work in a defense plant.

Seventy-two hours for a honeymoon was just too damned short, he thought to himself as the couple walked, arm in arm, the three blocks to the pier where the *Edward M. Hardy* was now tied up, awaiting its deadly cargo of ammunition. Once aboard, he had to force himself to switch roles, from new husband to first officer. He scarcely had time to wave goodbye to her from the foredeck as he supervised the loading of lethal cargo. He watched as net after bulging and straining cargo net disappeared into the cavernous hold, all the while casting an eye about the crowded pier for a last glimpse of his bride. In twelve hours the *Hardy* would be underway northward bound for Halifax, Nova Scotia, where it was to assume its position in the next convoy for an unknown destination.

Three and a half weeks and several thousand miles later, the scene of her gloved hands waving goodbye still troubled him.

The bridge of the *Hardy* was cold and very damp as Hale assumed his watch shortly after midnight. His first duty was to check on his men standing watch for any submarine activity. The night sky was mostly void of stars as the convoy played tag with the intermittent banks of fog. It was a perfect night for a submarine attack, just like all the other nights since they had left Halifax.

The rawness of the night air had already invaded the heavy wool of his coat. Pulling up the collar around his neck, he tried as best as he could to block out the night; perhaps a hot mug of coffee and a smoke would buoy his spirits. It was difficult to believe that the *Hardy* was only one of eighty ships plying the waters off southern Portugal. Within a few hours they would be making the turn south southeastward toward the Strait of Gibraltar.

Leaving the bridge, he opened the heavy steel door that led into the wheelhouse. Stepping through the portal, he turned and gently closed the hatchway behind him. Hale shivered from the dampness as he quietly checked the binnacle in front of the helmsman to verify their heading. The steady, low rumble of the deck plates beneath his feet was a reassuring feeling on this dank and lonely night. His next stop was at the large urn where he heard the gurgling of coffee that had been brewing for far too long. In slight disgust, he made a call to the steward to start a fresh batch. Next, he hovered over the chart table to verify the *Hardy*'s position with the navigation officer.

Yes, it was hard to believe that just six hundred yards away, on all sides of him, were the other ships from many nations, unseen and silent in the fog. For all he knew there could be submarines in and among the convoy right now. He had heard stories of the boldness of these sea wolves. On a night such as this they would ride on the surface, running their diesels to charge their batteries. The sound of their engines would be masked by the sound of the convoy. On the surface they could easily coordinate their attacks with their fellow submariners. This wasn't like the Great War. Oh no. In those days, they would surface alongside a vessel and allow the crew to abandon ship before they let loose with salvo after salvo from their deck gun, ultimately sinking the doomed ship. They might even pick up the survivors and transport them to a neutral port. That was a gentleman's war. *Now*, he thought, *they'd slip a few torpedoes into you and then leave you to die.*

While waiting for the steward to bring up the coffee, he chain-smoked three cigarettes while he nervously drummed his fingers on the chart table. It was then that he felt the ship heel over to starboard. Looking up to the ship's chronometer behind the helmsman, he noted with satisfaction that it was time to start zigzagging again.

Within a heartbeat the interior of the wheelhouse was lighted with a brilliant orange-white light. *How odd*, he thought. They were supposed to be in blackout conditions; no visible light was to show for fear of giving away their position, yet the light was burning ever brighter.

First Officer Hale felt time had been suspended until he was snapped back into reality. The mushrooming fireball spread in an instant until the shockwave shattered all the glass on the port side of the wheelhouse.

The roar of the explosion ruptured his eardrums; the heat seared

THIS DAY'S BUSINESS

and bubbled the exterior paint, starting numerous small fires on the outer walls of the *Hardy*'s superstructure. It took a moment to gather his wits and recover from the shock. The tanker vessel just a few hundred yards off his left side had erupted into a seething inferno. A quarter-of-a-million gallons of high octane aviation fuel lighted up the sky, turning night into day. Pulling back the cloak of darkness, the intense light revealed dozens of ships; they were starkly naked. The streaming fuel roiled as it floated on the surface, spreading swiftly as it mixed with the wakes of dozens of ships.

It dawned on every soul still alive that wolves were among the flock. Hale rushed to the left side of the wheelhouse and undogged the hatch leading outside. Where were the two men who had been standing the watch out there only moments ago? He stood trembling, alone out on the wing of the bridge. It was only then that he noticed that the flesh of his hands had been burned away from the intense heat that had cooked the hatch. The small fires on his ship had them silhouetted against the night. Looking again toward the conflagration, he searched vainly for survivors; there was little need.

The tanker either blew completely apart or melted away like a child's plastic toy in the inferno. There were only hell flames to be seen floating on the surface. He choked and gagged from the acrid smoke that was filling his lungs. At that moment the lookouts on the starboard side of the bridge started yelling in unison, "Torpedoes in the water." Hale ran through the open hatch, through the wheelhouse, and tripped over the body of the helmsman who had been struck by shards of splintered glass. Regaining his feet, he staggered outside to join those who were shouting and pointing wildly. The raw meat of his hands hadn't started to burn with pain until he lifted his binoculars in the direction of the attack. There were three of them, three white, foaming tracks just below the surface. Even with the blackness of the sea beneath them they stood out like contrails of death as they sped toward the ship. Hale had just enough time to grab the railing before him and hang on for dear life.

Oddly enough, he realized, as the torpedoes bore down on the vessel, the pain in his hands receded as he gripped the rails ever tighter to brace himself against the inevitable blow. A sickening thud could be heard reverberating up from deep within the bowels of the ship. A dud. It failed to explode. There was only an instant to brace himself again before the second and third fish struck. Again, there was the thud, thud as both torpedoes pierced the hull plates. A millisecond later both torpedoes, each carrying several hundred pounds of high explosives, erupted deep within the *Edward M. Hardy*. As the ship was picked up out of the water, it broke into two pieces amidships. The resulting concussion enveloped all who were on deck that night. Danny Hale, first officer on the *Hardy*, was catapulted almost a hundred yards through the air.

The explosion had broken nearly every bone in his body. He was alive only because his life jacket had absorbed much of the concussion. What wasn't broken was badly burned.

Alone, bobbing in a sea of unspent fuel and debris, he drifted with the current, just barely conscious. He knew he was in shock because there was no pain; there were only the final stages of hypothermia, which induced a sense of warmth and well being. He tried vainly to paddle his useless arms so as to reach some floating wreckage nearby, but it was futile.

As dawn was showing through the terrible night sky, there was nothing to see around him but charred flotsam. Hale knew from sad experience that the convoy had moved on. There would be a search for survivors, but the escort vessels, the corvettes and destroyers accompanying the convoy could not linger for too long; their task was to protect the living. Hell, there was nothing left to look for after those two explosions.

Hale thought of his new wife, of the life they would never have together, of the joys and sorrows they would never know. As he floated on his back feeling the waves and unconsciousness wash over him, he would never know that his widow would give birth to a son, that she, being so lonely that she would once attempt suicide, would, out of desperation, move back to North Carolina and marry an abusive, Bible-thumping drunkard. As he felt his final moments approaching, he attempted to make the sign of the cross; only then did he surrender his soul to God.

Finally, with the flume at their stern, the scattered and scarred would regroup and continue steaming eastward. On the left, to the

THIS DAY'S BUSINESS

north, laid Spain, a country neutral in name only because of the fascist victory in the civil war. On the right loomed the barren waste of North Africa. Only the vastness of the Sahara Desert and the Atlas Mountains broke the horizon.

Rommel's Afrika Korp had yet to be defeated at El Allemaine, and this doubled the threat to the convoys in the early days. Not only was the submarine menace still present, but now, the Luftwaffe, flying out of Libya and Sicily, was in a position to attack from the air. Like a punch-drunk fighter, the convoys staggered to the safety of the Suez Canal, which was still in allied hands. The canal offered only the briefest of respites because the shallow depths would not permit submarines to operate effectively. Once the transit was completed, the Red Sea opened up, and the menace from below would resume.

With their arrival into the Gulf of Aden, the escort ships and their charges split, forming two groups. The smaller of the two set course due east for Bombay on India's western coast. The remainder, the bulk of the convoy, steamed east southeastward past the island of Abo Al Kori for a highspeed run around the southern tip of Ceylon then due north directly for Calcutta, their destination.

Calcutta, the bung of the world if ever there was one, became the port of call for one of the larger armadas of merchant vessels. Flags of most of the free world's navies could be seen fluttering in the weak equatorial breeze. Where the city was choked with humanity, the harbor was choked with ships. Some were tied up to quays, disgorging their lethal cargo, the type of cargo that allowed one human being to butcher another. Many more, still several miles at sea, were queuing up for their turn at the docks while still others, their holds empty, riding high at anchor, awaited favorable tides and sailing orders for the return home.

The tropical sun, with its rays beating straight down at noontime, bounced off the steel deck plates causing a shimmering of the air. If one were to look through the heat waves, tiny mirages, puddles of water, could be seen on rusting hatch covers. The deck gangs swarming like bees around the hive directed and cajoled the derricks and winches while below decks, native laborers toiled in the holds, stretching and pulling at the cargo nets.

All were stripped to the waist; backs glistening with salty sweat. They grunted and strained and cursed the one-hundred-and-twenty degree heat. From the depths rose the materials of destruction. The jeeps, tanks, toilets, crates of surgical instruments, the beans and the bullets, all of it was pushed, rolled or carried onto cargo nets and pallets and then hoisted top side, swung over the railings and lowered onto the docks below. If the haul could roll it was swiftly moved to a staging area; if it could not roll it was just as swiftly loaded onto something that could roll then be taken away. The dockside ballet was every bit as choreographed as that onboard ship. At adjacent wharfs troop ships were off loading their human cargo. Those from the land of Glenn Miller and cheeseburgers were about to see how the other half lived. Every sense went into overload.

The eyes beheld strange men with strange attire, the ears detected a foreign tongue, the olfactories recoiled at the alien fragrances and the pores of the skin dilated in reaction to the God-awful heat and humidity. Chevron-sleeved soldiers barked orders, the rank and file obeyed, and everybody's back was soaked with sweat and stained with salt, all straining under the burden of steel helmets and seventy-pound packs. British soldiers could be seen guarding the waterfront from behind sandbagged emplacements; they had canvas tarps overhead to provide some protection from the elements. It was obvious that they had spent some time here.

The Greeks considered India to be the last outpost of the inhabited world, a land filled with marvels and strange peoples all with exotic customs and manners...but to the average British Tommy, one whose sorry lot it was to be stationed there, it was the land of mystery, syphilis and shit.

The dry season is a misnomer actually; the dry is merely interspersed with the wet. Guaranteed, the sheets of rain could be counted on to arrive between three o'clock in the afternoon and what the British call High Tea. The heat would drive all sane people from the outdoors to seek shade and some respite from the stifling and suffocating atmosphere. Those with nowhere to go, and there were a great many, sat where their misery found them.

The lowest caste, the unclean, had only their numbers to amaze the newcomer. Wherever the eye settled on the wide boulevards of Calcutta they could be found. Dragging, crawling, limping, or just lying in their own misery, the burning rays of the equatorial sun would afford them little relief and even less shade. Later, in the

THIS DAY'S BUSINESS

afternoon, the angle of the sun's rays would ease slightly from straight down to one where shadows could form. The midday heat, which baked the dirt and cobbled streets such as a brick oven might do to a pot of beans, would begrudgingly release its grip. The streets, alleyways and bazaars would again fill up with the flotsam and jetsam of humanity on the lowest rung of existence.

The dead or the dying, there was little difference. Merely a heartbeat separated the two. Neither had hope, both had maggots and worms, and both lay where they fell. There were so many that even the Reaper couldn't take them all at one time.

Some would linger for days, maybe a week. The lucky ones were taken quickly, but all were ravaged by cholera, typhus, malaria, typhoid and dengue. Their sepulchers were the doorways and gutters of Calcutta's streets. The corpses and soon-to-be corpses would lie for weeks as mileage markers along the sidewalks where their putrefaction would only add to the fragrance of the open sewers lining the streets. The only constants were the oppressive climate and the unwavering certainty that tomorrow would be worse than today.

A line had been drawn in the sand. It was decided that Dhaka would be the place where Stilwell would direct his operations. The small city was chosen for the main buildup because it had established rail lines and roads necessary to move men and equipment. The topography provided a barrier of sorts, because it was located to the southwest of the Mishmi Foothills, the easternmost range of the great Himalayan Mountains. The view to the northeast was spectacular, especially at sunset, but what attracted strategists was the height of the ridges. At an average elevation of 22,000 feet, the east-west trending mountains were the crumple zone where the subcontinent of India had crashed into Asia some sixty-five million years ago at the end of the Cretaceous period. While Dhaka was still vulnerable from air attack, a followup land invasion would be incredibly difficult. It was the ideal sanctuary from which to extract revenge.

The convoy had taken on a permutation, from one of the sea to that of the land. The rail lines carried the tanks, the planes, and the heavy equipment. The bulldozers and earth movers went first; they were the vanguard for those who would later follow. All else went by road. Twenty-four hours a day saw the long snake of vehicles course its way from the docks of Calcutta, north on highway 6, through the city then left onto highway 34 to Dhaka. The momentum had built up; there was no stopping that which could not stop. Separated by intervals of two to three minutes, the six-wheeled vehicles relentlessly droned on, the axles protesting with each irregularity in the road.

The drivers had been ordered not to stop for any reason. If they broke down they were to pull off of the road and guard the truck against theft. Shoot to kill orders were issued. Officially, they were told to expect all sorts of trickery from the native population. Whatever was in the back of the trucks was certainly more than a wog could ever hope to acquire in this life, reincarnation notwithstanding.

One tactic was for a beggar to walk out into the street in front of a truck and appear to get hit. This served two purposes. First, the family of the "victim" hoped to receive compensation from the rich American army for their loss. Secondly, while the truck was stopped and the driver's attention was diverted, the cargo would be looted. The spoils were to be sold on the flourishing black market. Unofficially, the soldiers were told that a live wog was more trouble than a dead one, the theory being that a hospital cost more than a funeral and there was much more paperwork to fill out. It was considered a standard procedure that if a truck hit a pedestrian, the best course of action for all concerned was to jam the vehicle into reverse and stand on the gas to make sure the bugger was dead, then continue on their way; life was dirt cheap there.

As it turned out, the two or three minute interval between vehicles was an unrealistic target. There were too many people in the streets, too many carts and too many stray animals. Sometimes the trucks bunched up. That was all right with the drivers, who felt safer following the tail lights of a countryman.

The two-hundred-and-forty-first truck of the day left the checkpoint a tenth of a mile from the scene of its offloading. It had survived the voyage in good condition. The driver and his relief were wide eyed and alert but strained from the unfamiliar climate. The daily afternoon downpour had ceased only minutes earlier, and, as expected, the return of the sun brought the intense heat with its oppressive humidity.

Barely ten minutes and several hundred yards later, truck 241 turned onto King George Boulevard. The wide thoroughfare, built by

THIS DAY'S BUSINESS

the British nearly fifty years before, was clogged with donkey carts, sacred cows and people. With any luck, the driver thought to himself, they'd be quickly through the city and the eleven-hour trip would settle into routine. Truck 241 approached a knot of carts and people ahead. Slowing, the six-ton, ten-wheeled vehicle completed a chicane around the throng when the brakes grabbed; they locked up on the right, causing the truck to swerve left. The dusty cobbled road, wet from the afternoon rain, was too slimy to afford any purchase for the large, knobby, treaded rubber tires. As the driver tried to compensate for the sliding rear end, what little traction existed was lost without warning. The over-steering brought the ass-end around to the right into a crowd. The skidding wheels jumped the curb and squashed four people against the wall of a building that lined the street. Although the truck was not traveling very fast, less than 35 miles per hour, the effect of several tons of truck and cargo impacting a stone-faced building made a gore sandwich.

The relief driver jumped from the open door onto the cobble, and looked the few feet to the back. In disbelief, his knees going rubbery, he grabbed at the canvas tarp covering the sides of the stake bed and tried in vain to steady himself. The first wave of revulsion came as a surprise; the subsequent violent retching did not. With all he could muster within himself, staggering the few feet to the open door, he vaulted into the cab.

His ashen face mouthed the words, "Go, go, get out of here."

The driver, so taken by the events, let his foot slip from the clutch. The momentum threw his right foot off the brake and onto the gas pedal, marrying it to the floorboard. The truck lurched forward a few feet, causing the right rear wheels to spin against the human mire. In milliseconds the tread of the six-ply tires caught traction, and the truck bolted forward then roared away under full throttle, leaving the scene and the aftermath. One eyewitness, a seven-year-old boy, shivering in disbelief, saw his entire family killed. His sight was locked on the receding, olive drab tailgate with the words "U.S. ARMY" stenciled on it. He knew that somehow, somewhere the scales would be balanced; the visceral urge for revenge would be sated.

CHAPTER 2

Sweetner

The flight from Oakland held the promise of being long, boring and uncomfortable. The military was leasing civilian aircraft to fly their personnel to Southeast Asia. Not only could they get their troops there more quickly, but it turned out to be a de facto subsidy for those airlines that were experiencing financial difficulty. It was a sweet deal for almost everyone. The usual amenities of coffee, tea or me had been dispensed with because Uncle Sugar was not paying for frills. Northwest Orient configured their DC-8 for the densest seating plan. Each GI had a steerage class seat that made coach seem luxurious.

The "Bird with the Big Red Tail" flew to Anchorage, Alaska, for refueling and a crew change. Anchorage was in the midst of a whiteout with drifting snow and high winds. The troops were allowed to leave the aircraft and stretch their legs in the deserted terminal. What was to be a one-hour layover extended into three hours, then six, while the storm played itself out. There were no open shops, no magazine counter and no bar for a drink. To break the tedium there were display cases of Eskimo artifacts and artwork, which were for sale at outrageous prices. It mattered little, because if one were inclined to buy anything there was no one around to accept payment.

The leg from Anchorage to Tokyo had no ending. The gray undercast of clouds that concealed the Pacific Ocean seemed to scroll on without boundary.

Tokyo was a diversion of sorts. For reasons known only to Japanese customs officials, no one was allowed off the aircraft while it was being refueled. The authorities, however, graciously consented to let the ground crew open one door thus enabling the heady aroma of jet fuel to mix with the stale cabin air. A fortunate few were able to stand in the doorway and soak up all the culture that the seven foot by three-and-a-half foot portal would permit. Movement about the cabin was limited by a narrow aisle and two-hundred-and-fifty souls who, at once, felt the need to stretch and relieve themselves. Twenty hours of confinement neither slowed the growth of beards or the pastiness of teeth; the latter was aided by the stale cheese and liverwurst sandwiches served hours before. The lack of fitful sleep and too many cigarettes added to everyone's discomfort. The change in cabin atmosphere invading the plane was far from a subtle one. That which had been stale and dry was being replaced with the humid; the type of humid that the auxiliary power unit running the air conditioning, could not cope with. The glacial passage of time, at last, saw the departure from the leaden, ominous sky of Japan.

Mercifully, the end was in sight for most. The third leg of the journey brought much relief for the unhappy souls. A large sign at the bottom of the portable ramp called out, "Welcome to Naha Air Base." For the Marines it meant a few hours to sit around and wait on the scorching tarmac while they waited for an available C-130 transport to deliver them further south. To the Air Force guys it meant a few days of squadron briefings, paper processing, the issuing of weapons and gear. The most important benefit was time on the ground. It allowed the circadian clock to reset itself and get used to the idea that today was actually tomorrow and that yesterday was left far behind in the jet stream.

The new fish, as they were called, were shuttled by bus from the air terminal side of the base to the transient quarters. The anticipation of a hot shower and sack time held each weary traveler in the rapture reserved for a kid on Christmas Eve. The banter was light, and there was little spoken of the final destination. All thoughts of "Vietnam, Republic of" were kept in that small corner of the mind saved for the fears of which men don't speak.

David Eagen, already more than halfway through his enlistment, found himself overseas for the first time and struggling down the spotless hallway of an apparently deserted barracks. He had only to follow the sounds of the Rolling Stones loudly emanating from somewhere in the building. This was no open bay barracks that he had envisioned but more like a college dormitory with two men to a room. Stopping at his assigned quarters and the source of the music, he pried a thumbtack from the door and stuck a copy of his orders onto it. He noticed in passing that the door was witness to the pockmarks of many thumbtacks over time and mused at the number of men that had been there before. There was someone else's orders already there, and the hope faded for a room to himself. Turning the knob, he opened the door and hoisted the overburdened duffel bag forward and onto the floor. Before him stood his new roomie with only a towel around his waist, drying himself off after a shower.

Sweetner, on his second tour of duty and fresh from his R&R on Taiwan, was engrossed in his best (worst) interpretation of "Satisfaction." At five feet eight inches and one-hundred-fifty-five pounds, Sweetner's hawkish, skinny nose hung under thick, black-rimmed, tinted glasses. Contorted eyes and a gyrating mouth aided the falsetto of his voice, unsuccessfully trying to stay in sync with the rumbling 8 track on the desk. Jagger would have been appalled. Surrounding him was a fog of baby powder, which he applied in copious amounts. Seeming to be on the verge of rhapsody, the scene reminded Eagen of a dog rolling in the dirt. It wasn't until much later that he was to learn that Sweetner hailed from a long line of Baptist preachers. The hellfire that Eagen was about to experience was quite probably the result of too much brimstone in his background, but there were those who speculated that his family tree did not branch

THIS DAY'S BUSINESS

out too much. Indeed, Eagen wondered if he were rooming with the "Wild Man of Borneo."

"Hi, I'm Bobby Sweetner," the towel-clad singer said as he stopped to thrust out a hand.

"Dave Eagen," the new guy replied.

"Where ya'll from, troop?"

"Boston," Eagen returned.

"Oh, a Yankee. Well, there goes the neighborhood," Sweetner shot back. It was more a statement than a question.

"Yeah, but it's South Boston; does that count?"

Before his enlistment, Eagen had never been out of New England and was fairly insulated from the north-south crap that still pervaded in some circles. He was amazed at the bitterness that some people harbored more than one hundred years after the Civil War. When confronted, his tactic was to use humor to diffuse the situation. He had to use caution though, because it might be taken as an insult. Anyway, he was just too tired to go a few rounds with some redneck SOB.

"Awright," Sweetner laughed, "a man with a sense of humor. Where you headed?"

"Da Nang, Detachment two," the new guy replied. "How about yourself?"

Sweetner didn't answer at first; he somewhat drew it out.

"I'm with the Fourth; we pretty much rotate between Nha Trang and Pleiku, but lately we've been up along the Laotian border. The B-52's are starting to pound the crap outta the Ho Chi Minh Trail and tunnel complexes. Hairy, my man, very hairy. I've never encountered a spookier place."

The powder fog began to dissipate and Sweetner continued, "You better stock up on this stuff before you head down south; it's like gold."

Eagen did not yet realize it, but crotch rot and jungle foot were almost as debilitating as the clap. At least there was penicillin if one got the latter, but the only thing that could be done for the others was a liberal application of baby powder. The climate was almost caustic to human skin.

Eagen took the only cure for jet lag: a hot shower and many hours of sleep.

The following afternoon the paper shuffle began with standing in line for pay records, last minute shots, security clearances, weapon checks and the writing of a will. It had been all rote work up until then. Some clerk handed him a list of where and when to report. Eagen's job was to show up on time and in the right place, complete the task and get the required signature as a sign off, but that last item left him and everyone else feeling very uneasy. It was human nature that most twenty-year-olds never gave a thought about dying; one just assumed that he'd live for ever. For almost everyone, this was the first leak in the dike of immortality, and the mood was disquieting as each man withdrew into his own thoughts.

The third and final day of processing brought the required VD lecture at the base theater. No one could leave until they had endured this pleasure. A stern-faced medic gave his master of ceremonies rendition of the gruesome and quite graphic slide show. Uncle Sam was becoming alarmed at the growing number of horny young lads who were thinking with the wrong head and who were coming down with the most god-awful social diseases. Rumors were circulating about the "Black Rose," which was purported to be a strain of clap so virulent that the military would not let one back to the world with it. It was further said that the unfortunate souls that contracted were held in the Philippines in a special ward until various parts of their anatomy rotted off; only then would they be allowed to die. Two things were abundantly clear: one, the flesh pots of the Orient were far from everyone's mind...at least for the moment, and two, it was going to be a long year.

With the show over, the lights came up, and with a profound sense of the macabre, it was announced that the chow hall next door was open and that lunch was being served. Years later, Eagen would still remark on the irony of that one.

Later that afternoon, it was Sweetner who suggested a night of drinking and debauchery downtown because they were both scheduled to fly out the following morning. At 4:30 the next morning, two very hung over and thoroughly repentant troops waited for the tailgate of the C-130 transport to lower. The dampness of the night, still hanging in the air, invaded every corner of one's being. Even at this hour the recently laid tarmac was a hive of activity. Before the twenty or so GI's enplaned, preparations were underway for the cargo. On this flight it was a jet engine fresh from a major overhaul that was desperately needed at Da Nang. The humans would fill the void not otherwise occupied. Crude canvas seats, just wide enough for both cheeks, lined the sides of the fuselage. Comfort was left off the manifest because this was a cargo plane, and anything riding in the back, be it jet engine or human, was cargo. Upon takeoff, the plane was pressurized for the cruising altitude of thirty-three-thousand feet but not insulated from the cold or noise vibration coming from the four turbo prop engines. The four-and-a-half-hour flight found the two sorriest and most repentant troops with their heads in their hands, staring at the floor hoping that the end would come swiftly…both swearing silently, "never again."

Da Nang in that summer of '65 was quite a remarkable place sited right on the South China Sea. From the air, the beach and the sand dunes that stretched for miles contrasted sharply with the azure and malachite of the shallow waters below. One could easily form an image of a plush resort—well, someday, but not that day. The adjacent city was ancient, but the air base on its perimeter was very, very new and far from completion.

The final approach was a steep one; the idea was to keep the plane as high as possible until the last moment, then dive for the runway.

Sweetner gave Eagen the elbow to get his attention. "Hey, that's a very pleasant shade of green on your face. Sorta matches your fatigues," he said. "Get your flak jacket folded up like this and sit on it."

Following Sweetner's lead, Eagen awkwardly complied while trying to counter his balance against the plane's abrupt angle of descent. "Why?" Eagen dumbly asked, "and why are we coming in so steeply?"

Sweetner, yelling now over the roar of the engines, said, "In case we draw any ground fire on short final. You wouldn't want to get a lead enema, would you?"

The excesses of the night before and the radical movements of the aircraft all combined to have one inescapable effect on Eagen. Sweetner calmly reached over from the rack above and handed

Eagen a helmet; no explanation was necessary. The straining of the engines and the stress on the airframe hid the sounds of Eagen purging himself of last night's excesses.

With an obviously distressed and puzzled expression on his face, Sweetner preempted him by saying, "You didn't expect me to hand you mine, did you?" And, in a tone dripping with self-righteousness, he added, "Welcome to Hell, Troop."

The thud of touchdown was not all that bad. However, the deceleration, brought on by the blades of the turbo prop engines being suddenly thrown into reverse, caused everyone to lurch forward, restrained only by the thin webbing of the seatbelts. Eagen could hear the cargo netting protest as it absorbed the strain placed on it by the tethered jet engine. In a fleeting instant he thought of the mess it would make if it ever broke loose; the result would be rather similar to a fat, old June bug striking the windshield of his old man's Ford.

Sweetner wasn't much for goodbyes. Throwing his bag in the dirt next to the cargo ramp, he turned and thrusted a hand at Eagen.

"It's been real, man," he said. "I should be back in about three or four weeks; we can hook up and raise some hell."

As he was holding onto his hat, Eagen nodded in the affirmative. He was hunched over with his back to the prop wash of the near idling engines. The torrent of wind pulled at the sun-and-salt-bleached jungle fatigues that hung from Sweetner's slight frame.

He is a strange one, Eagen thought to himself. *Just enough over the edge to be interesting without being self destructive.* In a short span of time he had been supplied with more laughs than Eagen could ever remember. It wasn't so much a cavalier attitude, for that implied a recklessness, as it was a controlled madness.

Since the city was off limits after dark, the only place to have a cold beer in relative safety was at the NCO club. During happy hour when the drinks were flowing freely, the talk of his teammates would invariably get around to who knew who. The bar in the back room at the club was the crossroads of the four detachments while everyone was in-country. Controllers from one sector or another would, in the course of their work, be talking on a land line or radio telephone with controllers in adjacent sectors coordinating the movement of air traffic. As teams of controllers rotated in and out of their assignments,

THIS DAY'S BUSINESS

fire base to air base, to the direction center or back to the world, it was not unusual to pass through Da Nang and the back bar of the NCO club where the boys of the 60th Tactical Control Squadron held court.

It was there in the back room that reputations were made or shattered. Occasionally, the names of a few legends, the truly gifted crazies, were spoken with reverence. Sweetner was on that short list.

As it virtually is with every military base outside the Moslem world, when the eagle flies and the drinks are really cheap, one can be assured of an interesting time. The boasting and bullshit are bound to surface sooner instead of later, and so, in that spirit, the legend of Sweetner was given free flight. On one particular payday night, Eagen was well on his way to a glorious drunk, the kind where you have dime slots for eyes and you're doing chin-ups on the foot rail. One troopie was recalling an incident that had just occurred recently on Taiwan.

Eagen listened raptly because the story had the makings of one that Sweetner, himself, had been about to tell back in the barracks on Okinawa many months earlier. Before he had gone very far, Sweetner seemed to have second thoughts of continuing because he had not known Eagen well, had only just met him, in fact, and there might still have been repercussions over it.

It seems that Sweetner and another man were in this "tea house" where the local businessmen went to relax. The exterior of the building was quite typical of the new orient. Almost all new buildings were constructed of concrete instead of the more rustic bamboo that most people envision. It was the interior design where tradition was upheld. The long, narrow hallway separated the individual party rooms that lined both sides. Rather than having doors, the rooms had sliders. These sliders, like the walls, were constructed of translucent rice paper, which was wafer thin. The floors of each room were raised about eight inches above the floor of the hallway and were covered with tatami mats and pillows. In oriental fashion, all one's business or partying was conducted on the floor around a low, squat table.

It must have been payday night for the Nationalist Chinese too, because every room was engaged. Sweetner and his buddy were in an end compartment raising hell and entertaining a couple of Taipei's soiled doves. They were fired up on a particularly potent vintage of the local plum wine. The talk eventually turned to football. Sweetner commented to one of the doves, supposedly to impress her, that he had scored the winning touchdown at his high school Thanksgiving Day game. The poor girl, whose only link with American culture was the occasional business man and drunk GI on R&R didn't have a clue regarding the concept of Thanksgiving. However, not wishing to enrage her customer, she gamely nodded and smiled.

Where she screwed up was when she asked Sweetner, "Voosbol? What is voosbol?"

That is all it took. Sweetner looked about the room and eyed a small melon. His pal leaned over, picked up the fruit and tossed it to him.

Sweetner tucked it under his arm as he drunkenly stood up and dropped his shoulder. At once, a hundred and fifty or sixty pounds of buck-naked Sweetner crashed through the rice paper wall into the adjoining room. The momentum carried him onto the squat table in the center where he stepped in a large bowl of raw fish. The occupants of the room, who were otherwise preoccupied, had no time to react to the intrusion. Sweetner slipped on the gooey mess and rolled with the grace of a gymnast. With a guttural howl, he burst through the far wall, and then the next, until he had penetrated each and every partition in the place.

Somewhere in the melee, the melon suffered major structural failure. His return to the line of scrimmage saw him covered with melon pulp and various articles of someone else's clothing. Rice paper adhered to his sticky flanks as though it were peeling birch bark. Both Americans, clad only in their birthday suits, grabbed their clothes and escaped in the confusion out into the street. Left behind in the chaos were the curses of the offended and the indignant.

Another story surfaced, this time out of Bangkok. The Air Force personnel from the nearby base were being billeted in a hotel downtown. Sweetner had observed that Orientals were the most industrious people he had ever seen. They, however, liked to do one thing more than work: They liked to gamble. He said, in passing, one day that they were a people who would bet on the time of their own death. Give them a mongoose and a cobra and the bets would start flying. Even the kids learned young. While the elders were indoors watching two cocks rip each other to shreds, the youngsters were

THIS DAY'S BUSINESS

outside betting candy on a cockroach race. They'd draw a circle about three feet in diameter in the dirt. In the center they would place a couple of the starving bugs with numbers painted on their backs; the first roach to leave the circle would win. Cheating was accomplished by enticing them with food.

On one particularly hot and humid evening, when even the pace of war slowed down, Sweetner was in a doldrum. Life was getting dull. Counting on the penchant for betting, he organized a few of the hotel staff to have an olive race. The entrants were a few of the houseboys and maids who were enticed with a hundred-dollar prize, which was a hell of a lot of money at the time. The object was to get the olive across the finish line first. The route went the length of the first-floor hallway, up the stairs, and then the length of the second floor, then down the back stairwell to the start/finish line. There were only three rules. First, if the olive was dropped, the entrant would have to start over again. Second, the olive had to be placed between the cheeks of one's ass. Third, the last place finisher had to eat all the olives! As an incentive to keep going, Sweetner hired a menacing and thoroughly foul-looking young man to strut around with a cattle prod to dissuade potential quitters. It was a sick world, and Sweetner was a happy guy. The raucous cheering and heavy pre-race betting netted Sweetner the equivalent of several months' pay and a spot in the bezerkers hall of fame.

To the uninformed it seemed that Sweetner was out of control and in dire need of a padded cell. But, like many legends, there were more than a few stories attributed to him that just had not happened. Sweetner was, in fact, about as steady an individual as one could expect, given the insanity that was happening all around him. Getting strange every now and then was just his way of coping. Some drank heavily, some got religion; Sweetner got...weird.

Eagen thought it rather odd that Sweetner moved around a lot. One day he might be on a hilltop firebase near Pleiku; later, word would get back that he was up on the Laotian border calling in air strikes against the tunnel complexes that lined the Ho Chi Minh Trail. There were times when he wouldn't be heard from for weeks, and then one day he would just show up, getting off a chopper with a bunch of grunts that were coming back from the bush. It never occurred to anyone—well, not everyone—that Sweetner might wear more than one hat.

The daily grind of twelve-hour days and six-day weeks had worked their magic. In one respect it seemed that time stood still; yet the checkmarks on Eagens short time calendar moved steadily in the right direction. The date for his return to the world was near at hand. He was being discharged early. Since he had chosen not to reenlist, and seeing that the ranks of the war machine were swelling all the time, Uncle Sam considered those like Eagen to be surplus, a fact that delighted the living hell out of Eagen. Thanks to the GI Bill, college would allow him to pick up his life where it had left off. Although the military helped him grow up, he often felt that he was just marking time— not regressing, but surely not advancing.

With Eagen having a week remaining in-country, Sweetner was able to join up with him in Saigon for a last weekend of carousing and general hell raising before their paths were to diverge. Sweetner still had close to two years to go on his second enlistment. He had once told Eagen that he was considering making the military his home because he liked the adventure, but Eagen thought it was because civilian life would not tolerate his antics. Sweetner never once voiced any thought or opinion that someday the war would end. It was as though it would go on and on, as would his part in it.

The chopper pad outside the communications bunker at Da Nang was where they split up. The supply bird was bringing mail, ammunition and fresh replacements to some Garden of Eden up north near the DMZ. Sweetner was needed up there to train some marines in directing air traffic. It was bad enough that the NVA, from time to time, would shoot down arriving and departing cargo planes, but there had been more than a few near midair collisions. The grunts on the ground lacked the experience to keep things straightened out.

Sweetner volunteered because, as he told Eagen, "Life was getting dull."

The sullen, towering cumulus clouds that gathered just offshore were starting to release their afternoon deluge in a fine gray veil that didn't quite touch the water. It would only be a short while before the torrent crossed the beach and swept over the airfield, moving westward, drenching everything in its path. The wind from the approaching frontal boundary was joining the rotor wash of the supply chopper to lay back the grass and brush surrounding the

THIS DAY'S BUSINESS

helicopter pad.

The crew chief was as nervous as a cat shitting briars because the bird was loaded with a lot of bang, and a charge of static electricity was building up in the air from the rotor blades and the approaching storm. More than one helicopter simply disintegrated in flight from just such a cause. It was a time to be cautious.

"It's now or never, Sweets!" the crewman yelled over the cacophony made by the whirling blades and the engine. Already, lightning was boring holes in the atmosphere nearby. The handshake was broken, a tight hug with slaps on the back was given, one last look into each other's eyes was made and the spell was gone. Sweetner turned and jumped aboard. He took a seat on the floor next to the door gunner, facing outward with his feet on the skid.

Cradling his rifle in the crook of his left elbow and using his hands as a megaphone, he yelled to Eagen, "See ya in hell, Troop." He then reached out toward Eagen, giving him the Hawaiian good-luck salute.

In one smooth motion the chopper rose vertically while dropping its nose to gain forward momentum. Eagen just stood there, his face feeling the sting of sand and rotor wash, his jungle fatigues flapping wildly in response. Motionless, he stared at the rigid digit until it and its owner were no longer visible in the door.

Only when the basso profundo of the blades faded in the distance did Eagen notice that he was thoroughly soaked by the cloudburst. Deeply saddened by this goodbye, he turned and headed off in the direction of his bunker to pack; tomorrow the freedom bird was taking him back to the world.

Sorrow and joy—what a damned strange cocktail, he thought.

CHAPTER 3

Conjunction

Until recently, few stores in the area had remained open much past 5:30 p.m. The problems that had plagued other tired, old cities had engulfed Boston as well. How strange it might appear to the unacquainted eye that the downtown section of the city would be choked with humanity during office hours and then deserted by 6:00 p.m. when the evening rush hour subsided. The concrete canyons would fall silent save for the incessant wind and the wail of sirens from the paddy wagons returning to the Area 7 lockup.

All of that was slowly changing. A renaissance of sorts was taking place. The seed of revitalization was beginning to germinate and would, with time, blossom into the new Boston. Gone was Scully Square with its burlesque image. Even the famed Combat Zone was losing ground to a skyline that reflected legitimate business. The crown jewel was Government Center, a creature that was born from the union of state and federal monies. The Fanieul Hall Marketplace, which had been allowed to slide into decay, the type of decay that resembled Dickens' London, was seeing a restoration to its former

THIS DAY'S BUSINESS

glory. The introduction of trendy, upscale boutiques and salons was attracting the shoppers who would otherwise patronize the suburban malls.

This was an area that was being reclaimed from the seediness and neglect that tired cities inherit from time to time. In response to this phoenix, the restaurants and taverns were extending their hours so as to cater to the new urbanites.

The night was a rather busy one, not totally unexpected but more than the one that was anticipated. Weather forecasters had been calling for occasional light flurries. By10:30 that night, slightly more than two inches of dry, fresh powder had already accumulated on the ground. The Bell in Hand, a Boston landmark since 1792, located just up the block on Cambridge Street from Government Center, was alive on this particular night. The Bruins were up on the Rangers by two goals early in the third period, and the enthusiasm was infectious. Normally, the Bell was a lunchtime watering hole for the state office workers and the financial Brahmans of the State Street brokerage houses. Lately, however, it had been staying open to accommodate those who celebrated in the city's rebirth. While not as old or famous as the Union Oyster House a few doors down, the Bell was a great place to drop in during or after work.

Monty, the proprietor, had a foot in both worlds. His reputation for a first-class kitchen, at reasonable prices, appealed to the old penny-pinching Yankees and the free spending up-and-comers. It was also neutral ground for those on both sides of the legal system. Here one could belly up to the bar and rub elbows with the town's biggest bookies while off-duty cops tended bar.

As one old cop put it, "In here, you do nothing stupid."

The controlled chaos of the kitchen and simple dignity of the dining area both reflected and contrasted the landmark at the crossroads of the Hub. It was the type of place where you would not mind taking your wife or girlfriend...but not both.

For a year now, Eagen had been working part time as a bar back while he was completing his PhD at Boston University. He didn't need to work because the GI Bill and a partial scholarship from the National Science Foundation were taking care of the tuition with enough left over to live off campus in an apartment, which he shared with two other grad students. He had had enough of dormitory living in the military. Living the life of the impoverished student held little appeal for him; therefore, the job allowed him a degree of financial freedom. Having a few bucks in his pocket meant that Eagen could afford to run his old MGB and indulge his one passion: mountain climbing.

The time was nearing 10:30 p.m., and Eagen was at the end of his shift. The Bruins' game had gone into sudden-death overtime, and the bar crowd was on its feet, urging the Habs on. The last of the late diners had vacated to join the excitement at the bar. This left him pretty much alone with his textbook and his thoughts.

The clinking, clanking and plinking of plates against glass and tableware had left only the most lingering of sounds hanging in the air. The universal noises that go part and parcel in any crowded room where food is being served grew less with each departing guest. From Eagen's booth it was possible to look into the bar and see both televisions. The one on the right at the end of the bar and furthest from him had the game on. The other, nearest him, had some lame comedy going. All eyes were on the game. It wasn't so much the absence of noise in the dining room—for it was now empty of patrons—it wasn't so much the groans and cheers from the expectant sports fans at the bar—they were a distraction that could be filtered out. The centerpoint of Eagen's attention was the television, the one on the left, the one with the volume turned way down in deference to the game.

The mug of draught beer was raised to the horizontal as he was draining the contents. The low-level sound was registering on the emulsion that was the photographic plate of his subconscious. It stopped him in mid gulp. His eyes were locked in the thousand-yard stare deep beyond infinity and the end of the mug. The sounds weren't heard so much as sensed, a sound so deeply burned into the soul that it is taken to the grave.

Slowly and deliberately, Eagen's eyes scrolled into focus and engaged the scenes pouring forth from the picture tube. The lead story for the eleven o'clock news was being previewed while the program was in commercial. The color was of poor quality and rather grainy, thus reflecting the state of video technology. There was no mistaking the open door of the chopper; the old men of eighteen and nineteen were loading up some mothers' sons in makeshift

THIS DAY'S BUSINESS

stretchers, the IV bags held high. Rotor wash agitated the elephant grass in the foreground, partly obscuring the camera's eye. It could not discern the bugeyed expression or drum-tight facial muscles on the door gunner's face as he searched outward, arcing the machine gun left and right with futility, unable to return fire out of fear of hitting the grunts loading the wounded. It couldn't see the hits from small arms fire that the olive drab bird was taking as it sat naked and vulnerable. It could, however, capture the mothers' sons wrapped in their ponchos being loaded last.

The mug was trembling ever so slightly, setting up vibrations in the froth. The clinking of the glass against his teeth hurt just enough to break the spell. Eagen exhaled for the first time in what surely felt like hours. He set the mug down, lowered his eyes to the table and slammed the book shut. Only a passing waitress paid notice to the slight disturbance. Scenes that he had repressed, willed from his mind, came flooding back. With his palms flat on the table, he pushed himself up and away from the booth.

Gathering the textbook, he picked up the half-empty container and placed it in the gray bucket used for dirty dishes that sat on a nearby tray. It was nearly time to go; besides, the Bruins had just lost in overtime, and the crowd at the bar was pissed.

"Into each and every life a little rain must fall," Eagen thought to himself.

From the front door he turned right and headed down Cambridge Street toward Government Center, some three-or-four-hundred yards away, to catch the subway home. Turning up his collar to the snow, he hunkered into his down jacket.

The flurries had passed and what was in the air was more spindrift, snow kicked up by the wind lifting the loose powder on the surface. The tall buildings were creating a venturi effect with the wind. The damp and moisture-laden wind coming in off Boston Harbor was funneled, compressed and redirected up the narrow canyon ways of the streets into a hat-lifting, umbrella-wrenching gale. A snowplow passed him by on the left as he navigated his way along the frozen sidewalk. The grating noise and sparks from the blade biting into the pavement were his only companions on the deserted street this night. Looking up skyward, he could see ink-black holes in the gray, light-diffused overcast. Every now and again,

W.J. O'BRIEN

a star would hang motionless on the velvet backdrop of infinite space.

As Eagen approached the stairway leading to the subway platform, he glanced about him, looking for signs of suspicious activity. Boston, as large cities went in the early 70's, was not too bad for street crime. However, it was a far cry from the safety of the womb. Looking to his left across the street, he could see a lone figure leaning up against a support column in front of the State Office Building at 100 Cambridge Street. Whoever stood there was trying to use the shadows to his advantage. Eagen suspected it might be a mugger waiting to roll some drunk who stumbled out of the Red Hat, a bar frequented by dykes and fairies.

Although he was some distance away, Eagen still had an uneasy feeling about the shadows and felt more at ease descending onto the well lighted subway platform. From the Center, the underground line traveled to Harvard Square where he changed cars to the trolley, which ran to the Brighton-Allston line. Someone had once mentioned to Eagen that this route was the greatest show under earth. It was never described on any tourist map; the Chambers of Commerce flatly denied it, but, for twenty-five cents on any given late night, those with a sense of the macabre could witness every whacked-out, burnt-out, perverse freak of nature. These were the true "children of the night;" here, they were free to act out their tortured delusions or insanities.

Usually, the denizens provided an interesting diversion on the commute home. However, this night was a little different. Eagen had an uneasy feeling, one that he was being followed. It was that type of feeling that could not be isolated or quantified, nothing tangible. As he rose from his seat he hesitated, looking up, then down, the aisle into the adjoining cars. He couldn't see anything that looked out of place. *But here*, he thought to himself, *the outrageous and the abnormal is commonplace.* He was the only sane lunatic in the asylum.

At his stop, Eagen left the train and wasted no time ascending the sooty stairs to street level. He immediately sought the shadows of an adjacent doorway. There, he made himself "small," willing himself into near invisibility and waited. Minutes passed. Feeling foolish, he chastised himself for giving too much free reign to his imagination. Satisfied that he was quite alone, he continued on with as steady a pace as the snowy sidewalk would permit. He could see from the

THIS DAY'S BUSINESS

street that the lights were on in his apartment and a party was in progress. Eagen had forgotten that one of his roommates would be celebrating a birthday that night.

The music was loud as he approached the second floor landing; it was louder still when he opened the door to his third-floor apartment. Upon entering, Eagen dodged his way through the gyrating bodies, making smalltalk with those he knew, all the while heading for the kitchen that served as the bar.

His roomie yelled from just beyond the doorway, "Davey, someone called for you earlier."

"For me? Who wazit?"

"I dunno...said he'd call back later."

Rather than making a futile attempt at shouting over the din, he just waved back, acknowledging that he understood the message. It was time to party.

Morning brought with it a grayness, the very loud clanging of bells in the foggy distance and a god-awful hangover. Caught up in the party spirit, Eagen had consumed way too much. Hoping that he didn't make too big a fool of himself, he thought to himself, *I do shine on wine.*

Swinging his legs over the edge of the bed, and with his eyes still closed, he reached for the source of the clanging bells. Feeling the button on top of the alarm, he knew that it wasn't the alarm. Sweeping his hand further left, he groped for the phone. Missing his target, he knocked the receiver off the hook to the floor where the ringing immediately stopped. Moments later, he braced himself with his left elbow on his knee and his head in his hand. Shifting his weight to the right, he bent down and scooped up the receiver. A voice called out from the earpiece. It was too late though, because his next movement snared the cord, pulling the telephone off the table and onto the floor, breaking the connection. Throwing the now useless device over his shoulder, he let himself fall backwards onto the rumpled bed.

"Just a few minutes, just a few minutes more ,and then I can get up...I hope."

That day he needed a clear head. He was to drive down to Woods Hole and spend a perfectly miserable day doing reference work among the stacks in the Lillie Library at the Marine Biological

Laboratory. Since he was already two hours behind schedule, Eagen did not stop to eat breakfast, but instead chose to shower, jump into reasonably clean clothes and bolt out the door with his book bag slung over his shoulder. Standing on the front doorsteps to his apartment building, he inhaled sharply several times in quick succession in a vain attempt to come fully awake and rid the lungs of last night's excesses.

The dampness in the wind accentuated the occasional stinging of his face by the partially frozen ice crystals slicing through the air. Turning his collar up for protection from the elements, he pulled his face down into his jacket. Carefully negotiating the unshovelled walkway, Eagen made his way the half block to his infrequently used MGB. Pulling out from the space, he gave himself one last chance to chuck it all for the day and go back to bed where it was warm, cozy and quiet.

Duty before comfort won out. His thesis was due in two weeks, and he needed the finishing touches. The B.U. Library was adequate in its own right, but it was not specialized enough for his purposes.

In a bygone era around the turn of the century, it was considered the height of fashion for the ultra wealthy to build icons in their name and place them in the public trust for all to benefit. The Carnegies had given the city the public library system, the Mellons endowed a university and the Lillies donated to scientific research. It was seen, by some, as a way to salve the consciences of the robber barons of the industrial age; the benefits, nonetheless, were quite tangible.

The Lillie Library was jointly operated by the researchers at MBL and the Woods Hole Oceanographic Institution. The data gathered within these walls represented Earth Science investigations collected the world over. The chronicles and journals from long-past voyages were cataloged, annotated and bound together. The findings from these thousands of expeditions, many from the age of sail, awaited the curious mind. If it were a scientific paper, printed in any of a dozen languages, it could be researched there. Not only was there an abundance of information, but the normally quiet facility would be deserted on Saturdays. The overstuffed, leather-bound armchairs were very comfortable and conducive to relaxed study. The decor of the oak-paneled reading room was almost elegant and lent an air of dignity and a sense of history to the place.

THIS DAY'S BUSINESS

From time to time, Eagen would glance down at his shopping list of reference material and decide that he had gleaned as much as he could from the text before him. Reluctantly, he rose from his leatherbound comfort, stretched and went in search of further material. He knew of only two other people in the building: the security guard downstairs at the street level and a reference librarian who betrayed her presence in a back office by using the hunt and peck method of typing. Unlike a metronome, her attempts were erratic and were the only counterpoint to the hypnotic humming of the neon tubes lighting the building.

From an architectural standpoint, Lillie was the design of an earlier age that reflected its nautical heritage and deferred only to modern safety codes. The narrow spiral staircases linking the floors resembled a ship's ladder, and the aisles between the stacks were reminiscent of a gangway. There was, in fact, only one large stack of books and manuscripts rising from the floor to the ceiling. The floors were added, seemingly as an afterthought, so that the stacks seemed to protrude upward through the floors. The result was that one could look up or down onto the adjoining floors.

Lately, Eagen had been exercising his mind and had not been working out as much as he would like. The responsibilities and deadlines with school left too little time for ice or climbing. As a result, he was feeling sluggish. Fresh air, adrenaline and some altitude beneath his boots were the elixir he needed, but, for now, he would have to forego taking the elevator to the second floor and opt for the spiral staircase.

The raw, bone-chilling weather outside and the off-season lack of activity on the street added to the feeling of isolation inside.The normally darkened aisles would be lighted by single, stark-naked lightbulbs with pull strings placed every twenty feet or so. It was custom to light only that area in which one was working and to extinguish it as one moved on. With few outside windows to allow in natural lighting and with the sound-insulating properties of books and papers, the sense of isolation was heightened.

It is bad enough, Eagen thought, *that the sleet-laden clouds outside obscure the island of Martha's Vineyard from the bulkhead just across the street, but the visibility here inside is very somber.*

The stacks held the mustiness and smells of many summers and winters of being closed up for too long, and of bound paper that was impregnated with salt air. Eagen found the aisle he was looking for on the second level and hunted for the nearly invisible string to turn on the light. Finding his reference book, he heard what he thought were a few footsteps, footsteps that sounded as if someone were trying desperately not to be heard. Looking down through the stacks of books, there was little visible in the dim light of the first level. The same could be said for the third level above. Out went the light as Eagen stood motionless for a few moments. It must be one of the resident mice, or then it might be history talking to him. His heightened sense of isolation allowed him to write it off as nothing more than his own imagination.

Eagen turned left and walked to an outside aisle and sat down at a well worn surplus government gray metal desk that was placed next to one of the few windows on that side of the building. He started thumbing through the index at the back. A most curious thought invaded the back of his mind, one that made the hairs stand up on the back of his neck and tingle. The metal desk was cold, damp, and room temperature to the touch. In contrast, the chair was warm as though he or someone else had been sitting in it for some time. Was it his imagination or paranoia? Having no sound basis for the latter, he reached the uneasy conclusion that it was the former.

Sitting casually back from the desk, Eagen had his left leg crossed over his right knee. Inches from his left shoulder was the window pane that defended him from the phalanx of snow showers sweeping in off Vineyard Sound. The splattering droplets merged on the outside with the salt spray and low clouds. The view reminded Eagen of Impressionist art with its slightly out-of-focus scenery. Water Street, running left and right below him, was empty.

Sitting at the source of the only natural light in the area, he felt the spinal rush of a chill up and down his back. The dampness was invading his bones. He knew that relief could only come with a steaming bowl of seafood stew and three fingers of Jack Daniels.

Using the eraser on his pencil as a pointer, Eagen scanned downward to the topic on pages 512 through 547. Thumbing the pages with the book in his left hand, he reached the article "Coastal Sedimentation and Ground Motion" by Brock, Edward R. He needed to cite a source, and Brock, Edward R. signaled a futile attempt to find

THIS DAY'S BUSINESS

one. Considering that he had achieved virtually all of his objectives, he smirked and mouthed "c'est la guerre" to his own reflection in the window. *It is time to leave,* he thought. *I'll just put this book back, collect my stuff downstairs and then bolt.*

Eagen was barely in mid motion of getting out of the chair when a light, four aisles away, snapped on. Although he had been concentrating on the text, he should have been aware of someone coming up there. His inner voice chided him for this lapse. Time slowed to a glacial pace, every sense within him became alert, and his pulse quickened to the point where he was conscious of it throbbing ever so slightly in his ears. Breathing, which he had stopped, returned slowly. It was, however, the shallow type of breathing that does not even move the diaphragm, lest motion, any motion, give him away.

Placing the weight on the outside edges of his shoes, he made three steps away from the desk and away from the window light. Turning right, he moved toward an intersecting aisle. Slowly and with deliberation, trying to become one with the shadows, Eagen was within three feet of the light. Shifting his weight onto his left foot, he stepped into the intersection. Already facing to the right, he was prepared to look rather foolish if it was the librarian or fierce if it were trouble. Nothing!   *Behind you!* his inner voice pleaded.

What he saw, what he had steeled himself for, nothing could have prepared him for the vision that was just three feet away.

CHAPTER 4

Allison

She was scheming, vain, and quite spoiled, with a propensity toward throwing tantrums. Daddy saw to it that his "little girl Allison" quickly got whatever attracted her attention. She did, however, have two estimable attributes, which she rarely harnessed, beneath a tight sweater or peasant blouse. Allison carried her six-foot slender frame with the grace and poise of a professional dancer, and yet she could slouch like a bricklayer drinking beer when she was in her "slumming" mode. Her head of rich auburn hair, long and straight, was a striking and distinguishing feature of hers. It showed the type of care and management given at only the most exclusive salons in Boston. She stood in contrast to most of her contemporaries who, at that time, were just emerging from their Woodstock Generation cocoon with its accompanying dress standards. The most dressed down that Eagen usually saw her was in jeans, expensive cashmere sweaters, and jerseys. Being a slave to fashion, custom dictated that the jeans were impeccably tailored, and the jerseys were from only the most expensive boutiques that Newbury Street could

THIS DAY'S BUSINESS

produce. At a party or gathering she stood out. There was just no other way to put it. Her stature, poise, and general outward appearance exuded confidence, class, and money.

Allison Babbage was the only child of Jonathan and Helen Babbage of Dover and Beacon Hill, both bastions of the well heeled. She derived her outspokenness and drive from her father, Jonathan, who was a senior partner in a very old and revered brokerage firm on Boston's State Street. The firm was an old warren where the only color that was more important than green was old Yankee blue. If one did not establish a pedigree, one simply did not exist.

Anyone who did not know her well would think that surely she must have inherited her looks and athletic physique from her mother, but in truth, Helen was rather plain. One might even say that she was dowdy. When first introduced, Eagen thought to himself that she had an ass on her two axe handles wide. What Helen brought to the union was money.

There was no doubt about it: Allison was daddy's girl. The old man had it all figured out. Nothing was too good for his daughter. She would be seen only in the right company, always with the right circle of friends. Although he insisted, over his wife's objections, she attend public school. He felt that Allison would have to exist in a world where there were more common people than there were of those who had position, privilege, and power. Brushing elbows with the common ones would give her an appreciation of those who were socially a cut above. Paradoxically, he was adamant that his influence should see her enrolled at Wellesley College, just the place for a young girl of breeding.

Allison met Eagen one night quite unexpectedly on the Boston Common. A crowd had gathered for the annual lighting of the Christmas lights. This event, one of the oldest in the country, was held the day after Thanksgiving. It signaled the beginning of the holiday shopping season. The theme of a traditional New England Christmas was everywhere. The department stores were all decked out in the proper colors. Gobs of tinsel and mountains of artificial snow were the order of the day. Jordan Marsh, one of the earliest department stores in the country, was proudly touting the opening of their Santa's Village. It was a huge annual event for which the Tremont Street retailer was famous. It seemed as though the entire ground floor was transformed into one large fantasy of Santa's home at the North Pole. The lights, the colorful wrappings and trappings, the expensive toys, the crowds; it was Nirvana to a kid!

From his earliest memories Eagen could remember his aunt bringing him into Boston for the annual ceremonies on the Common, the tour through Santa's Village, and then the finale, the pièce de résistance: a hot fudge sundae at Baileys. Yes, these were the things a child, of any age, dreamed about. As the fantasies began to fade and Eagen grew older, the village at the North Pole became less important. Passage through the teen years had brought with it the realities of life and the building of a future. There just wasn't the time for the trivial. Life just seemed to get in the way.

On this particular evening Eagen found himself with extra time. His late afternoon class was canceled and he wasn't due at the Bell in Hand for almost three hours. His roommates were still out of town for the Thanksgiving holiday break, and so he decided not to go home but to catch up on the goings-on in the big city. He was reminded of the ceremonies going on over at the Common from an article in the Boston Globe.

Bypassing his usual stop, he went one station beyond to Park Square at the corner of Tremont and Winter Streets. Upon reaching street level, he found himself injected into the chaos. The daily ebb and flow of society going about its business entwined itself with the shoppers and gawkers. Eagen was a gawker. The winos, the weirdos, the celebrators of the season, they were all there. Just seventy-five or a hundred feet up from the walkway, the crowds were beginning to assemble. The mayor was there, the press was there, anybody who was anybody or thought they were was there. The pompous, the pious, and the circumstantial were there, and so was Eagen.

At first he saw them. It was just a motion caught in his peripheral vision, the type of motion that compels the eye to lock in. There were six or seven of them, their arms interlocked for mutual support. They were having a hell of a good time judging from the way they were carrying on. Eagen mused to himself that they resembled a bunch of drunken bedbugs. They were all dressed well in the uniform of those

THIS DAY'S BUSINESS

whose blood ran blue. The overcoats of the guys were black with a thin stripe of velvet outlining the collars; underneath they wore dark three-piece suites. The one on the far left held a magnum of expensive champagne, which he tried to pass to his compatriots. The women, elegantly attired in their dark coats and suits, showed evidence of gold jewelry and pearls. It seemed as if the gates of Harvard Yard had suddenly opened up and disgorged them. They were oblivious to the surrounding festivities, save their own. As they were walking by, Eagen, who was on the periphery of the crowd, could overhear part of their conversation.

They stopped long enough to observe the goings-on. Apparently they had come from a posh cocktail party on nearby Beacon Hill next to the State House and were on their way to Old City Hall where a performance of Handel's Messiah was to take place; then it was on to the Parker House for dinner. Judging by their apparently inebriated state, Eagen thought it doubtful they would make it that far. As they became disinterested with the ceremonies, several of their comrades-in-arms were tugging at the others and urging them to leave. The young female on the end wearing a black lamb's wool coat with a wide fur collar turned, caught one of her spiked heels in a crack in the sidewalk, and dumped herself, most unceremoniously, on her ass.

Seeing this, practically at his feet, Eagen squatted to offer assistance. The young men with her were no help. They found the whole thing amusing. Greeting her at eye level, Eagen asked her whether she was all right. He felt silly for asking such an obvious question but a little annoyed by her friends who were behaving like jerks.

"Yes," she replied, "I guess that I'm lucky. Just twisted it a little, I suppose."

He handed her the shoe that had come off, took her hand, and, on the count of three, had her upright and replaced her shoe. A brief snow flurry began, but Eagen had not noticed until the flakes started falling on his eyelashes; only then did he blink. *Damn, she's good looking*, he thought.

She smiled. "Thanks. I think that I've had enough for one day." She tossed her rich mane of auburn hair in the direction of the magnum.

"Allison," her impatient young companion whined, "stop flirting! We'll be late for the concert."

45

This had her friends laughing. And a few of the passersby who had slowed to see what was going on.

"Oh, don't piss your pants," she retorted. "You know I hate walking in these damn things." Brushing herself off and fluffing up her lost dignity, she went on, "Lucky for me, I didn't dirty up this new coat. Daddy just bought it for me, and he would just kill me if he saw it with mud stains. Thanks," she said to Eagen. "Nice friends I have, huh?" He slowly turned and eyed each one. The stunning girl with the rich auburn hair and the black lamb's wool coat walked away, saying to her friends, "We're late, let's go." The same lighthearted banter returned as she joined her friends. They locked arms again and off they went toward Old City Hall as if nothing out of the way had happened. Eagen just stared at her back with that long, straight hair swaying until she was lost in the backdrop of a busy city.

With a smile on his face, Eagen turned and walked to work. He noticed that his steps were lighter and his breathing a little deeper. He had been smitten, even if only for a brief moment.

It was a busy night for Eagen; lots of people were in the city that night and that meant that the restaurant business would be good, it being a Friday night and the holiday season and all. He did not have the time to think of her again until just before he was about to leave. There was more than enough work to keep him busy. At quarter to eleven, Eagen exchanged his apron for his jacket and walked out of the room from behind the kitchen and through the swinging doors that opened out into the dining area. Holding one side open for a waitress, they smiled at each other and then he headed out to the bar.

"A couple of beers for the ride home and then I'm outa here," he murmured to himself.

She stepped out in front of him and took him totally by surprise. "Hi, remember me?"

There was a three-second pause; he hadn't really been expecting to see her again. What were the odds? "Yes, how is your ankle, I mean, what are you doing here?"

"We were having drinks at the Parker House and then a late supper and then more drinks, until we had way too much and they asked, ah, told us to leave. We weren't ready to quit for the night so here we are. We've been here for the last hour. What are you doing here?" she said in a slightly tipsy way.

"I work here part time, but I'm getting off now. Care for a beer?"

"No. I've had much more than I should; besides, I should be getting him home." It was obvious whom she was referring to. Her crowd of friends was at a table having a good old time except for the one with his face on his chest. The young man's longish hair was askew, and his head was bobbing from side to side. It was clear to Eagen that the guy was smashed. When he was able to look up, his eyes looked like they were doing Cuban Eights in their sockets.

"Well, at least, can I call you?" he persisted.

"Sure, I'll give you my number. I'd like you to call," was her reply.

Eagen wasn't sure if it was the liquor talking or if she really meant it. *Only one way to tell for sure*, he thought to himself.

The relationship had been ongoing for about a year, and it was beginning to show strain at times because of the demands put on Eagen by her and his class work. She could be very demanding and given to tantrums. Social gatherings in Allison's circle of friends would come and go without Eagen. He would either be in a library somewhere or at work. Her friends had little use for academia. The exclusive colleges were for the socially prominent, and manual labor was seen as degrading; besides, who needed to work as long as the trust fund checks kept coming? On the other hand, Eagen found her friends to be equally distasteful, shallow, and parasitic. Weekends at the Hamptons or Christmas skiing in Chamonix with "Muffy," "Biff," or "Chad" was his idea of nowhere. By and large, he found her friends to be vacuous and of little redeeming social worth. It was a great sense of friction between them both. To add sand to the gears, her father had seen potential in Eagen. He was only one of a few of her friends who had any sense of work ethic. Viewing Eagen as a possible son-in-law, Jonathan Winthrop Babbage saw the best way of providing for his daughter. Eagen would join the firm as a very junior clerk, and with time, he would move up. All the while, "David, my boy" would be remolded and groomed. His daughter's future security and position in proper society was of paramount importance.

The subtle and sometimes not so subtle hints about his career and his relationship with Allison were starting to get on Eagen's nerves, especially at a time in his studies when he did not need the extra hassles. Her old man was becoming more vocal with his disdain for Eagen's chosen path.

"What will it ever build?" he'd ask. "What power and influence will you ever achieve?" he would often implore. Their few encounters were becoming more strained, and Eagen was becoming more adept at avoiding him. Evasion was not his strong suit; he preferred to meet challenges head on, but this was different. The whole business was really starting to eat at him, and the effects were splashing over into his relationship with Allison.

She called him late one night. Her parents were having a dinner party at their country home in Dover the following Saturday night, and as she put it, "There will be scads of important people there." She added, as an aside, that "Daddy and I would be very disappointed if you couldn't make it." There was something in the tone in her voice to suggest that the old man was going to give it one last try at winning over Eagen. Reluctantly, he accepted, more for her than the old man. Time to get the old suit out of mothballs and dust it off. On the whole, he'd rather be in Philadelphia.

The long, unkempt hair, the headband and beads threw him off, but there was no mistaking the nose and eyes. The light of recognition dawned in his eyes when he saw the shit-eating grin on the spectre's face. "Sweetner?"

"Yeah, you Yankee simpleton, who else were you expecting?" They embraced tightly with much back slapping. Eagen's look of surprise changed to a frown.

"You scared the living shit outta me. You should know better than to sneak up on somebody. How the hell are you? How did you find me?" Eagen blurted these questions out while still feeling the rush of being scared.

Sweetner responded with: "Well, if you let me get a word in edgewise, stop shaking me so damned hard, I'll tell you. First off, I had some vacation coming to me and decided to take it while I was in town; I knew you were here because I called this morning after you

THIS DAY'S BUSINESS

rudely hung up on me and talked to your roommate who told me where to find you."

Eagen, remembering the attempted answering of the phone call, looked sheepish. Continuing, Sweetner went on, "Finally, this is the twentieth century, and they do have bus service down here, you know."

Eagen rambled on, " Can you stay a few days? You can bunk in with me; one of my roomies is away, and you can have his room." And so the questioning went on in rapid staccato fashion.

"It must have been two years, hasn't it?" said Eagen.

"Closer to three, but who's counting?"

The reunion was vocal and coarse. It dawned on them both that this was a library and wasn't the sort of place to catch up on old times. He gathered up his papers and then they both bolted for the exit. Running for the MGB, Sweetner cursed the weather. The ride back to Boston was slippery and raucous. They both stayed drunk for the next two days, reliving the bad old past.

Saturday evening had come. Eagen left the city, heading into the suburbs and aiming for the country. He was driving with elan and pushing the "B" up and down through the gears. The roads were empty, and this lent itself to some pretty spirited driving. Sweetner's return elevated his mood to a level he had not felt in a long, long time. Even the drag of the evening ahead could not bring him down. Twenty miles outside Boston, he was in the rural and genteel countryside. This was a town of two cops and large estates. The split-rail fences and pastures gave way to the high walls and crisply manicured shrubs of the Babbage estate.

In that strange netherworld that exists between sunset and the onset of darkness, Eagen's headlights found the massive wrought iron gates that separated the great unwashed masses from those who lived by the sweat of others. The driveway, of several hundred feet in length, unfolded before him. Everything was in its proper place; the newly mowed lawn, the intricately sculpted hedges, and the copse's of white birches, everything felt the loving touch of an army of gardeners.

The great house was English Tudor in style, built in the nineteen thirties. The lights inside shone through the stained-glass panels with lead insets. They were attempting to beat back the night and the shadows that were inevitably advancing across the landscape.

The little two seater with its top down seemed out of place as it rumbled up to the line of cars in the large diameter circular driveway. The valets with their noses in the air looked down with disdain on so humble a carriage. Eagen thought that there were none so snobbish as the servants of the rich.

Pulling up to the massive granite steps guarding the large double-hung oak doors, he held up his hand to stop the white-jacketed snob from opening the driver's door.

"Just show me where and I'll park it myself." As an aside, he added, " I may have to leave in a hurry." The man pointed to a small gravel patch next to several Jaguars and a Bentley. He backed in, put up the top, and walked toward the granite steps.

Casting a disapproving look at the new arrival's attire, the doorman nodded curtly and pulled at the brass knob parting the great slabs of oak.

Once inside Eagen knew that he was out of his league. The ladies were all in gowns and the gentlemen were in black tie. It was the first time that he had worn a suit since his high school graduation, and he felt rather conspicuous.

Mingling and making small talk was such a pain in the groin, but it was the price of admission for a great meal. At least the night, no matter how dull it turned out to be, would not be a total write off.

"David, my boy," the elder Babbage called out. "There is someone I want you to meet." Bringing Eagen over by the arm to the slightly balding, mustached man, he said, "David, this is Marcel Chazzi. Marcel, this is David Eagen. He and my little Allison are very fond of one another. David, you should know that Marcel is the Deputy Minister of Finance and Development at the French Embassy in New York; he is also an old and valued client of our firm." Eagen shook hands and made pleasantries with the man.

"Marcel," Babbage continued further, "I've been trying to impress upon David here the importance of a financial career. It's really true what they say about money making the world go 'round."

"David," the Frenchman began, "you are a student, are you not?"

"Yes, I am, at B.U." was the reply.

"Ah," Chazzi went on, "You should meet my son, Emile; he's at Yale. I'm sure that the two of you will have much in common."

THIS DAY'S BUSINESS

Little did he realize how prophetic his words would become. Chazzi started looking about the room, standing on his tiptoes to see over the crowd. "There he is, with your Allison."

Eagen turned to his right in the direction the Frenchman was pointing. His son was much taller than his father and had about three inches on Eagen. Walking up to the younger man, he noticed that he had his arm around Allison, and it did not seem to bother her.

"Emile, come here, there is someone you must meet. You will find that you have so much in common."

As Eagen held out his hand, the younger Chazzi kept his right arm around Allison, all the while running his fingers through the ends of her hair. Chazzi looked a lot skinnier up close than farther away. Eagen thought that he looked fashionably emaciated. The nose was thin and boney, and his hollow cheeks and vacant eyes had the look of a heroin addict, no, of a serpent. Emile just nodded his head at the introduction. Eagen felt awkward with the rebuff but decided to show restraint.

"Your father tells me that you're at Yale. What year are you in?"

"Year?" the younger Chazzi came back. "It must be four or five now, I've lost count," was the bored reply. "I am a professional student."

With that, Eagen separated the two by taking Allison's arm in his and steering her away out of earshot of Chazzi. "Who is this clown?" Eagen whispered to her.

"Emile? Why, he's someone I met a few months ago. My father and his father work closely together. They introduced us. We're just good friends. You're not jealous, are you?"

"Slightly annoyed," said Eagen, "but jealous, no. Let's talk later after dinner."

Throughout the meal, Chazzi, who sat on the far side of Allison, made sure that Eagen saw that he was paying a lot of attention to her. He would touch her hand and his serpent eyes would flick at him, baiting him, looking for a reaction. The eyes were daring him to make a scene.

With dinner's end, the guests filed out for further conversation and drinks. Eagen pulled her aside and asked her bluntly, "What is going on here? What is he to you?"

"Really, David," she responded in a very bored tone, "he's just a friend; now be a nice boy and get me a drink."

With that said, Emile slithered up to Eagen and, in a mocking tone, said, "Allison has told me so much about you. Tell me, how does it feel to be a killer of women and babies?" Chazzi was really enjoying this cruelty.

That did it. Those were the buttons Eagen didn't want pushed. Chazzi was playing him like a concert violinist!

Eagen was ready to give him a hernia when Allison, sensing trouble, thrust herself between them. Through clenched teeth, he went right up into Chazzi's face and whispered so that both could hear him say, "Allison, you keep this pimp away from me!" He was livid.

Turning on his heels, he walked out and headed for his car. Climbing in, he started it up and revved the engine, then dumped the clutch. Gravel flew like buckshot, ricocheting off of the fancy paint jobs around him. Instead of going around the fountain by the driveway he went straight through a flower bed, leaving tracks as the tires burned sod.

After passing the gate, he settled down, a little. Ocassionally banging the steering wheel with his left hand, he chided himself for losing control. His inner voice was telling him that she was trashing him, and she had just used that pile of frog shit to do it. She enjoyed setting him up; they both enjoyed it.

CHAPTER 5

Betrayal

The Russian climbed out of the limousine and nodded to the chauffeur as he held the door open. "Vasily, remain in view. I'll be expecting company, and we may walk a bit. Have the car turned around, and you can follow me down the street." The elderly, heavyset Russian stepped over the curb with the driver's aid and planted his cane firmly on the sidewalk. With his right hand trembling slightly, he reached for the parking meter with his left. This gave him the needed boost to walk the fifteen feet to the front door of the Polish restaurant.

Once inside, he was greeted by the waiter who offered his free arm as a brace. "Mr. Sulkhov," the waiter greeted, "we've been hoping to see you again soon. It has been several weeks, has it not?"

"Yes, Gregory," the Russian responded. "It is my arthritis. It seems to be getting worse, not better. Springtime in New York is beginning to feel like winter in Leningrad."

Chuckling, the waiter helped steady the old man as they navigated the sparsely populated main room. When they reached the rear, he steered the customer to the right with his outstretched hand. "Your usual private dining room awaits you, sir," he said. "Will you be dining alone today?"

"Yes," Sulkhov said in answer to the question, "but today I am expecting a visitor at some point. See to it that I am not disturbed until I am nearly finished. I detest mixing business with one of the few pleasures left to me."

"As you wish, sir " said the waiter. The younger man was ready to leave when Sulkhov stopped him and asked, "Incidentally, Gregory, is your lovely daughter still employed here? I would very much like to have her serve me lunch."

"She is, sir, and would be most eager to enhance your dining pleasure." The waiter knew that the old lecher's tip would be commensurate with the amount of cleavage displayed by his buxom and more than willing daughter.

As his meal was nearing completion, the waiter entered and announced to Sulkhov that his guest had arrived.

"Excellent, excellent," the Russian exclaimed with enthusiasm. "Coffee and cigars, when you get an opportunity, Gregory."

The man was ushered in with little fanfare. "Come in, my friend, sit." The old Communist waved his right hand to an empty seat while, with his left, he wiped a blue, starched linen table napkin across his greasy mouth. "We have much to discuss." The new arrival pulled the chair back and sat down nervously on the edge, his hands folded in front of him.

The proprietors' shapely daughter poured them both coffee from a side table. Serving first one, then the other, she revealed much of herself to them both, safe in the knowledge that a fat tip would be forthcoming. Leaving the men, she closed the door behind her and departed quietly for the kitchen.

Both men had their eyes on the door, and when they were sure that they were alone, they looked at each other. The Russian picked up a cigar and appeared to be studying it in silence. His guest chose a cigar from the open box on the table, and pulled at the wrapper; his uneasiness was heightened by the silence between them.

Seemingly lost in the task at hand, the Russian carefully examined the cigar, slowly rolling it over and over and passing it beneath his nose to absorb its pungent fragrance. He pulled the chrome-plated

THIS DAY'S BUSINESS

clipper from his waistcoat pocket and delicately snipped the end. A lighted candle was passed between them, and they each, in turn, took several puffs.

There was a tension in the air, and it hung heavy as the blue-white clouds of smoke that billowed lazily in the air. Sulkhov opened matter-of-factly with, "The Americans are up to something. We don't know what it is yet, and that concerns us. If I were thirty years younger, you could brand me as paranoid; however, experience has taught me…"

"How does that affect me?" the new arrival questioned. "And what has put you on the scent?"

Reaching into the watch pocket of his vest, Sulkhov retrieved the gold lighter, which showed many years of use. Noticing that the nervous man was eyeing it, Sulkhov said with great pride in his voice, "Kruschev himself presented this to me just after crushing the Hungarian revolt in '56." Biting at the cigar, he spat the severed tip onto the floor. The guest watched as the Russian proceeded to relight the tobacco. "It's not a Cuban," he lamented, "but it will have to do for the moment."

Coughing from the surging clouds of smoke being produced across the table from him, the guest again asked, "How does this affect us?"

The Russian continued between puffs, "They are casting their net wide, discreetly, but wide. It seems that they are beating the bushes looking for mountain climbers with experience. Our sources worldwide tell us that they are looking for expatriates and have even made inquiries into those with a military background. Have you run across any such thing?"

"No, but I am only a low-level attaché. Such whispers generally do not reach my ears."

Sulkhov responded, "We have looked at the professionals, the guides, and adventurers and have exhausted those possibilities and are of the opinion that they might be looking now for a talented amateur."

"Very well," the guest continued as his cigar smoke joined the Russian's, "but I still don't see how this involves me."

"Come, we will walk now," said the Russian, "and I will draw you the map."

They left the restaurant together, and Sulkhov gestured to the chauffeur to follow him down the street with the limo. After ten or so minutes of pained walking, the street opened up onto Washington Square where the small park with its monument commanded the view. There was a sea of young humanity milling about. The anti-war demonstrators with their loud hailers were attempting to whip up the crowd into a frenzy. The pseudo intellectuals, hippies, and guitar-strummers were all there with their signs and posters. The cops on horseback were just trying to keep the lid on the garbage can without giving anyone an excuse to riot.

"Look at this street rabble, my friend; love and brotherhood, indeed. These fools don't know the first thing about socialism. They talk of revolution but know nothing of its sacrifices; still, they serve our purpose. We funnel a great deal of money your way to keep these spoiled bourgeois busy; no matter how ludicrous their demands or self serving their slogans, it's still our money that you are spending. Without our generosity and ideology, their pathetic bleatings would evaporate like a fart in a windstorm—and your influence with it, I might add."

Humbled, the Russian's companion acknowledged, "Yes, the Marxist revolution must continue here to hold back the imperial aggression elsewhere in the world. It is only a matter of time."

"Bullshit!" Sulkhov shot back angrily. "The words are claptrap; it is about utter and total domination." He caught himself, for he was beginning to rant. The outburst unnerved the attaché. Regaining his composure and lowering his voice several decibels, he continued in a more controlled manner, "Listen, you've got people that we pay well, and I'm looking for answers. These students, and others like them, they have sports collectives, don't they? Find out. Don't they have hiking clubs and the like? I know Harvard has one, Yale has one too, don't they? Find out. Use them," he emphasized, as he pointed to the rabble with his cane. "Earn your keep, Marcel, but do it discreetly."

With that said, the Russian signaled for his driver, who had been following them from behind the wheel. The big car with its United Nations Diplomatic Corps plates pulled up. Sulkhov got in and closed the door. The black tinted window slid down, and an arthritic finger pointed at the second man. "Remember, earn your keep." The limo drove on.

◇◇◇

THIS DAY'S BUSINESS

She cried and cried. Her apologies were loud and profuse, and Eagen, being a sucker for tears, forgave her. Sweet-talking her on the phone, he said "Allie, listen, this Friday night I'm throwing a party. I've finally finished my thesis, and I'm submitting it for review on Monday. Also, Sweets' vacation...you remember me telling you about Bobby Sweetner...his vacation is over, and he's heading back to Washington, so I thought it would be a great time to party it up. See you around eight."

A warm Friday night saw the windows open and the loud music flowing. Eagen's wasn't the only place that was in a festive mood. The colleges had only recently let out for the summer, and people were either celebrating the end of exams or were in the process of moving out of the apartments they had rented for the school year. Eagen's place was no exception, and by nine o'clock, the party was in full throb, but there was no Allison.

At ten thirty she showed up, no fanfare, no blaring of trumpets, she just appeared inside the doorway. Sweetner, who had been recounting one of his dirty stories for two Simmons girls, looked up at the door and then pointed with his index finger at Eagen, drawing his attention to the entrance. Coming up to his side, Sweetner asked, "Who is that?"

Eagen retorted, "That, my dear fellow, is Allison. Would you like to meet her?"

"Would I? I'd be after that like a badger going down a gopher hole!"

"Well, I'll have you know that behind that angelic face lays the soul of true pain," said Eagen.

It was then that he entered the door behind her. Sweetner said to Eagen, "Who's the schmuck with her?" Eagen didn't answer. He parted the gyrating bodies before him and walked right up to her. Sweetner decided to stay a discreet distance back and take in all the action.

"Allison, I thought that you were going to keep this slimy turd away from me. Instead, you bring him here. What gives?"

"David, Daddy's really pissed at you for tearing up his lawn last week, and I just stopped by to tell you that we, Emile and I, are leaving town for Tahoe to do some late spring skiing."

Chazzi hissed, "Don't worry, Eagen, I'll take real good care of your little Allison."

Eagen caught the snake in the center of the chest just below the sternum with a stiffened thumb. It took everyone in close proximity by surprise. "Get out, now, both of you. I don't know who to feel more sorry for," he said. "You both deserve one another. Get out."

The music was just loud enough that only three or four people were aware that anything had occurred. The snake and his consort were gone, and Sweetner was cooling Eagen down.

"Is he the one you were telling me about?" Sweetner asked. Eagen just nodded. "Well," Bobby continued, "if you touched him, I hope you wash with plenty of soap and hot water."

"Listen," Sweetner said later in the night, "there is something that we have to talk over."

CHAPTER 6

Preparations

The room was closing in on Eagen, and he needed to cool down. Making his way through the crowd, he headed through the kitchen and up the narrow back stairway to the roof. Up there he had room to breathe as the panorama of Boston unfolded around him. It was there among the old abandoned pigeon coop that he came to think or just to rest his mind. Sweetner followed a few minutes later but said nothing, leaving him alone with his thoughts. The half empty bottle of Wild Turkey passed between them in silence several times with both of them staring at the horizon.

Sweetner was the first to break the awkward silence. "Have you ever considered leading another expedition, I mean a big one, to a big mountain?"

Eagen held up the bottle to eye level to better gauge the remaining portion, then handed it to Sweetner. "Not lately," was the reply. Once again, silence overtook them.

"Well, would you ever consider it?" persisted Sweetner.

"Perhaps. I don't know. The Alaska trip was damned expensive and a pain in the ass to organize. Truthfully though, I could use a change right about now what with school and now this crap tonight. What are you getting at?" he asked.

Sweetner turned his back to the horizon and faced Eagen squarely, saying, "Davy, would you be interested in tackling a Himalayan peak? I mean, a big one?" Eagen took the bottle from his friend.

"Give me that thing. You're only supposed to sip this stuff, not chug it." Taking the bottle from Sweetner, Eagen put a nick in the end of the label with the inside edge of his left thumbnail. Handing it back, he said to Sweetner, "This much, and no more; otherwise, somebody'll be scraping us off the pavement below."

"Listen, I'm serious," Sweetner continued.

"So am I," Eagen interjected. "This stuff will have us both eating shit and barking at the moon!"

Sweetner just wouldn't let go. "Listen, listen to me for one minute. If you had the time and money, I mean all things considered equal, would you do it?" he said.

"Sure," Eagen came back, "who wouldn't? It would be a dream come true." Eagen was convinced that the Turkey was getting to his friend.

Sweetner came closer and, in a conspiratorial voice, said, "I know some people, people that I work for, who are looking to finance a Himalayan expedition, and they're looking for someone to lead it. Interested?"

Eagen looked at Sweetner, saying, "You never did tell me much about whom you work for."

"That's not important now," was Sweetner's reply. "What's important is that maybe you should talk to these people. Maybe you can connect and...who knows, there could be some high adventure in it for you."

God knows I could use some right about now, thought Eagen.

His friend took the bottle and knocked back a slug, saying, "I've got to get back downstairs. I was in the middle of impressing the hell out of two lovelies when you decided to play bouncer. Give it some thought. I'll be leaving in the afternoon, but you can call me later in the week. That will give me time to set up an interview."

Eagen nodded as he continued to stare into space, feeling sorry for himself and very drunk.

<><><>

THIS DAY'S BUSINESS

The intelligence officer, whose cover was that of an agriculture expert, was driving slowly through Queens in the city. Not one of the residents paid the diplomatic plates on the car any heed; "those" type of people were known to go down there, looking for some action. On that day, it wasn't companionship that brought the man into that part of town. He was looking for a box, the olive green kind that the Post Office uses in the city when they leave sorted mail for the carriers. This particular box, the one on the corner at the stop sign, was a bulletin board of sorts. The man was looking for a particular mark on the box, a scribbling, if you will. It was something that would make no sense to anyone at all, except to himself. If anyone at all would pay any attention, which was highly unlikely, it would be passed off as a child's doodling. It was there, a zero with a slash through it. It was only about four inches tall, but in white chalk against a dark background, it stood out. It told him that a message was ready to be picked up from a source. It did not concern the officer where the message was or who originated it; his superiors would have that knowledge. His task was to report what he found.

It was nearly an hour before sunrise on Sunday morning when a man drove out from Boston in the rusted Fairlane. Turning off Route 9 in Newton, he made his way onto Highland Avenue toward Needham. The night air was cool and damp, and the sky was beginning to glow with a rose-like hue in the eastern sky as night was giving way to dawn. Venus was shining brilliantly, high in the inky backdrop and was casting the faintest of shadows.

After crossing over Route 128, the man whose jowls hung over his collar and hid the knot in his tie turned right onto Spruce Street and followed it to the end. With a right turn, the rattling muffler fading in the distance was the only trace of his passage through that neighborhood at the base of the twelve-hundred-foot TV antennas. The only witness was a dog sleeping off the night on his master's doorstep. The mutt lifted its head at the sound of the Ford driving by. Displaying no further interest, he yawned, stretched, then resumed his doggy dreams.

Ten minutes further down the road, the car approached Echo Bridge Reservation in Newton Upper Falls. The Falls were a throwback to the days when mills had sprouted up alongside waterfalls to take advantage of cheap power. The mill had long since been abandoned, and the paths leading to the magnificent arched bridge, which spanned the Charles River, had been allowed to fall into disrepair. The forest was slowly reclaiming an area that was home to lovers, muggers, and thieves.

The man turned the rusty car onto the dirt road and rolled silently to a stop so as not to awaken anyone in the working-class row houses that lined the nearby street. From where he parked the car, he could look up the hill to Our Lady of Lourdes church as it took shape in the growing daylight. He wasn't there for Sunday Mass.

He was oddly out of place in a seedy, brown, double-breasted suit that had gone out of style twenty years earlier. His brown shoes were of the genuine plastic imitation leather type with smooth soles. Walking along the dirt path, he was unsteady because of the slippery shoes. Also, he sweated profusely, a product of his overweight condition and too many years on a knockwurst diet. The path led him to the iron bridge with its institution-green anti-corrosion paint. Before stepping from the path, he looked around him to check his privacy.

The bridge abutment helped support his bulk as he leaned against it to regain his breath. It was then that he noticed a young man, a hippie from the looks of him. The hippy was sitting up in the lotus position on the cobbled stones that angled downward toward the river. This appeared to be the young man's makeshift home, judging from the discarded clothing and odd bits of trash strewn about under the bridge. He was very obviously stoned and no danger to the man with the weight problem. Still sweating heavily, the man went to the steel plates of the bridge where they met the concrete foundation. Counting up four rivets and then over three more to the left, he started to turn the selected bolt. It came loose with his fingers and popped out. It was more of a threaded cap than a full bolt. The last three inches of threads had been cut off, and it took only two or three turns of the cap to remove it.

Behind and below him the hippy exclaimed, "Far out, man," when the fat man inserted his pinkie finger into the hole and retrieved a rolled-up slip of paper. "Hey, man, you got some spare change?"

Pig Man returned the threaded cap to its proper place and put the paper in his inside breast pocket. "Yahz," Pig Man replied in a heavy east European accent. "I have zome change vor you."

THIS DAY'S BUSINESS

The youth was delighted at finding a soft touch so early in the morning, in there of all places. Pig Man gingerly stepped and slid down the dew-moistened cobbles and approached the bearded hippy from his left. The man then reached into his right-hand suit pocket and withdrew the object. Before the stoned-out kid could react, Pig Man, in one swift motion that belied his bulk, had the palm of his left hand on the hairy chin so as to shut the mouth and seal the lips. His fat thumb and index finger pinched off the nose so no noise whatsoever could escape. The next move was to push his right knee into the kid's back. In Pig Man's hand was an ice pick, which he drove up and into the hippie's brain at the base of the skull. Death was instantaneous, but the body gave one violent spasm.

Sweating profusely now, the fat man broke off the thin steel spike, which remained embedded. He threw the wooden handle into the flowing Charles River, taking care to watch it float silently away. There was no blood, no muss, no fuss. He let the corpse topple forward and slide down the algae-covered stones into the tea-colored water where only his dead, calloused feet protruded. Pig Man returned to the car and drove off to report to his masters.

The following Wednesday night, Sweetner heard from Eagen. "All right," Sweetner excitedly called out. "I just knew you wouldn't let me down. I've already taken the liberty of talking to my people, and they want to see you here in D.C. on Monday. Can you make it?"

Eagen interrupted him. "But I'm submitting my thesis Monday morning."

"No problem, Dave," said Sweetner. "You just take care of business early. There'll be a round-trip ticket waiting for you on the Eastern Shuttle; they leave every hour on the half hour. We'll talk, have lunch, and then I'll have you back in Boston in time for rush hour traffic. Just let me know when to expect you, and I'll meet you at Washington National...okay?"

"Okay," was Eagen's reply. They both hung up.

What passed for the trunk in his '69 B model MG was filled with a box. It held the six copies of his thesis, one for each member of the review board. The twenty-five pounds of bound paper contained the culmination of eighteen months of perspiration. Eagen balanced the box on his raised, bent knee as he dropped the trunk lid in place.

Taking the elevator to the second floor, he paused to exchange pleasantries with a few of the undergrads he knew. The door opened, and he found himself in familiar territory at the Department of Geosciences. Making his way to the secretary's office, he deposited the box on a table next to the typewriter. Ellen Morgan looked up from the bulky electronic device. Eagen could never figure out how that little metal ball with the type on it could spin around so fast. The secretary filled out a receipt for the box and offered it to him.

"Oh, Mr. Eagen," she said, "Dr. Kohl and Dr. Weiss need to see you in the cartography lab as soon as possible."

"Ah, is there anything wrong?" asked Eagen. He was wary of any last-minute screw ups, and he didn't need the grief.

"I don't know," she went on. "They didn't say anything to me about it." He waved a thanks to her, and, with an anxious step, he went down the hall and turned into the cavernous map room.

At the large table in the center of the room stood Dr. Kohl, his faculty advisor, and Dr. Weiss, the department chairman. "Ah, Mr. Eagen, come in, come in. Have a look at this, will you? And tell me what you think." On the table Kohl was pointing to lay two large-scale geological survey maps that were slightly overlapped so as to be properly aligned. They were of the central and northern Pacific Ocean showing Hawaii to the Aleutian Islands of Alaska. Eagen came up to the table and leaned over, placing his palms flat on the charts.

"Mr. Eagen, I need your opinion on this, if you would be so good," said Weiss. He continued, "Late Friday night, the Mona Loa Volcano Observatory on Hawaii started reporting new eruptions from the Eastern side of the volcano. They're finding that the lava is becoming less silic, but the flow is increasing to about two and a half meters per hour from the south rim."

Eagen asked, "What is the oxygen content like?"

Kohl replied, "Stable, but there are elevated levels of sulfur dioxide."

"Hmmmm," Eagen mused. Then he asked, "Earthquake activity?"

"Yes, they're beginning to occur approximately fifteen to thirty minutes before each new eruption," said Kohl.

Weiss asked Eagen, "What is your opinion, and what steps would

THIS DAY'S BUSINESS

you take if it were your call?" Eagen gave the problem a few moments' thought and opened with, "First, I'd alert the authorities and have them stand by for a possible evacuation of residential areas to the south and east of the park. Since it is becoming less silic, in other words, the lava is becoming thicker rather than being runny in nature. That would suggest a volcano that is getting set to blow off, an explosion instead of a fountain of molten rock." He added, "But, I'm not a vulcanologist. Have we any seismograms?"

The advisor handed the strip charts to Eagen, who set them down on the maps and studied them in silence. Taking a millimeter ruler off an adjacent table, he made several measurements of the rectangular graph paper. The squiggley lines appeared to be something that was produced by a lie detector or a heart monitor, which in fact was very close in its interpretation.

"Well, we're at magnitude 2.8 to about 3.6 earthquakes on the Richter Scale." Doing some mental arithmetic, he continued, "If I had to hazard a guess, I'd say that they were occurring approximately 60 to 75 kilometers below the surface, but I'd need more data to confirm that." Dr. Weiss glanced at his colleague and said to Eagen, "That's pretty much what we concluded as well."

"Also," Eagen added as his fingers traced a line to the upper portion of the two maps, "I'd notify any receiving stations from Juneau to Anchorage and at Kiska out on the Aleutian Islands to be ready for increased earthquake activity of small-to-moderate intensity, and to play it safe, I'd be talking to the Japanese authorities around Kobe and Tokyo to keep an ear to the ground, so to speak…for a possible tsunami." Eagen was slightly embarrassed by his unintended pun.

"Yes," said Kohl with some introspection, "that is a consideration that might seem prudent." Rolling up the charts, Weiss extended his hand to Eagen and thanked him for his input. "The committee will be reviewing your submission, Mr. Eagen, and you will be notified of their findings." Eagen took that as his exit cue; he had a plane to catch.

As expected, Sweetner was at the gate to meet him. He was clean shaven and reasonably well groomed. Seeing that this trip was a down and back affair, Eagen carried no luggage. It did not take them long to find the interagency vehicle with the light green paint. There was nothing remarkable about the Plymouth other than it looked like a fleet car and had government plates. Eagen, who had never been to Washington D.C. before, was playing the irrepressible tourist to Sweetner's consummate tour guide, and enjoying every minute of it. On the dash of the Plymouth was a white rectangular sticker that proclaimed: "The authorized use of this vehicle is for CSC personnel only."

"Okay, Bobby, what is this mysterious CSC that you work for?"

Sweetner looked at him through his dark glasses. "There's no secret. It stands for the Commission for Scientific Cooperation. It's perfectly legit. We are a quasi-independent agency of the National Science Foundation. Whereas the NSF is wholly funded by Congress, the CSC can accept grants and donations from private sources."

Eagen, needing more than that to satisfy him, asked further, "Yeah, but what does it do?"

Sweetner's answer was cogent. "We take private monies and apply for matching grants from the NSF. Then, we look around the international community for a country that needs our assistance. If they're on our approved list, we make it happen." Seeing the puzzlement on Eagen's face, he continued, "Pay attention, dim bulb, and let me connect the dots for you. For instance, Nepal is looking for a better way to reforest the slopes in their high country to protect against soil erosion. They can't afford it, but they can't afford not to. So, they come sucking around to Uncle Samuel. Am I going too fast for you?" Eagen gave him the bird. Continuing, Sweetner went on, "We pony up some money, find one of our scientists who specializes in the subject and underwrite his research. It's a sweet deal all around 'cuz the host country gets a problem solved, the researcher gets a technical paper published on the subject, and Uncle gets the goodwill. It's a win-win situation!"

"And where do you come in?" Eagen asked.

"I, and others like me, make it happen; we put the deals together. I get country 'A' together with Scientist 'B' to solve problem 'C.' Got it?"

"Got it," was the response.

The government vehicle pulled up to the red painted curb marked "Reserved." Eagen found himself in front of a row of Georgian Townhouses. Even the streetlights looked the type that burned tallow candles.

THIS DAY'S BUSINESS

Climbing the six steps to the darkly painted door, Sweetner rapped on the brass bird's head that served as the knocker. Eagen noticed the highly polished plaque that announced to all concerned that this was the Commission for Scientific Cooperation—deliveries in the rear. The Samoan houseboy answered the door in his crisply starched white mess jacket and black pants. With a light of recognition in his eyes he greeted them both. "Good day, Mr. Sweetner, and this must be Mr. Eagen."

"Good day, Tomas. I believe we are expected."

"This way, gentlemen," directed the houseboy. They both followed him into the large, cool foyer.

"I could have used my key, but I wanted to impress you," said Sweetner.

"Please wait here and I will announce you," said the Samoan. Eagen, watching the departure of the slightly built man, looked back at Sweetner.

"He's also security here. One can't be too careful in this city." The questioning look returned to Eagen's face. Sweetner gave a knowing smile and said, "Oh, this isn't where I work. This is our headquarters. My office is in a rathole on the other side of town." Eagen was slowly fitting the pieces together.

"Gentlemen," the houseboy announced, "Judge Brooks will see you now."

They were ushered into an exquisite dining room of Colonial vintage. The Judge stood to receive his two visitors.

"Your honor," said Sweetner, "may I present..."

He was cut off in mid sentence by the Judge. "Mister Eagen, how are you? Thank you ever so much for coming today. Please have a seat." Brooks motioned to the grand mahogany table that was so highly polished that Eagen had little trouble seeing his reflection on its surface. Brooks went on, saying, "And do call me Richard. I'm afraid that the title is one that has permanently stuck to me; it comes from too many years on the bench. May I call you David?" Eagen nodded in the affirmative. "Allow me to offer you both some refreshment."

Tomas appeared as if from nowhere. On the sterling silver tray, he was carrying a large decanter of Irish whiskey and three glasses. The houseboy began to pour. "Lunch will be served in fifteen minutes, your Honor," the Samoan announced.

"Very good. We're all famished, I'm sure." The Judge raised his glass of the rich amber liquid and offered a toast. "To your health, David."

"And to yours," was Eagen's reply. With that ceremony played out, the former jurist exclaimed, "To business. David, what has Bobby told you of our little operation here?"

Eagen cleared his throat and began, "Well, he mentioned a Himalayan mountaineering expedition and that you were casting about for someone who could plan and lead it."

The Judge rose from his chair and went to a side table and returned with a small stack of magazines, laying them out on the polished table before them. Somewhat embarrassed, Eagen noted that they were back issues of publications in which some of his climbs were featured or noted.

"It is because of these that we need to speak with you. But, before we go any further, I wish it be known that anything said here must be held in confidence." Eagen nodded his acknowledgement. The jurist continued, "By now, you must be aware that we give scientific and technical aid to foreign countries, specifically underdeveloped countries who could not otherwise afford our expertise. We believe we have a need for someone with your particular talents." This he said while tapping a magazine with his index finger to press home the point. "I'm sure you are as concerned as we are over the rather large number of earthquakes that have occurred of late in the northern part of Pakistan, and I'm sure that you are equally aware of the great devastation and the toll in lives these quakes have exacted." Eagen again nodded yes.

"Pakistan, I'm sure you will agree with me, is a desperately poor country with precious few resources to throw at the problem. I am reminded of the morbid joke that goes 'How does a Pakistani farmer fertilize his fields?' The answer is that he waits for an earthquake and offers the use of his land as a cemetery! Seriously though, we have put together a proposal to help them. We, with the aid of the NSF and the assistance of the Pakistani government wish to put in place seismometers, the instruments that detect earthquakes. They would be built and installed by us, they would use solar energy for power, and the findings from these instruments would automatically be

THIS DAY'S BUSINESS

transmitted by radio to their government for their use in forecasting the quakes and aiding the recovery of victims. As it stands now, sometimes weeks pass before survivors from some of the more remote villages make it out to call for help. Your job would be to oversee the setting up of these remote sites. Hence, the need for your climbing ability and your technical knowledge. Your Professor Kohl has highly rated your capabilities. We intend to start out small with one site in place, and if the need is warranted, more could be added at a later time. The United States Government and the people of Pakistan would be most grateful."

Eagen was overwhelmed by the scope of the project and his role in it. All he could say was, "You know Dr. Kohl?"

" Oh yes," the Judge answered, " he has been of enormous assistance from time to time."

Tomas arrived, announcing that lunch was ready to be served. Brooks greeted the news by rubbing his hands together in anticipation. He went on, "I realize that this would be a serious undertaking for you, and we want you to give your answer a lot of thought; but the timing will be critical. We must expect it soon. You can give your answer to Bobby as he would be your liaison with us for the project."

Eagen stammered, "What can I say? I'm humbled and honored by your choice, sir; I accept."

"Excellent," cried the Judge, "I knew it, I knew we could count on you!"

"There is only one fly in the ointment, however," said Eagen. As the platters of baked, stuffed crab with scallops in wine sauce were being placed in front of each of the three, Brooks was pouring another glass of Irish for each.

"And what could that possibly be, David?"

Eagen looked rather nervously at Sweetner and then Brooks. With a feeling of being torn in different directions, he began, "I'm supposed to be prepping for my oral exam, which is scheduled to come up in four weeks. How soon do you expect this project to begin?"

The jurist looked over to Sweetner to provide the answer. "We'll need to leave the States by Labor Day."

"Labor Day?" Eagen almost choked on his drink. "That's less than three months from now, and it will be the onset of winter at those altitudes. My PhD is of the highest importance to me, sir. Failing the oral is out of the question; I've worked too hard to lose it all now, and besides, there just isn't enough time to throw this together."

A knowing and conspiratorial smile passed between the two other men. Sweetner said, with a shit-eating grin, "You've already had it, chump, this morning, remember? Professors Weiss and Kohl were there. Weren't you?" Brooks was all smiles and Sweetner was laughing his ass off at the dumbstruck expression on Eagen's face.

"David," Brooks continued, "people think that the U.S. Government is damned near omnipotent, that all we have to do is wave a magic wand to make things happen. There is no magic wand, but we can sometimes influence the course of events, and we try very hard to reward those who work with us. You passed your oral exam because you earned it and because Dr. Kohl has worked with us before. We merely speeded up the process. As for the thesis, I would expect that it will be favorably reviewed. Again, that is all due to your own effort. By Christmas, I would expect that the name David Eagen, PhD would be a fact. Congratulations!"

CHAPTER 7

The Nuts and Bolts

Sweetner had not been kidding. Rush hour traffic from the airport through the Callahan Tunnel was miserable. Even the top down on his car and a pleasant June afternoon could not shake the bad taste left in his mouth when dealing with the daily grind. How anyone dealt with this rolling parking lot day in and day out was beyond Eagen.

A full hour and twenty minutes later, he found a space for his car within walking distance of his apartment. He was elated and relieved to know his hard work had paid off, honored and pleased that he had been chosen to undertake such a project, but at that moment, he was also tired and sweaty from the travel. All he wanted was a shower and a cold beer.

Being the only year-round resident of his building, the other tenants having moved out, he found the walk up to be quiet until he reached the landing before his apartment. The sound of furniture being moved was his first indication that something was amiss, but since he was at the door of the apartment below him, which he knew to be vacant, Eagen considered that it might be the landlady cleaning up. Another step or two brought with it the sound of breaking glass. This time he was sure. It had originated above him, from his place. The front door was slightly ajar, and the sounds of things going bump in the day grew more loudly as he approached.

A burglary in progress? he thought. He was pissed; someone was going to get his ass in a sling as a result!

Waiting at the doorjam, he paused to let his breath catch up with the adrenalin rush. There was the sound of muffled voices and footsteps treading on broken glass. With an economy of movement, he slid through the partly opened door. Taken completely off guard, the female turned with saucer-wide eyes.

"Allison." It was a statement more than a question. The look of shock was all over her face. He started to move deeper into the room as she intercepted him.

"David, David, I'm sorry, I'm so very sorry," she implored. Her arms were around him, but it was not a gesture of endearment; rather, she had him in a bear hug. She was blocking his approach all the while begging forgiveness.

"How did you get in here?" he stormed.

Stammering, she blurted out, "I still have your key. David, let's go for a drink and talk this out." She was desperately trying to turn Eagen around toward the door. He wasn't buying any of her bullshit. The bitch was running interference for someone.

From the way the place was trashed, he knew who that someone had to be. As he pushed her aside, she still clung to him, vainly attempting to slow him down. Eagen had her by the forearms, as much to deflect her long, sharp nails as it was to gain the needed leverage to toss her clear. He wasn't interested in her just yet. His eyes followed the trail of debris that was strewn about on the floor behind her. Eagen was once and for all going to settle the hash of the one responsible for all this. Heading for the door to his bedroom, he fended her off as she wildly tried to cling to him. He half turned to knuckle her in the face.

A sharp voice called out from the left of them both. "Eagen," came the hiss, "where did you come from?" The acidic words just sprayed forth from his venomous lips. If a snake could smile, Chazzi was smiling.

On the bureau by the door Eagen spotted the intruder's car keys,

THIS DAY'S BUSINESS

carelessly left no doubt when they had assumed they wouldn't be disturbed. Eagen feigned a lunge for them. Chazzi, anticipating the grab, reached for them. Eagen didn't want the keys, he wanted their owner. The serpent had been suckered. Eagen's left foot was sharply directed at the inside of Chazzi's left kneecap. It snapped with the sound of a pencil being broken in two. The knee buckled and began to cave in from the lost support. With little resistance, Eagen carried through with the kick. With his weight rolled back on his right foot, he spun around to his right, keeping his elbow in high and close. Chazzi had pitched forward just enough that Eagen's elbow impacted the serpent's jaw just ahead of and below the ear. The sickening crunch was quite like that of a styrofoam cup being crushed. The frog was pole-axed.

David bent over the crumpled form as he grabbed a fistful of hair from the back of the head; with his other he grabbed for the belt. Picking up the limp sack of shit off the floor, he used Chazzi as a battering ram against the partly opened front door. The portal bounced so hard that the resulting energy sprung it open wide and cracked the molding by the lock. With nothing to impede his progress, Chazzi was flung out the door. His momentum carried him down four or five of the washboard-like steps; his face making contact with each.

Taking several quick breaths, he returned to Allison.

She was clearly terrified beyond words. *Good*, he thought, *that's just the reaction I want. I don't want her to forget this, ever. Payback is a bitch.* She backed away from him until she was stopped by the wall behind her. Eagen approached her with doom in his eyes. He had her by the throat with his left hand but didn't squeeze, although the thought had occurred to him. He needed her alive to pass on a message. He lifted her up by the neck so that she had to stand on her tiptoes to breath. She was starting to loose control of her bladder. His face was contorted in a rage as he went eyeball to eyeball with her. Gesturing with his right thumb over his shoulder in the direction of the door, he said, "You tell him, you tell him that if I ever see him again, ever, I'll kill him where he's standing, understand?"

In her terror, she could barely nod yes. Continuing, with his right finger poking her cheek for emphasis, he said to her, "As for you, the next time I see you I'll cut out your heart and feed it to a wolf." As he flung her toward the door he sent his right foot up between the cheeks of her rounded ass. The effect lifted her a full three inches off the floor. He made a believer out of her. In minutes the adrenaline was beginning to wear off, and the resulting hangover was setting in. What were they doing here? What were they looking for?

◇◇◇

"Marcel, come, join me." The Russian patted the seat next to him on the park bench. "Relax," he continued, "we are just two old friends having a quiet chat on a beautiful day." The attaché was clearly nervous, his eyes ever darting about.

"I said sit." It was a command this time. "We've received the list of names that you passed on, and we're running through them now. Our man had better be on it…for your sake."

The meeting was bringing a bead of sweat to the Frenchman's upper lip. He fumbled for a handkerchief; all the while his eyes never once stopped moving. The Russian had no appetite for such amateurish behavior and disgustedly produced his for the man to use.

"Take it," said Solkhov; the man complied. Only after the attaché had wiped his mouth did the Russian add, "I've only used it once." With that, the now green-faced man dropped the linen cloth, and Sukhov laughed coldly. The old master enjoyed making people squirm, especially the weak ones. In parting, he added, "If there are any further developments, you will let me know. Won't you?"

The reply was, "Yes, yes at once."

"Good," the Russian came back. "Just so long as you understand me. Now get out of my sight before I become ill." Marcel lost no time in blending in with the crowd.

Sweetner's call was very upbeat. He impressed the need to get the planning off the ground. Eagen told him that he was going to need the particulars, that he was largely in the dark on a number of points. Sweetner suggested that he join him in D.C. for several days and that he, Sweetner, would make the arrangements. The plane tickets

THIS DAY'S BUSINESS

would be waiting at the airport.

Sweetner was there to meet him at Washington National just like the last time. This time the talk on the way to the Georgetown house was of adventures yet to come. At a light, while waiting for traffic, Sweetner matter-of-factly said, "I've got some information on your friend, Chazzi." Eagen shot a glance at him. Sweetner was looking for some type of reaction. "I've done some checking. You know, a call here, a whisper there. It seems that our boy is some sort of honcho with the SDS, the Students for a Democratic Society, a nasty bunch of creeps." Eagen was only interested in the word "is," as in, "he is still alive." For a short while he had feared that he might have killed Chazzi.

For several days afterward, Eagen had scoured the Boston papers to see whether a body, a badly beaten body, had turned up. Nothing.

With the light turning green, the government car continued its journey. Sweetner continued, "The report I got said that…" He paused for a moment, pulling a slip of paper from his shirt pocket and referring to it. "…That when he was brought to the emergency room by some friends, he said that he had slipped on a bar of soap while in the shower." Sweetner gave Eagen a shit-eating grin and said, "Accidents will happen."

"You know," Eagen countered, "a man can't be too careful these days."

"Fer sure," said Sweetner in his best valley talk. "I gather that his jaw was broken in six places and will be wired shut for several months. There's more: they had to pin his kneecap together. I don't suppose that he'll be doing the Watusi anytime soon."

Well, nice things happen to nice people, after all, noted Eagan. He noticed that Sweetner made no mention of Allison.

Sweetner used his key this time; it was more expedient and far less pretentious. Tomas was inside awaiting them both. As before, he had them wait while they were announced to the Judge. They were shown into the library this time, and His Honor entered right behind them with a number of large maps in a travel tube under his arm. A moment later, Tomas came in, wrestling with an oversized easel. Brooks motioned Eagen to have a seat, and they exchanged pleasantries.

In contrast to their last meeting, the Judge was in a business mood.

Sweetner pulled up a high-backed chair with his arms resting on the back and his legs straddling the seat. Tomas worked the room efficiently and silently, appearing this time from a side room with a large tray of sandwiches followed by a steaming pot of coffee. This was to be a working lunch.

The "few days" became ten, and then Eagen stopped counting. At the Judge's insistence, he moved in to the Commission's townhouse in one of the better neighborhoods. The fact occurred to Eagen one fine day that things were definitely looking up! He was living rent free at a nice address, and had great food and someone else to cook it. All he had to do was to plan and execute a mountaineering expedition to a place he'd never been and with people he'd never climbed with, much less met, and then return to tell about it.

From experience, Eagen knew that climbs of this magnitude usually required nine months to a year of careful, methodical planning. He had two. Even his own small climb in Alaska had required four months from inception to fruition.

The author of a short article at the time wrote of his last trip and offered the possibility of hasty planning as the cause for the team's failure to climb the west ridge of Mt. Hunter. Eagen was sensitive about that, but he had little control over the timing of the trip. The seismometers had to be in place before the onset of winter in the Himalayas, which could be as early as October. Conditions would then be impossible, and their next opportunity would not come until the middle of the following April when the jet stream and the soul-stealing cold released its grip.

One could expect a brief window of fair weather before the monsoons arrived, but that would be mid July. Too late, way too late. The Judge was emphatic on that point.

"The Government of Pakistan is most anxious to set up this network of monitors," he told Eagen at several points in their discussion.

With considerable foresight, or perhaps it was insight born of the frantic weeks that he knew lay ahead, Eagen had packed a few extra things and remembered to bring a briefcase jammed with every piece of paper from every trip that he had ever planned. This was the starting point for the planning. Every trip was unique but there were constants. Some of these topics included the weather, the route, food,

THIS DAY'S BUSINESS

tents, clothing, and so forth. One could easily come up with half a dozen others. These and many more were questions that were yet to be addressed and resolved. Half of any expedition was in the planning. The remainder was just getting there and doing the climbing. Late in the day of his first day back in Washington, Brooks laid out the whole project for Eagen.

It had been decided by the Pakistani government scientists that the seismometers should be placed somewhere along the Karakoram Range of the Himalayan Mountains. After much deliberation and consideration by leading experts, it was agreed that the exact placement be at or near the summit of the mountain known as Gasherbrum IV. The name and Roman numeral was a taxonomy, a means of identification. It meant that this mountain was the fourth highest in the Gasherbrum group of mountains, which is a subset of the Karakoram Range of the Himalayan Mountains.

The maps were of World War II vintage but were useful nonetheless. Eagen knew, overall, that the general appearance of land features could be expected to remain nearly the same even after thirty years, whereas other features were more transitory. For instance, the fifty-ton boulder nestled in a stream bed might not be there after the next spring snow melt flooded the streams and washed away all before it. On the other hand, the valley depicted on the old maps could be expected to remain until erosion wore it down or some other cataclysmic event occurred to destroy it. What the maps could not tell was the current elevation of the snow line or at what height the glaciers, those frozen rivers of ice, began. More up-to-date information was needed.

Tomas brought out the easels with the photo enlargements on each one. They were black-and-white glossies, at least three feet on a side. The first was a grainy and slightly out of focus shot of Gasherbrum IV. It was actually a copy of a print that had been taken by Walter Bonati on the first successful ascent of the peak in 1958. It was only of use for planning in the general sense.

The other two were completely dissimilar and taken from a slightly different perspective. They were sharp in focus and of high contrast, which lent depth and dimension to the land forms. They were clearly aerial photos taken from a very great height. This enabled an accurate assessment of the conditions along the line of march for the expedition, and more importantly, this would aid in planning a route up the mountain and a suitable location for the installation of the seismometers. Although nothing was said up to this point, Eagen took it as a given that a shot at a second ascent of the world's twenty-first highest mountain would be a bonus.

Brooks took notice of the fact that Eagen was intensely studying the aerial photos with a magnifying glass. With a touch of pride in his voice, he said, "Beautiful, aren't they? They're from an SR-71 Blackbird spy plane. I find them to be quite remarkable." Eagen nodded in awe. He continued, "To answer your next question, I'm told that they were taken from an altitude of well over one hundred thousand feet, and that information stays in this room. Understand?" Eagen clearly acknowledged the sensitivity of the information. "Excellent, very good," said Brooks. "Now, to a thorny issue."

Eagen still had his face in the magnifying glass, studying the black and whites as the Judge dropped the bombshell. He looked uneasy but sounded resolute as he spoke. "On the issue of team members, I realize that you would prefer to have your own people on hand, people whom you've climbed with in the past and that you trust. However, there just isn't the luxury of time in this affair, I'm afraid. We've chosen a group of our people who, although not as experienced or accomplished as you, are none the less skilled and competent in their own right." Eagen started to interject when Brooks held up his hand to stop the interruption. "David, please. This one is not negotiable."

The jurist crossed the room and took up a chair alongside Eagen. The act was symbolic of a doting father imparting wisdom to a beloved son. "David, this project is most vital and of great interest in high places just up the street." His right index finger was pointing over his left shoulder in the general direction of Capital Hill. No names were forthcoming. "By your successful completion of this project, which, incidentally, has been named 'Aurora,' you will make this part of the world a safer place. I'm not talking political instability here, although there's more than enough to go around. The American people are short of friends in this part of the world, and as you are no doubt aware, our image is somewhat…tarnished. This project will go a long way in restoring some of the shine and goodwill with our ally. The whole of the region is a powder keg and there are any number of

THIS DAY'S BUSINESS

interested parties with lots of matches. Anything that can be done to alleviate suffering must be done."

The Judge's argument was positively compelling, and his points were well made. Eagen conceded that it was their ballgame, and they, the American people, were paying the freight and therefore calling the shots.

"Now," continued Brooks as he opened the portfolio that lay before them on the coffee table. "here is your team." The three 8 by 11 glossy photos came out of the folder first followed by a brief biographical history of each man. "You'll be meeting these characters this afternoon," said Brooks as Eagen picked up the first file. "They are now or have been at one time instructors at the Army's Mountain Warfare School; they know their business."

Scanning the background sheets, Eagen silently half read off the data.

Cloutier, Maurice, "Mo," SSgt, U.S. Army
Born: Oct 17, 1951, Coventry, VT.
Instructor, Mountain Warfare School
Communications Specialist, Weapons Specialist

Packard, Lawrence, SSgt, U.S. Army
Born: Dec 27, 1950, Ft. Lewis, Washington
Former Instructor, Mountain Warfare School
Survival Instructor, Medical Specialist

Baxter, Timothy, SSgt, U.S. Army
Born: April 3, 1951
Instructor, Mountain Warfare School
Intelligence Specialist, Engineering Specialist

Among the three photos there were few differences. The ages, the experience, and other biographicals were all similar. Of course, the faces were the single most distinguishing characteristics between them. There was, however, something different about Baxter' s picture. Had they met? Had Eagen somehow seen Baxter's somewhere before? No, that wasn't it. There was something different about Baxter. He could not reconcile what was out of place. Eagen dropped the file on the table as Tomas entered and whispered in Brook's left ear.

"Ah, good. Show them all in." Turning to Eagen, Brooks said, "We have a Mr. Avooram joining us today. He's from the Interior Ministry of the Pakistani Government. Mr. Avooram will be our liaison here before we leave, and then someone else will pick up the ball when you get over there. Also, if I am not mistaken, that rowdiness you hear in the hall should be your team. A word of warning: They may seem like average fun-loving college kids, but each one is totally dedicated to his craft. If you lead them as I know you can, they'll be with you every inch of the way."

Mr. Avooram entered first, and the Judge gave him the same warm greeting that he had given Eagen. Brooks showed the representative of the Interior Ministry to a comfortable seat at the large mahogany table. Introductions were made with Eagen. Next came the team. First came Packard, then Cloutier, followed by Baxter. Again, the rituals of greeting were observed. It was at this point that Sweetner joined the meeting. He had been out and about on his own business for most of the day.

It was a typical hot and very humid day in Washington, and the room where the seven men were meeting was a study in contrast. The blinds were drawn, and the air conditioning beat out its low-frequency hum in a valiant effort to keep pace with the elements outside.

Brooks opened the meeting by giving Mr. Avooram the floor. Avooram, 37, was of average height for a South Asian. His dark eyes and complexion showed that he enjoyed the climate. It was very much like his own in Karachi.

"Good day, gentlemen," he began as his eyes swept the room. "Judge Brooks has informed me that this is the first opportunity everyone has been together, so I'll be as brief as possible." Eagen noted that his English was as impeccable as his tailoring. Mr. Avooram must have been brought up there in the States—schooled there at least.

The Pakistani official went on. "I need you to know that my government takes very seriously its responsibilities regarding the welfare of its citizens. It is, I suppose, the will of Allah that one of the newest and poorest of countries in the world should be visited from

THIS DAY'S BUSINESS

time to time with such misery. As you are no doubt aware, each year we lose approximately five hundred people. All too often, we lose many tens of thousands to these earthquakes. It is indeed unfortunate that my beautiful homeland is located atop one of the world's great unstable regions, both from a geological point as well as political point of view. This scientific equipment that you will be installing is, I am told, to be placed very high on the mountain." Avooram pointed to the large panoramic photograph as he continued. "This will entail great risk to yourselves, risks that we are not technically capable of assuming ourselves. We can, however, assist you in every way possible. We will open all the doors that need opening to speed you along the way." Here, he paused for a few seconds and then continued. "As you might have heard, our bureaucratic system of government can present a formidable challenge if one wishes to accomplish anything in a timely manner. You will have the assistance of an experienced army officer while you are in my country. This officer will be the official representative. I must say, with all candor, that the region you are about to enter is a very volatile one. It is an area where the boundaries are being disputed by at least three countries and possibly a fourth. For the moment, the world court rulings have favored Pakistan, but we are not optimistic about the future. We are less than a decade away from our last war, and there are many old scores left unsettled. The whole of the region is a potential flash point. This is why we severely limit access to the area. When we must, we have someone from the military acting as an advisor. We are trying to prevent any accidents or misunderstandings that might escalate into an armed conflict, no matter how brief. Now, as a small token of my government's appreciation for your assistance, I want to present each of you with this Rolex watch. I am told that they are the finest chronometers available."

With that said, he produced five of the precision timepieces from his briefcase and presented them to each of the team. Now they were truly a team. "I'm passing out my card to each of you so that if you have any questions or require any assistance you are to call me at this number. If I'm not there, someone will know where to reach me. Before I leave, is there anything that I can do for you? Questions anyone?"

Packard raised his hand. "Sir, Pakistan is a Moslem country, is it not?"

"Yes, it is," came the reply.

Once again Packard asked a question. "I'm told that one can't have any alcohol there; is that so?"

The Ministry civil servant thought for a moment, his brows furrowed in thought. With his right index finger he pointed so as to underscore the exclamation. "Ah, yes. There is a provision in the law that allows for nonbelievers to possess and consume alcohol. There is a simple form to fill out, which you present with your passport at the time of entry. I'll have the forms sent here, and we will process them. As long as it is for your own consumption, there is no problem. Anything else? No? Very well, I must be off. Once again, feel free to contact me at any time."

The Judge was the first to speak. "Thank you, Mr. Avooram, thank you for coming." With that, the Pakistani departed the room with Tomas escorting him to the door.

"Well," the Judge continued, "I guess it's official. You're a team. I realize that this is a sudden introduction, but time is of the essence, so I'll turn the meeting over to David."

Eagen remained seated as he began to speak. "I want to welcome you all on this climb. Unfortunately, we haven't had the opportunity to climb together before…" He stopped in mid sentence and slapped his hand down on the table, and said loudly, "That's it. Curly…Curly." The others in the room looked at Eagen as if he had snapped. To each one of his new teammates, he pointed. "It was the hair that threw me off," he said as he pointed back to Baxter. "Moe, Larry…and Curly."

It would appear from a short distance away that Tim Baxter, in addition to being heavier than the other two, appeared bald as a cue ball! In fact, his head wasn't shaven but was very closely cropped, and his deep suntan gave the appearance of being bald. The laughter around the table was loud. From that moment on, Tim Baxter was referred to as "Curly."

Eagen knew that it was time to get down to business. "Your Honor, the first thing that we're going to need is a secretary. There are too many odds and ends that need attention, and I'm a big believer in checklists. That way, very little gets overlooked or forgotten."

"Done," said Brooks. "We'll have one in here in the morning."

THIS DAY'S BUSINESS

"Second, we'll need a place for headquarters, somewhere to take delivery and to store gear."

Brooks began, "Why don't you just do it all here? There's a large, empty cellar below us, and there's room for all of you to stay here. What do you say?"

Looking at his new team nodding their heads in approval, he said, "That'll be great, sir. It seems the logical choice. Okay, here are your assignments. I've tried to align our needs with your experience. There will be daily meetings to iron things out and to keep track of our progress. We'll need a working plan in less than ten days, because in seven weeks, we leave. Moe, I need you to plan our radio needs and to tackle the oxygen situation. Although Gasherbrum IV, at 26,000 feet, isn't as high as Everest or K2, we will need to install the scientific package at or higher than 24,000 feet, and that is going to be hard work. We can slowly adapt to climbing without oxygen, but I feel that we should sleep with it to maintain our strength and to maintain an appetite. Larry, you'll be our doctor. Your hands will be full with that assignment because not only will you have our health to deal with, but that of the entire expedition, porters and Sherpas included. So, prepare accordingly. You'll need to prepare a list for a medical kit with those criteria in mind. Curly, I hope that we won't need your intelligence..." (This brought waves of laughter from Moe, Larry, and Sweetner) "...I mean your background," said Eagen wryly. "It's your engineering skills that I'll need. Ladders will need to be rigged to cross any open crevasses and fixed roped must be in place on the steep sections to help us carry heavy loads. Also, you lucky devil, you will have the food detail. Taking into account our nutritional requirements as well as our likes and dislikes will be a formidable task. I suggest that you start with a questionnaire to poll everyone involved.

"Sweets, I didn't forget about you, old buddy." The sarcasm was dripping from Eagen's tongue. "You'll have the treasury and be responsible for paying the bills and keeping the books. You and Curly will be the pay masters for the porters; good luck on that one. Tomorrow, the work begins. I'll have lists drawn up for each of you as soon as the secretary gets on line. These are based on my last two expeditions, so they'll save you a lot of time and aggravation. I'll be taking over the procurement of equipment. Speaking of which, if you have any preferences or recommendations, feel free to let me know. If we encounter any roadblocks, and we will, we'll work them out together. Questions?"

Once again it was Packard with the hand up. "Yes, I have one: Do we get Wild Turkey for this trip or just the local stuff they sell to the tourists?" Larry elbowed Moe, who thought the whole thing was ridiculous.

The Judge interjected at this point by saying, "I think that we can find room on the list for a case of Wild Turkey." Packard looked with pleading eyes at Brooks. "All right, two cases." Larry's victory was well received by all.

Eagen cut in, "Well, we probably won't die of thirst." This kept the tempo of the meeting upbeat.

Sweetner, who had not spoken much since his arrival, said suddenly, "I'm hungry. Let's go out for dinner and a few pops." A unanimous vote was taken, and the meeting came to a close.

With the addition of Mrs. Hanson, the team secretary, the day-to-day planning of the trip was taking shape. Her twenty-two years of making sense from chaos for several succeeding administrations was pivotal in making progress. Without her herculean efforts, the team would never have gotten off the ground.

Everyone eventually settled into a routine. Mornings were for assembling a game plan; the afternoons were for brainstorming the needs and wants of the team. Two sticking points kept cropping up. The first involved the amount of oxygen needed. The original estimate of one bottle per climber per day was changed to two per day and was eventually revised upward to three when the high altitude porters were factored in. The various manufacturers were contacted and their specifications noted. In the end, an American company was selected over the Italian and French ones. Although previous expeditions had successfully used the French designed bottles, the valves and regulators were not compatible with the American designed A-14 mask, which was deemed superior by virtue of its flexibility and fit. In very low temperatures, the condensation formed as a result of heavy breathing during physical exertion caused other less flexible masks to become clogged with ice buildup. Often, the flow of life-giving oxygen would be interrupted by ice, and the stiff mask could not provide a proper seal against the face, thus wasting a precious commodity. Although the American oxygen bottles were slightly heavier, they were more robust and reliable. Further, they were available.

Food. Now there was a sticky wicket. Mutinies have started because of food; people have resorted to cannibalism from the lack of it. That was always the trickiest part of the planning. Eagen had heard of one ill-fated trip that had ended prematurely in its attempt to climb a peak. In fact, the way Eagen had heard the story was that the team never got to Base Camp before failure struck. It seems that the clown who had overseen the menu was a strict vegetarian and health food fanatic. Needless to say, the menu reflected his choices, and the screw up was not detected until it was too late.

To safeguard against such a calamity, a series of seven menus was drawn up. The master menu reflected the needs of those at Base Camp and at the higher camps. It was decided that at Base Camp there would be at least one cook and a helper on duty. Large Coleman stoves of a type similar to those used for family camping would be employed in addition to the main stove that was fueled by liquid propane. Since there would be more people at basecamp at any one time than at the ones higher up, there would be more luxuries. However, luxury was a relative term. It meant that there would be lightweight camping tables and chairs and a few gas lamps in the big community tent, a decadence unheard of higher up the mountain.

The final lists were drawn up in just seven days because of the long hours put in by everyone. On July second, a meeting was held with all members present. It was here that Eagen laid out his final plan to the Judge.

Reuters, in their afternoon dispatch from New Delhi, noted the passing of well-known adventurer and mountain climber Chandler Moss. Moss, 41, heir to the vast Moss fortune, was discovered murdered in his tent along with two native guides. Robbery appeared to be the motive for the slayings, which district police said were committed several days ago. No further details were forthcoming.

The July third edition of the Manchester Guardian reported that popular rock climber and noted author Terry Bisset of the Lakes District died of injuries sustained in a climbing accident. Mr. Bisset, 29, made numerous and daring ascents in Chamonix, France, over the past four years. He was planning an expedition to the Peruvian Andes in November according to his family. Mr. Bisset suffered a broken neck while climbing alone on cliffs that he had known since he had been a youngster. There were no witnesses to the accident, which was reported to the Lakes District Constabulary. A Wednesday funeral was planned.

Everyone, including Judge Brooks, was present for the meeting. A plan had been formulated, and parts of it were implemented already. Now the hard work was to begin. Supplies and equipment had to be acquired, sorted, and repackaged. The final phase would begin with everything being shipped out in advance so as to arrive on time in Karachi, Pakistan.

"Okay," began Eagen. "In no particular order, let me give you the plan." This he directed to everyone, but his briefing was mostly for the benefit of the Judge. All five of the team members were in such close contact with each other on a daily basis that everyone was in the loop. Eagen went on. "Each of you has the latest maps of the region, which are guaranteed to have been outdated twenty years ago. Because of the urgency of the situation, we'll be ready to depart on Tuesday, September sixth, the day after Labor Day. The gear must go out air freight no later than August fifteenth so as to arrive and clear customs. Although I don't anticipate any problems there, we can't take anything for granted when dealing with third-world red tape. We'll depart Dulles on the sixth on TWA and lay over in London. The following day we'll leave for Karachi by way of Athens and, I might add, return the same way. Once in Karachi, we'll need three or four days to clear customs and acquire all permits. Also, this is where we'll pick up the bulk of our locally purchased food and equipment for the porters. From Karachi we then fly to Rawalpini where we meet our sirdar or head porter and the military liaison. We'll send out the word that an expedition is hiring porters.

"This brings me to the makeup of the expedition itself. We are

THIS DAY'S BUSINESS

planning on five climbers or sahibs, one hundred and forty porters, ten of which will be selected for high altitude, one sirdar, one liaison officer, one Base Camp manager." Eagen looked up from his notes at Brooks, saying, "We still have to resolve that issue." Brooks, for his part, was taking notes on his copy of the checklist and nodded at the mention of someone to run Base Camp.

Without looking up from his writing, Brooks interjected, "I have someone in mind for that."

Going on, Eagen said, "Add to the list two cooks." Eagan shuffled through some papers to find the next topic.

"Under the heading of oxygen, Moe has calculated that we'll need one hundred bottles. If we are conservative in our use then there will be just enough for those in the lead to use for climbing and everyone above twenty thousand feet to sleep with."

"Incidentally," Moe cut in, "we have an appointment at Andrews Air Force Base next Tuesday to be fitted for oxygen masks and have a session in the altitude chamber."

Eagen went on, "Food. For planning purposes, I'm counting on ten sahib's for forty-five days. I'd rather have too much than not enough because there's no way to really gauge our appetites. The tendency is to lose it the higher one goes while some can eat til they bust. By the way, Sweets, there'll be no ham and lima beans allowed on this trip."

This brought a smile to Sweetner's lips. Both he and Eagen had not-so-fond memories of the C-ration delight that would gag a maggot.

Continuing, Eagen went on. "The sooner we buy the food in bulk, the sooner we can package it up. That can be time consuming. This brings me to finances. This is where the rubber meets the road, as they say. We'll need a checking account for purchases here and one in Pakistan to pay the porters." Once more, the Judge jotted a note to himself. "There are just two more items for now. Let's see here," Eagen mused as he consulted his notes and lists. "Radios. We will need one at each of the four camps and one with the lead climbers. This is in addition to the Base Camp radio that must be of at least twelve watts power so as to reach all camps if possible. There should be at base a shortwave radio capable of reaching the U.S. mission in Rawalpindi."

Putting his pen down, the Judge said, "The Pakistanis informed

87

me yesterday that they'll supply the high frequency radio, but it must remain under their control for security reasons."

Curly leaned over the table to Moe, and in a stage whisper, said, "Paranoid buggers, aren't they? What do they think we're going to do? Order up some hookers and then stiff them for the bill?" That sent the meeting off on a tangent of laughter.

At that point, Mrs. Hanson entered the room with a very worried look on her face. She handed a slip of paper to the Judge who read it, and in turn handed it to Eagen. The team leader dropped into his chair with disbelief in his eyes.

Paraphrasing the note, he said, "The company supplying us with the oxygen was hit with a devastating fire of suspicious origin. As you know, oxygen burns extremely hot, and the building where our bottles were being stored prior to shipping was totally consumed. The good news is that we only lost one third of our order." The news was crushing to all in the room.

The Judge excused himself from the meeting, saying that he was going to contact a second source supplier for the government. At this point, Tomas wheeled in a cart with a steaming pot of coffee and a platter of freshly baked tollhouse cookies. Gathering his thoughts, Eagen continued, "As far as equipment is concerned, make a list of what personal gear you have and what you need. I've been in contact with an old climbing buddy who now manages a mountaineering supply cooperative in Seattle. I gave him a brief rundown of our requirements, and he assures me that if they don't have it, we don't need it. We'll need to be out there to be fitted properly." Christmas in July, thought the stooges! Picking up where he left off, he said, "Since you four appear to have so much energy lately I thought that you should do some climbing while you're out there. Since Sweetner has never climbed before, we'll be enrolling him in a mountaineering school at the same time."

The thought of the self-confident Sweetner dangling at the end of a rope over a precipice was more than the stooges could bear. With his image and dignity in shreds, Sweetner rendered his teammates the good luck salute. Although the ribbing was in fun, inwardly Sweetner wondered just how he would react to the dangers ahead.

The Judge returned and poured himself a cup from the steaming pot. "Good news," he said. "We have another source for the oxygen,

THIS DAY'S BUSINESS

but it's going to be tight on the delivery. On a different note, David, while your merry little band is off on holiday climbing, you'll need to be in Pasadena, California, at the Jet Propulsion Laboratory to be checked out on the scientific package. NASA has come up with a design, which they've been successfully using on the moon, and the word from the Apollo guys is that they're easy to install and set up. The engineers at JPL have assured me that with some slight modifications the package should be ideally suited for our needs."

Although Eagen was looking forward to some climbing with the guys on Mt. Rainier, he knew that there would be plenty of climbing ahead in the days to come. Besides, he thought, the idea of getting his hands on a state of the art scientific grade instrument, which was designed for use on the moon, was too much for him to pass up. Eagen reminded everyone that there would be only two weeks left to assemble all the gear when they returned to Washington. Time was getting very short, and there was much work yet to be done. Every nut and bolt had to be accounted for and dealt with because it all had to go out the door on August fifteenth. Eagen, for his part, was filled with worry. He knew that it was a long way from Georgetown to the Baltaro Glacier, and the way was strewn with pitfalls. The butterflies in his gut were having a dogfight now, but they too would vanish once he set foot on the mountain.

CHAPTER 8

Rawalpindi

The oxygen arrived, finally. In fact, the second source shipment arrived before the main order. However, it was not until the morning of August fifteenth that the original load appeared, double parked in front of the townhouse. There was a shared feeling of anxiety among the team as the delicate cylinders were unloaded. Without the precious gas, the odds of completing the objective would grow quite remote.

The climbing gear had arrived several days earlier than expected. It was a surprise to all when yet another truck pulled up. The cellar floor was covered with boxes, canned goods, and sealed bags. Every household utensil imaginable was on the floor somewhere. It was so crowded that aisles were formed, stretching from the old boiler to the rickety back stairs. That was when the main floor, including the Judge's office, became the new warehouse. It gave everyone a chance to unpack it, sort it all out, and then assign it a box with a color-coded number.

THIS DAY'S BUSINESS

The food was all purchased locally at several grocery wholesaler warehouses. The easy part was the buying. That was just leg work, tracking it all down. The hard part came when it was time to repackage it. It was determined that all of the perishables would be purchased in Pakistan from local vendors. The remainder would consist of canned goods, freeze-dried items like noodles, and various sundries.

No matter what it was, if it were to be carried on the back of a porter, it had to be re-packed in a rectangular container that weighed no more than sixty pounds.

The General Services Administration was able to put the team in contact with a supplier who could provide containers that were made of heavy-duty, wax-impregnated, corrugated cardboard. Each box was color coded and numbered in a scheme according to where it was destined and what it contained. A green label meant that the contents were to be used on the approach march to the mountain. Yellow showed those items that were bound for Base Camp, and red was for anything above Base Camp.

Because of the last-minute delivery of the oxygen, only a random sample of the bottles was made to verify that each held a full charge. As it happened, Railway Express had to wait several hours until the last cylinders were palleted and loaded onto the truck. At four-thirty in the afternoon, the padlock was on the door of the semi tractor trailer. For better or worse, the first leg of a very long and perilous journey had begun.

The next phase of training was about to begin. Sweetner and the stooges were off on an all-expense-paid climbing holiday, while Eagen flew out the same day for Los Angeles and the Jet Propulsion Laboratory in Pasadena. All were to return to Washington just five days before their departure date, thus leaving the Judge alone to think his dark thoughts.

The trip to Pasadena went without incident. Eagen secured a room at the Holiday Inn a short distance from the famed campus that orchestrated the Apollo moon landings. He had to pass through no less than three security checkpoints on the modern campus, each one leading him deeper into the bowels of the cavernous building where the future of space travel was being designed.

Once inside his destination, two armed guards escorted Eagen from the first station where he was identified and issued a security badge to the third, and finally to the laboratory at the end of a very long hall. There was but one door in the full length of the long corridor. No offices, no pictures on the wall, no water cooler, just the single glass security door with the coded, push-button electronic lock. The guards, whose demeanor suggested that they were serious professionals, neither spoke nor exhibited any sign of congeniality. Their function was to limit or deny access to anyone who did not belong. This ritual occurred twice a day for Eagen, once when he arrived in the morning and again when he departed in the late afternoon. It was an occurrence to which one just had to adapt.

It was in the lab that he met the scientific team who designed and built the seismometers that were flown to the moon and installed by the Apollo astronauts. The scientists led him into an airlock that resembled a street-level revolving door to an office building. As the glass-walled chamber began to pressurize slightly, it revolved and opened into another room where several others were preparing for their workday.

Eagen was handed a sterile gown, mask, booties, and dark goggles. With the exception of the goggles, all were to be worn in the clean room where the seismometers were assembled. The elaborate precautions taken were necessary for two reasons. Dirt and dust and other environmental contaminates could destroy the delicate microelectronic circuitry of the equipment, and secondly, there was the possible contamination of other worlds to consider.

Since these instruments were destined, at some point in time, for the moon and beyond, NASA did not want any contaminates from Earth, be they biological or otherwise, to take hold elsewhere. So, the over-pressurization of the airlock was to keep dust out, and the dark goggles were to be worn while the small chamber was scanned with a burst of ultraviolet radiation to kill off any bio contaminants. The clean room was actually four hundred times more sterile than any surgical suite.

The delicate instruments were in various stages of assembly being readied for deployment on future missions to the lunar surface. Of the six that were in specially designed foam cradles along the back wall, it was only the last two that were complete. It was these two that Eagen would train on and take with him to the mountains.

THIS DAY'S BUSINESS

The scientific team welcomed Eagen as one of their own. They were ranging in age from twenty-four to thirty-five, and most of the seven had recently been plucked from the ranks of academia and given the keys to the biggest toy chest in the kingdom. These young and very bright people were given a task to design equipment that would withstand the vacuous and bleak conditions of space, and register and record moonquakes.

In his work in the lab, Eagen learned about the care and feeding of the instrument. The engineering team was quite possessive about their equipment. In their good-natured way, they let Eagen know that these seismometers were still their instruments and that Eagen would only be the guy who installed them. Obviously, they were very proud of their creations.

In the course of the week, Eagen learned that the team would be installing not one but two of the instruments, the second acting as a backup should the first fail for whatever reason. He learned the assembly and test procedures necessary to ensure a functioning instrument. The two scientific packages, when crated, would be three feet long, about the size of a large duffel bag, and each would be housed in a thick, dark grey, aluminum, casket-like case that weighed a shade over sixty-five pounds. They were designed to be carried in a sling by two men or by the straps for a single-man carry. Upon assembly, each instrument package was hermetically sealed to repel moisture and dust. They were to be opened only at the time and place of installation. Both packages were to be flown out to Pakistan via military aircraft and delivered to the residence of the American ambassador in Pakistan for safekeeping until they were released into Eagen's custody.

Just before signing out for the last time, Eagen attended the mandatory security debriefing. A senior civilian manager for the whole instrument lab pointed out that the electronics involved were of such sophistication that there might be unscrupulous parties that would seek to profit by their possession. In other words, they were delicate and valuable. Thus, it was easier and safer to transport them on the normal military courier flight.

As he was about to leave the building, one of the junior scientists, a recent Stanford graduate, pulled Eagen aside and asked disturbing questions. He wanted to know why NASA was willing to part with the two seismometers that were scheduled to fly on the next Apollo mission.

"Didn't you know that the replacements would not be ready in time for the launch schedule? Didn't you know that the delay would cost quite a few million of their research dollars? What is so important about 'Project Aurora' anyway that it couldn't wait until other packages were ready?"

Eagen could feel the guy's frustration. Eagen knew that he wouldn't like one of his experiments thrown off for someone else's benefit. It bothered him that there was no explanation that could placate the dedicated scientist. Any complaints would have to be taken up with a higher authority because this decision had been made at the State Department level or higher.

The last few days before departure were spent in a frenzy of last-minute packing of personal gear. The big items were safely on their way to Karachi. It was the first time in weeks that anyone relaxed, except, that is, the Judge. The outward appearance of tranquility was a façade; he was the type that sweated the details. That was a comforting feeling to Eagen. He was glad to have someone backstopping him on the big decisions. There were just too many details for any one man to keep track of. In a week, he would already be chin deep in whatever adventure lay ahead, and that was not the time to discover an oversight or suffer a miscalculation. All the planning had to be done right.

He caught himself staring out the windows overlooking the street. His musing took him back to the days of agony in grammar school at the end of the year. After the last test had been finished, he had had to wait for the nuns to mail the report cards home. Would he pass onto the next grade or be doomed to spend time in the purgatory of summer school thereby screwing up the entire vacation?

The next day was the big day; however, that night the Judge and the entire team enjoyed an early Sunday dinner of roast turkey with all the trimmings. Tomas had slaved over his stove since early morning to prepare the feast. During the dinner, the Judge announced that the airlines had called earlier. The original plan had been to lay over one night in London until the following morning; this was due to the lack of seats on the connecting flight to Karachi. As it happened, a small tour group of Muslim clerics had canceled at the

THIS DAY'S BUSINESS

last moment. The agent mumbled something in passing about an incident of food poisoning at their hotel in London. The team could save eight or ten hours by taking the earlier British European Airways flight out of London. As a bonus, the reservations were for first-class seating. Eagen insisted. He had already traveled down that path before and knew that the extra comfort provided up front was well worth the expense on a long trip.

He had not expected anything of the sort. None of them had. There was nothing secretive about the project but little was said about it outside the team, several friends and climbers from BU's Alpine Club, and a few relatives of the stooges. Mountaineering had yet to succumb to the disease of commercialism. A mountain, any mountain, was climbed for the experience, the purification of the soul, and, as George Leigh Mallory had put it forty years earlier, "Because it's there." Since the project was already funded, no one had to go out and raise financing. This meant that few people, even among the climbing community, were aware of its existence. Therefore, it came as a pleasant surprise to the team that a small crowd of about fifteen well-wishers appeared at the departure gate to see them off. Everyone, even Brooks, posed with the team for the obligatory family photo album shots. The moment had arrived.

London was a breeze. The State Department had greased the wheels with Her Majesty's customs service, and the team was escorted into a V.I.P. lounge while their check-in luggage was transferred from TWA to BEA.

The lounge was too dark and quiet at this empty hour of the morning. Sweetner and Larry broke free from the gloomy decor and made their way next door to the bar where the two proceeded to devour Bloody Marys. The rest of the group found the overstuffed couches and stretched out. Within two hours, they were on the second leg of the journey. Next stop, Athens.

They would be in the air for two hours and fifteen minutes with a short turn around; Karachi lay 2,967 miles and four-and-a-half hours to the east.

Somewhere over the Mediterranean Sea, someone was getting restless. Eagen, who had the row to himself, heard low, muffled laughter coming from the stooges, two of whom were seated directly behind him. Turning around in his seat, Eagen peered back at Moe and Curly. It was easy to see who the conspirators were. But, of what were they guilty? A glance over at Sweetner on the right side of the cabin showed him holding his finger up to his lips, thus telling Eagen to shut up and watch what was to unfold.

It seemed that earlier in the flight, the lads had been trying to score points with the stewardesses in first class. They had learned that one of them was very new to the job. The boys were ready for some sophomoric fun. Curly was watching the flight attendants in the back. When he saw that the new girl was near the annunciator panel, he signaled to Moe who, with a big grin, winked at Eagen and reached up and pressed the button to summon the flight attendant. Curly, who had the window seat, began to feign airsickness.

As the new stewardess arrived, Moe played the role of the compassionate friend. In his best stage whisper he said, "My friend here appears to have a queasy stomach. Is there anything you can give him?"

The stewardess reached up into the overhead compartment and retrieved two barf bags, which she then handed to the ailing Curly, who appeared to be quite distressed at that point. She informed Curly that she would return in a few minutes to retrieve the bags. As she turned to depart the cabin, Sweetner struck up a conversation with her. This was a ruse to keep the young flight attendant in close proximity to Curly's sound effects. The ringmaster made the appropriate noises into the bag for everyone's benefit. Unbeknownst to anyone, hours earlier he had opened a can of beef stew and poured the contents into a plastic baggie and kept it in his inside breast pocket. As he bent over, supposedly blowing lunch, he placed the baggie in the sick sack.

The stewardess returned, and a much-relieved Curly started to hand over the bag. Moe intercepted it and rather loudly began to inquire about Curly's eating habits. Sweetner, who was behind the attendant, had his back against the cabin window and his stocking feet up on the empty seat alongside him. He was twitching with anticipation and ready to piss his pants over the gag. While the poor girl stood there, Moe began to question Curly about what he had been eating earlier in the day. All the while he had his hand in the bag, fingers searching for a delicacy.

"That's it. That's what I was looking for!" he exclaimed. With his

THIS DAY'S BUSINESS

fingers he removed a chunk of cooked meat with the gooey gravy dripping off it. "No wonder you were sick, you fool. You eat so damned fast that you can't chew your food, and your stomach can't digest it completely. Look at this perfectly good piece of meat going to waste!" With that, he plopped the morsel into his mouth, chewed once or twice, then made an obvious swallow. The new girl and two passengers rapidly left the cabin with their hands over their mouths.

"Find him!" roared Sulkhov. The veins in his neck were bulging out, and the spittle was forming at the corners of his enraged and contorted mouth. There was a pause in his voice as he hunched over the desk. Slamming his large, peasant hands down, he lowered his eyes to the newspaper that was tightly clutched in his fists. Only deep, controlled breathing brought back color to the old Russian's face. Raising his eyes to his subordinates in the partially darkened room, he spoke slowly and with deliberation; he was a man barely able to contain his intense anger.

"Find him and bring..." He stopped in mid sentence as the lightbulb of inspiration suddenly flashed on. "No. Wait. Better yet, locate him and we'll pay him a visit." The Russian relaxed his grip on the crumpled paper and threw it with force back onto the desk.

Several hours later an aide to the old Communist appeared from a side office and handed a sheet of paper to Sulkhov. The message was quickly read and action was called for. Reaching for the intercom button on the side of the desk, he barked his orders.

"My driver and bodyguard. Now."

The minor clerk at the end of the wire snapped into motion. Two calls were made downstairs. By the time Sulkhov reached the front lobby, his ride and protection were waiting for him. Great was the respect and fear that the Stalinist commanded, even after all those years.

It took a few minutes for the arthritic old man to settle himself comfortably in the deep leather of the limousine. With a rap of Sulkhov's bare knuckles on the glass partition, the driver lowered the soundproof barrier and turned to his superior.

"Gregor, we need to find this man, and this is where we might look first." Sulkhov handed the file jacket to the bodyguard who opened it and studied the black-and-white photo of Marcel Chazzi. To Gregor, the chauffeur, he gave a slip of paper with Chazzi's probable whereabouts written on it. A map was consulted, and comments in Russian were passed between Gregor and the overweight and sweaty bodyguard in the front passengers seat.

"Gregor, we will need to take all the usual precautions."

The driver nodded and spoke. "Yes, Comrade Sulkhov."

The obsidian black limousine smartly left the curb and proceeded in the direction of La Guardia Airport. They were driving around the Queens section of New York City in a random fashion in order to shake off any tails. It was routine for the FBI's stakeout squads to provide surveillance on anyone observed leaving the Soviet Trade Mission. It was the squad's task to find out who they were and to catalog their movements. At the corner of 81st Street and Ditmars Boulevard, the limo swung into the multilevel parking garage. The attendant on duty directed them to level six where they should find ample parking. The vehicle wound its way upward on the ramps, passing each level in turn. Stopping at level four, the stately Lincoln passed the filled rows of commuter cars and pulled up behind a Chevrolet panel truck whose occupants immediately got out. The three men from the embassy car quietly exited their vehicle. While Sulkhov and his bodyguard were assisted into the van through the sliding side door, the chauffeur took off his black uniform hat and tunic, then put on a light tan jacket, which was handed to him by the van driver. He slid behind the wheel, started the truck up, and the three embassy men drove off, downward toward the street. They had been vigilant. There was no need to suspect that anyone had followed them to that garage, but one could never be too sure. With Sulkhov and the bodyguard out of sight in the van, the driver left the building and headed northwesterly out of the city on Interstate 87.

After three hours of highway driving, the van turned off onto Route 213 for High Falls, New York. It was there that the windshield began to record the first spattering of rain. The sky ahead was growing darker with each passing mile as the sporadic bolts of lightning announced the passing of a cold front.

With the bodyguard consulting a roadmap and offering directions, the van slowed and turned down a narrow dirt road,

THIS DAY'S BUSINESS

which ran for a better part of a mile into the woods. Gregor stopped the panel truck just short of the clearing where a modern-style log chalet had been built. There were no other cars visible from the Russians' vantage point. With a nod from the chauffeur, the bodyguard slid open the side door, stepped out, and walked the seventy-five feet to the house. Lowering his three-hundred-pound profile by keeping the woods to his back and a shrub or two between him and the house, the henchman softly slipped up the front stairs onto the porch. He took note that even on this grey, rainy day, there were no lights on in the house; however, there was music coming from somewhere toward the back. With his right hand he swept aside his suit jacket and retrieved the Ruger Mark II 22 caliber pistol with a four-inch-long bull barrel. Peering left and right of the door into the darkened windows, the large man was perspiring heavily by now. Satisfied that he was not being observed, he waved to the van, which silently rolled into the driveway. The driver stepped out and joined his sweaty companion at the door. He now had his uniform cap and tunic on and looked every bit the image of a chauffeur. The gunman, hiding to the left of the door, reached into his left hand suit pocket and retrieved a cylindrical object that appeared to be an extension of the barrel. Threading the suppressor onto the Ruger's barrel, he nodded to the man in black. Gregor rapped on the glass with his gloved hand. The bodyguard cocked the auto pistol.

"Darling, there's someone at the door. Do you want me to get it?"

The two Russians were now aware that Marcel Chazzi was entertaining a lady.

"Wait a minute, I'm coming." The voice of the unidentified female called out from somewhere within the structure. Moments later a hauntingly attractive brunette, in her early twenties, opened the door to the stranger as he tipped his cap.

The fat man used this opportunity to kick open the door and thrust the suppressed automatic up toward her at eye level. The blood drained from her face, and she fainted in a heap in the doorway. Pig Man was first through the door. Wherever his eyes went the pistol was pointed. Gregor picked up the young woman and entered next. Chazzi was on the second-floor landing, frozen in his tracks, not knowing what to make of the scene below him in his living room. With the subdued daylight flooding in from the open front door, all he could recognize were two dark forms, one holding a gun and the other, his girlfriend. The one with the gun pointed to him, ordered him down the stairs slowly and to sit down on the couch. Chazzi began to whimper and babble something about having little money to steal. The diplomat's knees went to rubber, and he nearly stumbled twice as he approached the first floor.

Gregor crossed the room and dropped the benumbed brunette onto the couch next to the French diplomat. He was thoroughly frightened, and she was starting to regain consciousness. Sulkhov made his dramatic entrance as a fresh peal of lightning and thunder rolled across the adjacent hills. He casually walked across the room, stopped just short of the coffee table, and stood silently. Chazzi started to get up, but the chauffeur was by now standing behind the seated man. He placed both of his large, gloved hands on the small Frenchman's shoulders and pushed him down. Chazzi was held firmly in place with such sufficient force that he could feel his spine begin to compress.

As Pig Man trained the barrel of the Ruger on his forehead, the diplomat voided his bowels where he sat. Too frightened was he to speak. The old Communist took the folded newspaper from under his arm and threw it down onto the coffee table before Chazzi. Leaning over, he pointed with his gloved hand to the photograph on page six of the Worcester Telegram. "Who is this man, and why haven't we heard of him?" barked Sulkhov. Leaning over Chazzi, Gregor kept his right hand heavily on the Frenchman's shoulder while he scooped up the paper and held it up so that it could be read by his prisoner.

Stumbling and searching for his words, Chazzi spoke his son's name. "Emile, he, he told me not to have anything to do with this man, Eagen, or he would be killed." Taking furtive glances at the photo and article about a Boston mountain climber heading off to Pakistan, Chazzi's eyes darted back to Sulkhov. "I was only trying to protect my son. I would've told you. You must believe me."

With both of his hands balled tightly into fists in front of him, Sulkhov continued, "We paid you a lot of money, Monsieur Chazzi." Glancing about the room and then back to the brunette, he returned his gaze to the diplomat and continued, "You seem to have done well with it."

THIS DAY'S BUSINESS

In his defense, Chazzi stammered "I never took a franc of it, Comrade General. All of it went to your projects, I swear by all that is holy..."

He was cut off in mid sentence by the old man who asked dispassionately, "Where is your son now, monsieur?"

The Frenchman was distraught and losing control of his voice. He could only answer the question by lowering his eyes and shaking his head. Sulkhov knew that action was called for or he would lose this man to a stroke. "Pietor Ilyich," he called to Pig Man. He nodded in the direction of the sobbing girl on the couch. She had recovered sufficiently to wrap her arms about her head and assume the fetal position. The large, sweaty man with the smile on his lips came behind the couch and handed the pistol to the chauffeur. Gregor walked around to where he could cover the Frenchman. Pietor Ilyich Kamaroski lunged at the sobbing girl. His fat-knuckled hands were around her throat. He pulled her bolt upright and off the couch so that she dangled a foot off the ground, while her arms and legs flailed away. She was held this way until she ceased to struggle. The lifeless form was then dumped in a heap at Chazzi's feet. His eyes nearly bugged out of his head. Having tried the stick, Sulkhov now tried the carrot approach.

Looking about him, he pulled up a chair to the couch and leaned closer to Chazzi, only to be repulsed by the stench surrounding him. Gregor, seeing his superior recoil at the smell, joked, "It must be some new French aftershave lotion, Comrade Sulkhov." Pig Man came to the chauffeur's side and retrieved his pistol, his eyes never once leaving the Frenchman.

Once again, Sulkhov spoke in a calming tone. "Marcel, where is your son? He has much to explain."

With his face buried in his hands, Marcel could only steal a glance at the lifeless form on the floor before him. "I can't, I can't."

The Russian now was clearly losing his patience with his prisoner. He snapped his fingers in Kamaroski's direction. The pressure wave from the barrel of the suppressed Ruger registered a *pop*, a noise little louder than a champagne cork being released. The low velocity, twenty-two caliber short bullet jumped from the muzzle, and Chazzi's right kneecap exploded. The howl of pain radiating from the chalet was muffled by the pouring rain and the roll of thunder echoing off the distant hills.

"Marcel, this is most distressing and, quite frankly, very distasteful for me as well. Tell me now and the pain will go away."

This time, with little left in him, Chazzi could only shake his head. *Pop!* His left kneecap disintegrated just as a loud clap of thunder roared overhead. The Frenchman stiffened quickly, removing his arms from around his knees and clutched his chest. He began to gag as he swallowed his tongue. The magenta-like hue in his face turned a deep blue as the tortured eyes rolled up in their sockets. Marcel Chazzi lay over on his right side and slid quietly off the couch onto the floor at the feet of his dead lover. He was beyond further pain.

With a look of disgust on his face, the General surveyed the day's work that lay on the floor and said, "Fortune smiles on us, Comrade Chazzi. We might yet hold the trump card."

Kamaroski and the chauffeur went about the business of setting the fire. As General Sulkhov returned to the van, the gas jet in the fireplace was turned on full. A wad of plastic explosive about the size of a golf ball was pressed onto the valve, and a blasting cap with a timer was inserted into it. For good measure, an oil lamp from the mantel was taken down and the contents poured over the corpses. The two, finishing their grim work, left the chalet, turned the van around, and departed down the narrow dirt road. They were confident in their craft to know that the explosion, the resulting fire, and the rainstorm would remove all traces of their passage. As the van turned onto the two-lane blacktop, a muffled roar in the distance was heard. The surrounding forest and storm conspired to hide the carnage from view. The scene would not be discovered for another ten or twelve days.

The cabin door in the first-class section opened with a slight whoosh, allowing the stale air out and the rancid air in. As each passenger stood in the cabin doorway, they were quickly assaulted with the sights and fragrances of Asia. Everyone who deplaned had to walk down the rickety stairway to the pavement below. Sweetner and Larry, who had been cooped up for too long, needed to use both hands on the hand railings because of the jet lag and the long hours on

THIS DAY'S BUSINESS

the go. Assembled around the bottom of the stairs was a small knot of people, who were the welcoming committee, and three photographers from the local press.

Alan Lloyd, standing a good two inches taller and twenty pounds heavier, thrust his hand over the crowd and directly at Eagen. "Mr. Eagen, I'm Alan Lloyd, Special Assistant to Ambassador Van Arsdale. Welcome to Pakistan."

Handshakes and pleasantries were exchanged, and photos of the team were taken, followed by a short question and answer period. Within minutes, the team was whisked through Pakistani customs and toward the departure gate for the last leg of their journey. Lloyd had flown down from Islamabad that morning just to greet the arriving team. He was an easygoing sort, thought Eagen, quite efficient and personable judging from the way their arrival was handled. Lloyd told everyone that the baggage was being collected and would be transferred to the flight leaving for Rawalpindi.

The Air Pakistan BAC-111 had seen better days but was apparently airworthy. Eagen noticed as he was boarding that the ground crew, while going about their business, appeared as professional as anywhere in the world he had seen. Lloyd used the one-hour-and-twenty-minute flight to bring Eagen up to speed. He noted that the supplies from the States had arrived without incident and that each pallet had been inventoried. Both scientific packages had arrived as well and were being stored in the garage at the ambassador's residence. In the course of their conversation, Lloyd mentioned that he was to be their Base Camp manager. He was telling Eagen that he was looking forward to the challenge and for a chance to get back up into the mountains. It was then that Eagen remembered where he had first heard of Alan Lloyd.

"You were on Nuptse in '64, weren't you?" asked Eagen.

"Actually," said Lloyd, "it was 1959 and it was Lohtse, an adjoining peak to Mount Everest."

Eagen was suitably impressed. "Were you successful?" Eagen asked.

Lloyd exhaled slowly through pursed lips as he gave thought to the question. Wistfully, his mind's eye raced back more than ten years in time to the icy slopes of the world's fourth highest mountain. Could it really have been that long ago? "I suppose we were," he

103

continued. "We didn't make the summit, but everyone returned alive. We were on the mountain at the same time as a small group of Japanese climbers. Apparently there was an accident, badly injuring two of their Sherpas. Although the Japanese were competent climbers, their few numbers made the rescue and evacuation all the more complicated. Since we were a larger and better-equipped group, we went to the aid of fellow climbers. By the time the evacuations were completed, the monsoon season arrived with its heavy snowfall at higher altitude, and when we were in a position to move upward again, it was too late. There was just too much snow."

The flight into Islamabad went without incident, and the Embassy staff made light work of offloading the luggage. Silence passed between the two for the ten-minute journey to the Ambassador's residence. As the four identical grey Jeep Wagoneers were about to turn left into the diplomatic compound, Lloyd pointed out the team's living quarters for the next few days as they wound down from their long trip. The next three days would be used to gather the fresh food and supplies from the local merchants, finding enough tarps for the porters to use as shelters for the trek into Base Camp, and, if there were time, sightseeing.

The stooges were the first ones up the next morning, followed by Sweetner and then Eagen. All were groggy and very stiff from the long ride. After breakfast with Lloyd, everyone assembled at the motor pool to inspect the shipment of goods. The limousines and all other vehicles were parked outside because the canvas-covered pallets took up much of the four-bay garage. What surprised Eagen the most were the Marine guards. There were three of them at the front of the building and three more inside. All were in a relaxed but vigilant state.

Lloyd sensed Eagen's curiosity at the presence of the guard detail. Heading off any questions, he opened with this thought: "Judge Brooks asked the ambassador if he would be extra careful with this shipment since a lot of people were interested in the results. The ambassador in turn asked me to oversee the arrangements. Everyone agrees that this scientific project is important enough, and so, I felt it appropriate to provide the proper security." Wryly, he added, "Things have a way of growing legs over here, if you catch my drift."

The team went about its business of tracking down their personal

THIS DAY'S BUSINESS

gear such as sleeping bags, ice axes, and so forth. All were boxed up and inventoried, all were destined for some poor beggar's back.

Day two in Rawalpindi found the stooges, with an interpreter from the embassy, out scouring the bazaars for their needs. Eagen, Sweetner, and Lloyd met with the Sirdar, a Mr. Shastri, who had come highly recommended with a reputation for keeping his porters in line. Later that afternoon, the supplies from town began to arrive. The stooges, with the assistance of some off-duty Marines, began to weigh out and repackage the bulk goods. It was a long day that ended for all shortly after dinner.

The third and final day was just as hectic as the previous two; however, the effects of jet lag were diminishing as everyone settled into their new time zone. Negotiations with the head porter, Mr. Shastri, were completed, and he left the Ambassador's compound before nine in the morning. He was to fly to Skardu and arrange for the hiring of the porters.

Shortly before one o'clock that afternoon, two military jeeps from the Pakistani Army arrived at the main gate. The Marine guard on duty checked the papers of the soldiers and then called his superior to announce their arrival. The reinforced steel security gate opened electronically, and one jeep entered the compound. The other vehicle was an escort for the military liaison officer who was to oversee everyone's safety. No one was allowed into the Baltoro region without a military escort. This was because the area was still hotly contested by two other nations, and artillery duels between the claimants were not unheard of.

Major Gujral stepped from the jeep with his highly polished jump boots and crisply starched dark brown uniform. The beret on his head was tipped jauntily at an angle, giving him a brash and daring appearance. From the way the enlisted men unloaded his luggage and fawned over him, it appeared that Major Gujral had a high regard for his station in life.

Curly, who witnessed the major's arrival, wondered how this recruiting poster of military might would hold up under the stress and strain that lay ahead. Upon meeting the major, Eagen's first impression of the man was that he was a dilettante, and a useless dilettante at that. Sweetner took an instant dislike to the man when he announced to all concerned that he would require three or four

105

porters to attend to his personal needs while on the trail.

At Sweetner's insistence, Eagen took Lloyd aside and asked, "Does this asshole know what he's in for? I hope he doesn't expect someone to draw his bath for him."

Lloyd could only shake his head in sorry amazement, saying, "I have to take what they give me, just like everyone else." Eagen felt that this guy could cause more trouble than he was worth. Reading Eagen's thoughts, Lloyd continued, "As far as I know, we're stuck with him. I just hope he doesn't get in the way."

Sweetner didn't trust him. Someone like that would likely try to save his own skin in an emergency, and to Sweetner, that made him dangerous. A long time ago, Eagen had learned to trust Sweetner's instincts. Major Gujral would bear watching.

CHAPTER 9

Skardu

He was wide awake that morning at five o'clock. Eagen's inner clock was adjusting to the local time zone. Fifteen minutes later, as he lay in bed, the movement of machinery and men brought him out of a light stupor.

"What the hell's going on outside?" Rising and pulling apart the curtains at the front window, he could see straight ahead from the guest bungalow and slightly to the left. The front of the motor pool was blocked by a semi tractor with a flatbed trailer. A forklift driver was engaged in loading the expedition's supplies from the garage to the truck.

Joining the commotion outside, Eagen found Lloyd and the stooges supervising the loading while Sweetner was still in bed. He, apparently, had not quite fully recovered from his jet lag.

First came breakfast and then the pack-up for the airport. Although the local police were there to provide a motorcycle escort from Islamabad to the airport, Eagen wanted two of the team with the scientific packages at all times until they were safely aboard the plane. Sweetner and Moe volunteered. They left straight away to procure a vehicle and a driver. One last inspection of the load was completed as it sat covered with tarps under the Martian-pink sky of dawn.

Eagen gave a look around him. Almost three hundred and sixty degrees they stretched, the brown foothills of the grandest mountain chain on Earth. Sunlight was just striking the tops of this barren topography while the valley below, holding the twin cities of Islamabad and Rawalpindi, were still submerged in the shadows of last night.

The convoy departed the U.S. Embassy compound in the diplomatic enclave and turned south onto the Khayaban-Suhrawardy road for the airport, no doubt under the watchful gaze of the Russian and Chinese embassies. One hour later, the rest of the team left with their bags for the airport.

It was quite small. One would believe that an airport serving the capital city of a large country would be more expansive, busier. In contrast, the airport at Karachi was many times busier and larger. The one-story cement block building, recently completed, was already in need of light maintenance. Even the control tower was still under construction. Before reaching the terminal Eagen could see the aircraft. There were two of them sitting on the ramp, one behind the other. Even at a distance, their silhouette revealed them to be FH-227 Fokker/Fairchild, a twin-engined, high-winged, turboprop aircraft that had seen service throughout the world. The four embassy vehicles drove past the front entrance and came to a stop at a heavy gate in the chainlink fence. Honking several times, the driver waited until the attendant unlocked and slid the gate open. The convoy of four drove out onto the tarmac and pulled up just short of the first Fokker.

As everyone gathered around him at the jeep's tailgate, Lloyd was handing out the boarding passes to each team member. They were able, with Alan's influence, to circumvent the check-in process and load the baggage directly onto the plane. Both aircraft were of the Mk 300 variety, Eagen thought, judging from the large cargo doors fitted to the forward cabin. The freight handlers on both aircraft were accepting cargo while the passengers were loading from the rear stairway. He began his own walk around of the nearest bird. The

THIS DAY'S BUSINESS

fresh paint covering the aluminum skin proclaimed AIR PAKISTAN, but the ghosts of three other airlines and at least two other countries' air forces could be seen peeking through the the watered-down pigments. This plane had been bought and sold more times than a New Orleans whore on payday night.

Lloyd addressed the team as they assembled at the foot of the stairs. "They've added an extra section to accommodate our band of merry men and an organized pilgrimage to one of the holy mosques near there. They'll put our team, most of our freight, and some passengers on our flight, then the rest of our stuff and the tour on the second plane." The four bladed, jet-driven engines began, ever so slowly, to turn over as the cockpit crew initiated their startup checklist.

With the noise swiftly intensifying, Lloyd suggested that everyone get aboard. The team filed into the cabin just as the right engine began to belch raw fuel and fire up. The door slammed closed behind them with a hollow thud, and then there was a scramble for the seats. This was no class seating. The forward half of the cabin was segregated by a moth-eaten cargo net that instilled little confidence. It seemed incapable of holding it's own weight let alone several tons of freight. The last of them were seated just aft of the netting as the breaks were released. A bit of power to the left engine brought movement to Air Pakistan flight 1752 and 1752A. Moments later, the second section began its slow lumber out to the runway. The first plane carrying the team with their gear taxied out onto the runway for its final runup while the second section did the same on the taxiway. There was little chance of a collision at an airport that saw only six or seven flights a day.

The crew stood on the brakes while the captain, in the left seat, reached for the throttles and pushed them forward to the stops, causing both engines to run up to full power. With the takeoff checklist completed, the first officer was ready to release the brakes when a series of pops, originating from the right engine, were heard and felt throughout the aircraft. The throttle for that engine was pulled back, almost to idle. The Fokker slowly limped it's way to the end of the runway in order to taxi back to the gate.

Meanwhile, the second section rolled into position on the runway numbers. The crew repeated the same procedures as the first. When the brakes were released, the Dutch-built, twin-engined workhorse leapt down the tarred strip. Although the second plane wasn't as heavy as the first, it required two thirds the length of the runway to get airborne. The departing flight climbed and then banked to the northeast with a steep right turn to avoid surrounding mountains.

Inside the ailing craft, the six Americans looked to each other for an explanation for their return to the gate. The announcement from the PA system was hopelessly garbled in an undistinguishable tongue. Its sudden bleating startled the two goats and some other livestock that didn't appear on the manifest. The cacophony of protests filled the cabin and added to the confusion. At the gate, a scaffold was rolled up to the right engine. Two airline employees ascended the stairway to inspect the engine. After a few minutes of poking and prodding, an argument ensued with much shouting and gesturing. The confrontation ended with one man slapping the other. The loser returned a few moments later carrying a cardboard box. Eagen could not tell whether it was oil or hydraulic fluid that was being added to the ailing engine. It could have been chicken soup for all he knew.

Only fifteen minutes behind schedule. Not bad considering their reliability problems, thought Sweetner.

Both engines were turning and the crew appeared satisfied that all was well. They repeated their actions of earlier. While at the gate, Lloyd found six empty seats in the small area between the cockpit and the cargo deck. The plane was taxiing for takeoff as the last of the team dove for a seat. Sweetner claimed as his own the jump seat that folded down into place from the lefthand bulkhead wall. He had the best seat in the house, being situated between and immediately behind the crew. The engines were up to full throttle now, their song biting into the dusty heat of the midmorning. Momentum built up slowly, then much faster. The halfway point on the runway was reached quickly, then two thirds. Three quarters of the tarred surface was already behind them, and the nosewheel had yet to lift off. A flock of birds at the far end scattered every which way to avoid their big aluminum cousin that seemed hell bent on running them down. Flight 1752 was clearly feeling the effects of the heavy load in its belly.

With less than three hundred feet remaining, the high winged aircraft vaulted skyward. Apparently the crew wanted plenty of

THIS DAY'S BUSINESS

flying speed before committing themselves. The plane climbed slowly until the landing gear was brought up. Less drag equated to more flying speed. The delayed flight executed a climbing righthand turn, mimicking its earlier sibling. Like the other plane, this one climbed to the assigned altitude of twenty thousand feet. At that height they would be above all but the highest of mountains in the area.

Sweetner was strapped into the jump seat. It had no back at all, so he leaned forward, hanging monkey-like from the grab bars that protruded from both the left and right bulkheads. At twenty thousand feet, they were above the haze and pollution that was trapped in the broad, dusty valley somewhere below. This was everyone's first opportunity for a glimpse of the largest phalanx of mountains anywhere. Everyone in the compartment behind Sweetner was peering out the one cabin window. They were all searching for the mountain giant, K2. They planned to use it as a reference point in locating Gasherbrum IV, which was a known distance and heading from it. Sweetner, with map in hand, was conducting his own search by looking out the copilot's window. He picked up on the fact that the crew never spoke English up to that point.

He got the first officer's attention with a question. "Is the weather at Skardu good enough to land?"

The man in the right seat brought his soot-black eyes up to the speaker. His broad, round face and dark complexion beamed a grin, which betrayed a gold-capped tooth at the front of his mouth. His answer was an enthusiastic, "Yes." He kept nodding almost stupidly.

"Will we get there on time?"

Again, the answer was the same: "Yes."

Sweetner was getting suspicious of those two. "Are you a needle-dicked, egg-sucking ferret?"

Again, the bobbing of the head. Sweetner turned in his seat and put his mouth up to Eagen's ear, saying, "Yin and Yang here can't speak a word of English. It's supposed to be the international language for all aviation. No wonder they were having an argument over the map. They can't read it!"

Eagen did not want to hear that! A quick glance back into the passenger compartment revealed that almost everyone was heavily working their worry beads! Hmmm.

The flight proceeded uneventfully for the next two hours. When the navigational instrument began to receive the radio beacon at Skardu, the first officer began calling out the distance to the beacon to the captain. The nearer they flew to the signal source a mileage counter would tick off the distance. At a point in space exactly fifteen miles out, the crew retarded the throttles in front of them. The copilot reached down by his left foot and rotated a wheel which activated the flaps. This gave them better control of the plane at slower speeds. They began to descend from twenty thousand feet. Descending into the cloud tops at fifteen thousand feet, they immediately began to encounter turbulence. With a fixed rate of descent, the FH227 Mk 300 would cross the radio beacon, inbound, at ten thousand feet. At a distance of 3.2 miles inside the beacon and on final approach, they stepped down to eight thousand feet.

This was a tricky approach. Even on a clear day, the surrounding terrain provided unpredictable and sometimes violent turbulence, something that Sweetner was experiencing at that very moment. His seat offered little in the way of support, and the effects on him were akin to riding a wild rodeo bull while blindfolded. As the landing gear was extended, the grinding and bumping noises of the mechanical and hydraulic parts faded when the wheel struts locked into place. A feather-like touch on the controls was called for there.

The plane slowly settled down, the rhythm of flight marred only by the occasional microburst of turbulent energy. There was nothing to see outside the windshields but the bright white of the clouds. Sweetner later described the experience as being submerged in a bottle of milk with a very bright light being shined on it. Being solidly in the clouds since leaving fifteen thousand feet, one could easily induce vertigo by staring outside for more than a few minutes. Sweetner forced himself to concentrate on the instrument panel. But, as he would infrequently look up, the brightness would give him a headache just over the eyebrows and at the base of the neck. It occurred to him to carry his sunglasses on the return trip.

To compound the difficulty of landing at that airport, it was not built in the Skardu valley, proper. The town sat at approximately seven thousand feet above sea level in the flat Skardu Valley which is about twenty-three miles long and a scant six miles wide. The airport

THIS DAY'S BUSINESS

was built upon a plateau, or flat table of land, that rose six hundred feet above the surrounding countryside. Occasionally, on the approach, the whiteout would change to a dark grey as the plane was pelted with heavy rain and hail. Swiftly, they flew through the area of precipitation, restoring the diffused light outside.

On short final the first officer was calling out the distance and altitude to the captain who was flying. They were picking up more turbulence as they approached the ground. Without warning, the lights appeared to go out. The bright, milk-white clouds changed to coal black. The first officer yelled out something that sounded suspiciously, to Sweetner, like "Fire." As he looked out the left window slightly behind the pilot, he could see what appeared to be tongues of flame coming up from the ground seeking to envelope them. The crew executed the missed approach procedures. The throttles were rammed forward to their stops, and the landing gear was retracted.

Slowly, very slowly, the Dutch-built plane responded to the new inputs. Clawing its way skyward, the wheels barely missed a radio tower at the end of the airport boundary and about two hundred feet to the right of runway centerline. Somehow, they were two hundred feet off course. But Sweetner was watching the localizer instrument. All the way down the approach, every indication was that they were on course. Could they trust their navigation equipment anymore? If the fire on the ground had not been spotted at the last moment, they would now be a permanent addition to the landscape. Apparently the fire, whatever the source, superheated the surrounding air thereby burning off the fog and mist just enough to alert the landing aircraft. They had very nearly flown into the debris path and subsequent crash site of flight 1752A.

The crew was definitely spooked as the plane made the climbing turn back to the radio beacon for another try at the approach. They had every reason to be concerned because they had flown this approach often before in good weather, and they alone knew just how close their wingtips were from the surrounding hills and ridges. The turbulence was with them again as they climbed higher. Once again, they were established on a long final approach to the runway. As before, the first officer was calling out the airspeed numbers and the distance, while the captain concentrated on flying the aircraft. At about the same point as earlier the engine throttles were retarded, the landing gear was extended, and the flaps were set for landing. At the slight crosswind, the plane began to yaw slightly. The captain made his course corrections, and the descent into the milky void began anew. They were less that two miles from touchdown when the troublesome right engine, the one that had delayed their departure earlier, belched loudly, spewing smoke and dirty black oil. Now they were really in trouble. They were flying blind into a dangerous airport that was ringed with tall mountains. They were flying an approach with navigation equipment that was apparently unreliable and misleading. They were flying this approach in a stricken bird with a sick engine that could catch fire or explode at any moment. Sweetner's asshole was puckered tighter that a miser's grip on a dime!

As the power to the right engine was retarded, the left engine throttle was advanced to full power in order to maintain flying speed. Down they went, down the invisible, electronic highway. Just two hundred feet from the edge of the runway, they broke out of the clouds and were once again off course to the right. The flight could not go around again; they were committed to the landing. The captain gave a quick jerk to the control column in front of him. There it was! They could see it now. The woods and grass beneath them was all ablaze or scorched from the passage of a rolling fireball. Chunks of twisted and shredded aluminum were everywhere. The wheels touched down with a screech and a thud. The Fokker was landing fast and hot. At this point in a normal landing, the crew would have thrown the propellers into reverse thrust, directing the engine's energy forward. This would sharply reduce their speed and shorten their rollout distance. Without this maneuver, the only option available to the crew was to stand on the brakes and lock up the tires.

The screeching of rubber against tar was deafening inside the cramped cabin. As shredding rubber was being ejected off the wheels, the tires on the right side blew out with an explosive jolt. The medium-sized twin began a ground loop on the runway. The aluminum bird shuddered as it came to a stop on the far righthand edge of the tarmac. The cabin doors and emergency exits were popped open, allowing the dazed and shaken human cargo to evacuate.

THIS DAY'S BUSINESS

They were all alone out on the edge of the runway. The clouds were parting just enough so that everyone could see the black column of smoke a half mile away. Looking around the airport, Lloyd could not see any other aircraft parked near the shack that served as the terminal. As the team gathered around him, Lloyd, and everyone else, was coming to grips with the horrible reality that thirty-four souls and a third of their oxygen were the source of the conflagration.

The forest, what was left of it, was charred. The ground for a hundred yards in every direction was scorched and blackened with soot. There was nothing, nothing left at all. The grass fire and smoke obscured the carnage as the team approached the crash site. They were sickened by what they saw. Insulation, aluminum, and body parts were scattered everywhere. The scene was still too hot to go near. Rescue was futile, for there was no one left to rescue from this inferno. In the distance, the lone wail of Skardu's only fire truck could be heard as it wound its way along the dirt road to the airport. The utter feeling of helplessness invaded the psyche of those who trembled at the perimeter of the conflagration.

Eagen and Sweetner had been there before; it was somewhere near the Laotian border, but it was there. The carnage was similar, the total destruction was the same, but this was different. This was not the jungle being ripped asunder by a devastating B-52 strike; this was Pakistan, and something terrible had just occurred. Lloyd was testing the limits of his composure; he had no frame of reference, no neat pigeonhole for his bureaucratic mind to file or retrieve what he was seeing. He was stunned and unable to come to terms with the horror that was unfolding around him.

Somewhere from beyond the veil of smoke came the relief. The army outpost had been alerted, and it was their sorry lot to clean up and restore order. As in the fire back in the States, the oxygen fueled the firestorm. Everyone and virtually everything had been consumed by the hell at the end of the runway. Lloyd brought the team back to their stricken bird. In spite of all that was happening, this was no time to leave their supplies unguarded.

Three hours after the wounded Fokker skidded to a halt, a vehicle finally arrived. Major Gujral, the Army liaison officer, had the driver pull up smartly in front of the team. His authority and jurisdiction in this incident were total. He spoke only with Lloyd and scarcely acknowledged Eagen's presence. The major spoke rapidly in his native tongue to the American consulate officer. As swiftly as he drove up, the major loaded his exalted self back into the jeep and departed in the direction of the smoke. Lloyd was regaining his composure with the aid of the Wild Turkey that Moe had recovered from somewhere within their carry-on baggage. For the first time in a half hour he spoke.

"His supreme highness has informed me that the plane will be offloaded shortly and that we can begin selecting porters in the morning. The Sirdar, a Mr. Morarji Shastri, has started to put the word out to the villages that we are hiring. With any luck, we should be on our way in forty-eight hours."

The sunrise was beautiful, thought Sweetner, but it did little to stir his soul. There were still a few small fires that had yet to be extinguished although the ground-hugging fog did its best to envelope them. In the night, the wind shifted direction and filled the valley with the stench of unburned jet fuel and roasted human flesh.

CHAPTER 10

Base Camp

The gray, chilly mists of dawn added their somber tones to a new day. Shock and dismay still hung heavy in the air, much like the fog and juniper smoke from the campfires. Eagen was up first, then gradually, the others. He made his way the few feet from his tent door to the stockpile of crates and boxes that held the essence of the trip. It was his favorite time of the day. It brought with it a certain clarity to the mind and peace to the soul. The events of the past few weeks were already spinning a stifling web of anxiety and self doubt around him. Had they planned for every contingency? Had they overlooked anything? Who could have foreseen yesterday's crash? Would the loss of the precious oxygen doom the climb before it started?

These questions and many more were weighing on him that first morning as he walked among the still sleepy camp. However, he knew that the unfolding day would surely be a long one, and his self doubts would vanish with the selection of the first porter. Looking about him, he could sense that a whole twenty-four hours would pass before one pound of equipment was carried one foot. This was what it was all coming down to, wasn't it? Getting supplies moved. From a remote and dusty outcrop of his mind, Eagen expressed the hope, the fervent desire that despite all that could go wrong, and all that would go wrong, the whole thing would work itself out in good order. He was amused by the thought of bringing a sense of cosmos to all this chaos encamped in an area slightly smaller than half a football field. He and the team would rely on the judgment of Gujral and Shastri to select the ones to successfully and safely carry them to Concordia and beyond.

This was his first time among them, and he had little experience in sizing them up. They were an eclectic lot, those Balti people. Their features were a genetic road map of history. The genes of the Middle East, of Europe, and of the Orient were engraved on their weathered faces and etched into their earthen hands. It was they and not the land that marked the passing of empire-builders from Ghengis Khan to Alexander the Great.

They kept to themselves in huddles, where this village did not mix with those of that village. Clan stayed distant from clan. Although a trained ear could discern the subtle differences in dialect, the eye would register only that which they had in common. The Baltis, to a man, all wore the same heavy, loose-fitting woolen clothes in the heat, cold, rain, or snow. There were hundreds of them. By Eagen's estimate, close to five or maybe six hundred of them. Many were barefoot, and a great many more brought the entire family, although those would not be hired.

As for the hiring, there was a protocol to all that. The large semicircle was formed by Gujral's soldiers who carried four-foot long wooden canes. They were to mass the throng into something that resembled a line and then maintain order. Anyone who jumped the line would swiftly feel the wrath of those in uniform. At the center lay the small mountain of supplies, which were closely guarded by several armed troops. A portable folding camp table had been set up using the pile as a backdrop.

The major, looking resplendent in a crisply starched dark brown uniform, was to be the authority figure at the proceedings. It was his presence that lent the governmental stamp of approval to the whole effort. In the middle sat Alan Lloyd. As Base Camp manager, he was ultimately in charge of the expedition. No one was hired, not one

THIS DAY'S BUSINESS

pound of gear was moved, without his approval. However, in the matter of hiring, he deferred to the recommendations of his Sirdar and Military liaison officer. To his left sat Sweetner, whose role as paymaster was to obtain a thumb print from each porter and issue to each a pay record. Shastri, the Sirdar, stood at the table and acted as interpreter, inquisitor, and devil's advocate. Gujral's sergeant would point to the swelling throng with his cane and motion the prospective porter in the direction of the table where he would list his qualifications and have his suitability judged by the Sahibs. Eagen kept busy by assisting Sergeant Mustafa, doing some photography, and by staying out from underfoot. His role in all this was to begin anew once they left Base Camp. But for the time being, he was the passive eye of the camera lens, taking it all in. Larry, meanwhile, was giving each one selected a very brief physical checkup.

A number of the Baltis, it seemed, had various ailments such as pneumonia, tuberculosis, and dysentery. These were not suitable for the long, hard work ahead, and so were sent away. It was agreed upon by the team that they would eventually need two hundred porters, up from the original estimate done in Washington. A further fifty were added to carry all the locally purchased supplies and equipment. With the sun climbing higher in the sky and burning off the accursed fog, the selection process ever so slowly began. And along with the brightening day came the heat and the rising dust kicked up by the hundreds upon hundreds of feet and hooves as they marched forward in line.

The crowd had been assembled for some three hours and were now becoming restless. Eagen felt relieved that Moe and Curly were babysitting the boxes and that Gujral's men were on hand to maintain order. Frustrated with the pace of progress and tempers growing shorter with each passing minute the crowd finally had enough of waiting around. They wanted everyone hired and they wanted it done now.

The Baltis were getting quite vocal and some were becoming belligerent. Several tried to jump the line only to be beaten back by the stinging blows from the canes. They were quickly degenerating into an angry mob. Eagen thought to himself of a scene from an old western movie where the townspeople became a vigilante mob; at least no one was brandishing a rope...yet. Shastri's pleas for calm and order were going unheard. They had ears only for their village elders who were quite adept at whipping up their charges into a frenzy on a moment's notice.

Gujral stood up sharply, almost upsetting the light table before him. He barked a command, and his soldiers waded into the mob with their clubs swinging. This bothered the three younger members of the team because their culture did not allow this. The others, however, had been to the third world where reason and order were oft times the exception rather than the rule. One particularly unpleasant-looking fellow was making the loudest noises. He was attempting to foment a riot. Because of his agitation, there was talk of seizing the supplies. The team could only look on in embarrassment; for they did not want an international incident to jeopardize the operation, yet they needed the cooperation of these people. The soldiers zeroed in on the loudmouth and subdued him rather forcefully. This only served to enrage those around him.

Things were turning from bad to shit very quickly. Moe and Larry were on their feet, and the soldiers guarding the stockpile made an obvious gesture of chambering a cartridge in their rifles. Gujral raised his arms in a futile attempt at regaining some control over the throng. Realizing his wasted effort, he too waded into the crowd, pushing aside those who stood in his way. As he approached the Balti, the man sensed his chance to gather support from his fellow porters. Becoming loud and abusive again, he spit on the shirt of the career soldier. Gujral calmly and deliberately unsnapped his holster and withdrew his revolver. Pointing it within inches of the man's face, the major dropped the hammer on his life. The reaction from the crowd was predictable and immediate. The sea of faces that had at one time pressed inward on Gujral now opened up to a circle of thirty feet in diameter, leaving the major with his revolver pointed at anyone and everyone. The body at his feet was still twitching spasmodically as the crimson fountain puddled up in the dirt. The major stepped over the corpse and backed away to the table. The Sahibs were dumbfounded; no one moved for fear of starting more violence. Gujral reclaimed his seat with a renewed air of authority and self importance.

While the mob shuffled back into a line, the major leaned over to Lloyd and spat out the words, "Communist troublemakers. The hills

THIS DAY'S BUSINESS

are riddled with them." Lloyd was speechless.

They were a mob no longer. In fact, to Sweetner they seemed quite docile, almost relieved. Most just wanted to get back to the business of doing business. The sudden cooling of tempers allowed the selection process to pick up where it had left off. To the sergeant, Gujral ordered the body removed at once and that he bring up the next applicant. To underscore his position, the major kept his revolver on the table at the ready for all to see. There were no further disruptions of the business at hand that day.

By four-thirty in the afternoon, all two hundred and fifty porters were selected and assigned a load. Those who would be running the camps, such as the cook boys, were hand-selected by Shastri, who had employed them all before on other expeditions. The many who were not chosen were sent packing with the not-so-subtle urging of Gujral's men.

Eagen was amazed at these people. How could they, who struggled just to eke out an existence, walk so casually away from death? What was it that drove these people to survive in this harsh land? *Another day of disturbing scenes*, thought Eagen. Perhaps the sweat and strain of the next week and a half would pull all these events into focus.

It had rained all night, bringing a dampness to the soul and skin alike. All were awakened before dawn and the preparations for the journey were begun. Each porter was assigned a load that he alone was responsible for. In very short order, the camp was broken down into its elementary components and destined for someone's back.

The plan was for the Sahibs to carry a light rucksack with only their personal gear to sustain them for the day's march. All else would be carried by a porter. Initially, everyone on the team felt a little uneasy about this, but gradually realized that the Sahibs were here to climb a mountain and needed to conserve their strength for as long as possible. The Baltis, for their part, were without a clue or motive. They couldn't explain why these strange foreigners would want to do something so unproductive, so pointless as climbing a mountain. Although the reason for the outsiders' presence was explained, the Sahibs had the impression that the Baltis had yet to make the connection between their own well-being and what was about to be accomplished. The sense of "winning this one for the

Gipper" just wasn't there.

Who can blame them? thought Curly. There was no feeling of loyalty to a government that cared little for them. The concept of one nation, a Pakistan, was a totally alien one to these people, who lived in the world of clans and tribes.

For the next nine days, the routine would fall within narrowly defined parameters. Everyone would be up well before dawn making breakfast and preparing for the day ahead. At sunrise they would be off for a destination few had heard of, much less traveled to. Each day's camp would be sited in a suitable location by four o'clock in the afternoon. This allowed the stragglers to arrive before dark.

Earlier, it was determined that two Sahibs would be out in front scouting the route to the next camp, two would stay with the science package at all times, and two would be at the tail end dealing with the stragglers. Those in between would be taken care of by Major Gujral and his men. Moe and Sweetner were the scouts for the first day and so were on the trail a good hour before the first porters awoke. It was quite impressive to see well over two hundred men with their loads head out of camp on that first morning.

Crate after numbered crate was checked off as each porter and his burden walked by Lloyd and Sergeant Mustafa. The heavy loads, such as the seismometers and the oxygen, were carried by horses and ponies. The porters, in addition to their assigned loads, brought with them sheep, goats, and chickens to supplement their food source. It was a real traveling circus then.

It seemed like days since anyone had remembered having seen the sun; however, that point did little to subdue the enthusiasm of the porters, who were glad to finally be on the road and making money. The feeling of well-being was in the air, and the unpleasantries of the past few days were but a distasteful memory.

From the first porter to the last, the line stretched for over a mile and took several hours for it to move through an area. The initial obstacle was at a place about two hours' walk from their encampment and on the outskirts of Skardu. The Indus River had to be crossed. Fortune was smiling upon them that day, for there was a narrow, wooden suspension bridge that had been in place before the dawn of time. The porters, when they first saw the structure, were apprehensive about using it with their heavy and unwieldy loads.

THIS DAY'S BUSINESS

The soldiers, however, spaced out the load bearers so that they did not bunch up or overstress the span. One by one they gingerly tested the boards. Satisfied that they might hold the weight, each Balti inched out farther across the river. Eventually everyone was across and safely on the far side. It was a great beginning to a first day.

Eagen was on the trail again, happy and alone with his thoughts. The path and his rucksack were becoming an extension of himself once again as he felt his tense and tired muscles stretch and respond to the demands of the trail. This was the first time in weeks that he was not in the company of others. Hours seemed to pass without seeing anyone, and then, from time to time, as he stopped to gaze back down the winding path, he would catch glimpses of porters as they rounded a curve or crested a hill. But, by and large, he was alone.

The trail ahead was an obvious one, even to a blind man. Hardly anyone could fail to notice the path that betrayed the passing of hundreds of feet and hooves. It was here, on the trail, that Eagen was able to lay back in his mind and admire the scenery such as it was. He employed an old climber's strategy to wile away the tedious hours of walking. He was able to put his wits in neutral and let his subconscious do the plodding along. This left his mind free to wander off or to tackle some administrative or logistical problem.

The march had taken them through orchards of apricots and peaches; among patches of pine and birch; through groves of fragrant spruce and juniper. It was for this and more that Eagen considered himself a lucky man.

The first night's camp was among a boulder field. The house-sized rocks provided a wealth of protection for the porters, who were fending off the damp breezes that flooded into the lowlands in the late evening. With the largest open area being taken up by the supplies, there was no room to set up the large community tent. Therefore, every one of the team pitched their smaller mountain tents. The groans that resulted from aching muscles were soon replaced by the deep snoring of the exhausted.

At sunrise they were off. It was a scene to be repeated until they reached Concordia a week into the future. The conga line treaded the path in a lifeless desert of exposed sandstone and blowing sand. Occasionally the porters would break out in song to see them through the difficult walking. Yet, at other times, there would be silence from all as the eye concentrated on the delicate way underfoot. Eagen, ever the geologist, was looking about for suitable rock samples to catalog. It never occurred to him that with each specimen saved, the heavier his pack grew. That night in camp, safely tucked away in his tent and snuggled up in his sleeping bag, he lit his candle lantern and began a rudimentary cataloging of his samples.

Red sandstone, he thought, *Probably of the Miocene Era. Yesterday outside Skardu there was igneous rock everywhere and that's volcanic in origin. This must be part of the Kohistan Island Arc, the group of islands formed between Asia and India before they collided.* His eyelids were growing heavy from the day's hike, and he was feeling the sandman's handiwork. He blew out the candle and reveled in the blackness of the night. His last conscious act for the day was to burrow deeply into the womb of his sleeping bag. Just before the tide of sleep washed over him, he thought of the fifteen miles walked the day before and the fifteen miles they had completed that day. They would be lucky to make half of that from then on as the path wound its way up into the foothills. The way was sure to become more chaotic and more challenging.

The Braldu River was the next hurdle to be surmounted. This was the river that they would follow for the next sixty miles to its source, the Baltoro Glacier. But first, they had to reach the far bank in order to take advantage of easier walking. To remain on the near side was to add at least three days to the march because of the difficult terrain.

They could hear its angry and tortured flow before they could see it. The river was flush with the meltwater from the glacier many miles distant. The milky brown water boiled with turbulence as it tossed boulders and rocks as if they were stage props.

The scouting team of Curly and Larry found another suspension bridge just around a bend in the trail only several hundred yards from where the porters called a halt. They started to huddle in small groups as several of them gestured wildly. The Americans could not understand what was getting the porters all lathered up, but with so many pointing to the racing waters and the bridge, there eventually left little doubt. Lloyd made his way past the head of the line for a closer examination of the problem at hand. After an hour of inspecting the questionable structure, he and the team walked back to the throng just as the last of the loads arrived on site. Only three

THIS DAY'S BUSINESS

things were clear. It was a bridge; it was suspended, and it looked dangerous as all hell.

The porters wanted no part of that bridge-crossing business. It was the typical rope suspension type that was seen the world over. There were two ropes at armpit height for hand holding with a third one of larger diameter for the feet. Lloyd was quite reluctant to send someone over on it, much less risk a load.

The major and Shastri were called forward to confer with the Sahibs. Lloyd needed to know the alternatives. He was frustrated by Shastri's report that this was the only bridge for twenty miles. It was there they had to cross, and they apparently had to do it over this bridge. Understandably, the porters were becoming upset, for they had not signed on for anything quite that dangerous. Some were beginning to talk of dropping their loads and leaving for home. The Americans could sense another outbreak of violence coming on, and they wished to defuse the situation before it got out of hand. Besides, they could not afford to lose any porters because each and every load was vital. Their options were discussed and weighed in a sometimes heated and animated way.

Gujral was starting to speak again of shooting a few of the porters as an example to the others, and Shastri was for abandoning the whole thing, paying off the porters, and going home. Neither choice was acceptable. In the end, it was decided to offer the Baltis an extra day's wage just for the dangerous crossing and an extra half day's wage for every day spent on the glacier ahead. There was continuous negotiating back and forth with the porters making absurd demands that were not possible to grant. In the end, it was agreed that two days' pay would be given to cross the river because it would be encountered again on the way home, and an extra half day's pay for every day spent on the glacier. The porters were attempting to milk the deal for all it was worth. But there were limits.

The three strands of rope were weatherbeaten and rotted in a number of places. No one relished the idea of using it; however, the bridge was the only option they had at the moment. The plan was to send one man across roped up. In keeping with his lead from the front style, Eagen volunteered to go first. A half hour later, he was in his climbing harness, weaving a figure of eight knot through the attachment loop. The rope was merely a psychological safety device, because if he did fall into the river, the current would sweep him away quickly, and he would be powerless to do anything about it. It ran so swiftly that he would most likely be sucked down into it and dashed to pieces on the hidden boulders. If he somehow managed to stay afloat, the freezing cold of the ice water would numb his limbs and he would die in minutes from hypothermia. The rule for survival was an absurdly simple one: do not fall!

Eagen was screwing up his courage and trying to keep his knees from knocking as he climbed the few rock steps to the point where the ropes were anchored. Leaving terra firma resolutely behind, he reached for the two-hand ropes and put a death grip on each. Leaning forward, he slid the instep of each boot sole slightly farther out ahead of him. Thus began one of the wilder experiences of his life. Foot by painstakingly slow foot, he slid his way along the rotted old rope. As he applied his weight with each new stride, the strands beneath his feet would stretch and sag like a played-out rubber band. He had to maintain his balance and resist the urge to pull on the two upper-hand ropes, for they too would stretch or snap if he pulled on them. By then he would be out of balance and would fall the fifteen feet into the frothing liquid ice.

Midway out on the river, the mist from the day had turned to a spitting snow, and he was starting to squint from the wet flakes hitting his eyelashes. The spray from the river below was soaking him to his knees, and the roar from the rushing water was deafening. All those sensations were adding up to one intimidating feeling of isolation although over two hundred pairs of eyes were locked on him. As cold as he was, Eagen could tell that he was sweating profusely from the concentration and fear. His sense of tunnel vision left him room only to focus on his foot placements and nothing more. It took forever, it seemed, to make the crossing. In the end, he was soaking wet and shivering almost uncontrollably. He had all he could do to make the rock steps on the far side and sit down. It was the longest hundred and fifty feet. Curly was next, then Lloyd. Each one kissed the ground when he got off.

It was one thing to get a lightly loaded and physically fit man across the water; it was quite another thing altogether for an unmotivated, heavily laden porter to attempt the crossing. It was deemed too hazardous for the porters and impossible for the horses

THIS DAY'S BUSINESS

and ponies. Another way would have to be found. Curly brought one of the camp radios with him while Moe, on the far bank, had another. The roar of the river made communicating with the far bank nearly impossible. It was Major Gujral who came up with an alternative plan. The main body of the expedition would move upstream several hundred yards to a sandy beach where they would wait until shortly before dawn when the day's meltwater was at its lowest and slowest point. They would then ford the river using some of the climbing rope as a safety line. Curly volunteered to go back over the rope bridge to the main body. On his return to Eagen and Lloyd, he would reel out the main safety line from a spool attached to his day pack. With tension applied, this line would be secured at both ends. Upon this cable they fitted a pulley. The plan called for the porter to attach himself to the pulley by a sling around his body. A second line was tied to the sling so that the porter could be hauled along the length of the rope if needed, guided by the pulley. Once the far shore and safety were reached, the line and sling could be retrieved for the next crossing. The horses and ponies would require their handlers to prod and guide them along their way. Alan and Eagen, on the far side, prepared themselves for a soaking wet and thoroughly miserable night without a tent, sleeping in their rain gear.

Well before first light, the entire caravan was ready. It was judged that the river conditions would never get any better. Curly was the first to cross. Carrying just his rucksack and the rope secured to his climbing harness, he switched on his head lamp and waded into the liquid ice up to his knees. Using ski poles for balance and support, he let out more than a few whoops and hollers as the water climbed to his crotch. The Balti people learned a few new words of English that day! Bracing himself against the current in the semidarkness, the spotlight pierced the gloom just enough to let him see the swiftness of the flow around him. Sometimes it was better not to see the big picture. He could feel the drag on his body as his pockets filled with rock flour, the sediment left from pulverized rocks that were suspended in the turbid waters. The riverbed beneath his boots was being pulled away from underneath him. He was delicately trying to pick his way through the ever-present undertow. It was impossible to read the surface of the water for clues of what lay beneath. It would not do to stumble on a hidden rock or slip into a hole. Even with the added stability of the ski poles, it would be too easy to topple over and disappear. At midstream his legs were going numb, but the bottom was relatively flat and free from obstructions. This allowed him to move faster, until he flopped into the waiting arms of Eagen and Lloyd.

The line was stretched as tightly as possible and secured at both ends. Gingerly and with much hesitation, the first porter went, then the second, then the third. They were all terrified and rightly so. In the dark of a foggy predawn, one could only see a foot or two ahead. Because of the frigid water, legs would quickly go numb. This made the footing all the more treacherous. All around them the current was just waiting for a misstep to bowl them over and take them away.

As each one made it across, Eagen and Lloyd were waiting to assist the harried porter up onto dry land. The four-footed porters had the least trouble but the same could not be said for their handlers. Moe crossed with the Balti and his horse that was carrying the boxes, while Larry and Gujral's men escorted the pack animals that were carrying the oxygen.

Lloyd remained on the far bank to encourage and direct the porters to high ground. He would not allow them to huddle up after the crossing. Instead he directed them to keep walking so they would warm up faster. It was not a popular decision with them, but Lloyd knew that if they did not keep moving, their leg muscles would cramp up. They had to keep moving to stay warm. Lloyd sent Sweetner ahead alone to scout the way to the village of Bardomal, which was the next campsite. He made the hike over easy terrain in excellent time and was back to the river before the the first fifty porters had crossed. In talking the situation over with Lloyd, it was decided to push on through all the way and clear the last major hurdle, the Braldu Gorge.

The walls of the gorge were very steep in places and quite sharp in contrast to the broad, flat plain they had just left behind. The switchback trail led upward in a zigzag fashion, almost touching the base of the dense, somber clouds. That was barely a goat track some two feet wide and studded with loose rock underfoot. Those foothills, like mountains everywhere, were disintegrating pebble by pebble under the influence of gravity and the climate. From time to time, a loose chunk would go zinging by, sometimes plummeting straight

THIS DAY'S BUSINESS

down to the river below and sometimes ricocheting off the walls above.

Although the porters were heavily laden, they seemed to have little trouble negotiating the steepness. In contrast, the horses were a source of concern. They seemed to have a better sense of danger than their human counterparts. At times they would balk or hesitate when a very narrow or steep portion of the trail was reached. More than once the long train was held up on very exposed terrain when a pack animal or human came down with a case of the jitters. It would take more than a few minutes to calm the situation down. The soldiers were stationed at the worst places to keep everything moving.

It was long after dark when the last of them stumbled, tired and cold, into camp at Bardomal. There was little sign of relief in the eyes of the trekkers. Everyone was beat. They had completed ten long miles over some of the toughest terrain ever. Later, as Sweetner looked out from his tent, he remarked to himself that the usual bonfire in the Balti camp was missing that night. Everyone was wet from the constant mist; they were all weary and just plain miserable.

The Sahibs gathered around a small campfire and took each other's council. Shastri was quite insistent that the porters be given the next day off to regroup and dry out their clothes. Lloyd agreed and then disappeared into his tent for the night. Soon he was adding his contribution to the crescendo of snores that rose up from the camp.

The temperature had dropped overnight, and the fine mist that had been their constant companion for days was sharing the sullen grey sky with intermittent wet snow. The porters kept to themselves, huddled beneath their tarps for most of the day. They passed the time by drying out their clothes over smokey wood fires and by making chapattis that they would consume in the days ahead. The Sahibs had the main tent erected where they secluded themselves until supper was served. Both cooks were kept busy fussing over the gas propane stoves.

On the morning of the sixth day, Larry and Curly set off before three o'clock. They were to scout ahead for an anticipated campsite eight miles away. The trail was flat and wide with few obstacles. The air at this altitude had dried out considerably, and the sun was fruitlessly attempting to burn off the ever-present cloud cover. They were now able to see up into the side valleys where fields of poppies, and what appeared to be violets, were spotted. Every now and again, a breeze would carry the scent of grass, which could lighten the most burdened of shoulders.

The main body of the trek arrived in Paiju at around two o'clock in the afternoon to the great excitement and curiosity of the few inhabitants. It was now the middle of September, and at almost eleven thousand feet altitude, the growing shadows chased the plunging temperatures. It was the first time that Eagen donned a heavy sweater underneath his rain jacket. Although there was still daylight left, everyone agreed to stay put for the night rather than press on. The days ahead would be short in the distance gained due to the difficult condition of the trail. That evening the Baltis scoured the sparse groves of birch and poplar trees for firewood. That would be the last opportunity for gathering.

A further journey of one hour saw the first of the porters through the boulder field. It was a maze of rocks that would rival the finest hedge groves of any French palace. Lloyd and Major Gujral were out in front by about an hour. They were the pathfinders who left strips of surveyor's tape on the rocks as a trail marker for the Baltis to follow. Without them making the mistakes, and then correcting them, the expedition would quickly grind to a halt with everyone following false leads.

At ten thirty in the morning, Sergeant Mustafa and three of the first porters came upon the scouts. Lloyd had everyone dump their loads and rest. There was to be a meeting of the entire expedition. Lloyd was kicking his boots at the loose rubble at his feet. With the surface scraped bare, the greyish white ice crystals could be detected. They had arrived at the foot of the Baltoro Glacier.

Again the camp table and chairs were brought out in a replay of hiring day. Handing a clipboard to the sergeant, the major directed Mustafa to locate and set aside specifically numbered cartons and to arrange them in order before the Sahibs. The porters were lined up before the table with the cane-wielding soldiers hovering nearby to keep order. Each porter was issued a pair of high-topped sneakers, a cheap plastic rain jacket, sunglasses, and woolen mittens. This was not called for in the verbal contract back in Skardu. If anything, it was a bribe to ensure that there were no slow-downs or strikes between

THIS DAY'S BUSINESS

there and Concordia. Lloyd liked to look upon it, with tongue in cheek, as a small token of the team's goodwill for the people they had hired. In any event, the nights would be colder at a little over twelve thousand feet, and those who were barefoot could not be expected to walk on ice and snow in that state. Any way one looked at it, it was still baksheesh.

They were entering the most strenuous and desolate portion of the trek as they camped at Udorkas. The deserted village was nothing more than a loose collection of goat herders' shacks that were abandoned until the spring. They were situated on a grassy slope about three hundred feet above the glacier, which, with its openness to the landscape, offered little to block the incessant wind. With every human finding shelter from the elements, the camp was quiet for the night. Many minds pondered the next day's route, which would involve the crossing of numerous subsidiary glaciers, climbing up and over a Byzantine and chaotic array of rocks and boulders, and dealing with the cold. Sometime in the night, a light dusting of snow covered the camp.

Sweetner stirred in his sleeping bag until his nose was free of the feathered caccoon. He was aware that it was damned cold outside and he had to piss like a horse. Facing the inevitable, he gritted his teeth and did the unthinkable. He unzipped from the warmth that surrounded him and prepared to put on near frozen clothes. Pulling away the flap of the tent made him wince. The first breath of air was so cold and devoid of moisture that it hurt his lungs to breathe.

Further, he was nearly blinded by the intensity of the sunlight. His foggy brain realized this possibly meant that a stretch of clear weather had descended over them. He finished unzipping the rest of the tent flap and rolled out onto the glacier and a totally cloud-free morning. Sweetner stood up and twirled himself around three hundred and sixty degrees. There were mountains everywhere, huge mountains. Up until then, the low cloud cover had revealed only the bottom third of those giants. Previously, his only scale of reference had been the glass and steel peaks that formed the canyonways of New York City. It was quite probably the nearest thing to a religious experience for him. All that could escape his enraptured throat was a long and drawn out, "Wow."

Without realizing it, the previous night they had camped in the

131

gloom and fading light beneath the ice-covered, fluted walls of the Trango Towers. The Towers were a complex of granite spires that pierced the skyline at twenty thousand six hundred feet.

He called the others out from their sleep to marvel at the scenery. The cooks, who had been up an hour earlier preparing breakfast for the team, handed each one a steaming mug of tea to ward off the cold. Maps were laid out on the table as the Sahibs tried to pick out landmarks from the surrounding peaks. It was a fairyland of pink and white that bathed the granite walls around them. To the south, they could spot the Masherbrum Group of mountains with their summits averaging twenty-five thousand feet high. But no one could find K2, the second highest in the world, or their destination, Gasherbrum IV. As the sun was clearing the lower hills to the east, the growing intensity of light, which reflected off so much snow and ice, soon drove everyone to the tents in search of their dark goggles. There was a feeling among the team that if they made haste today they might reach Base Camp at Concordia by nightfall.

Sweetner and Eagen were the first out of camp and on the road by several hours. They were tasked with finding a suitable location for Base Camp. Along the way they placed bamboo wands in the ice to mark the route for the porters to follow. They also had to locate and mark any obvious crevasses. These were the ruptures in the ice caused by the stress and movement of the glacier. They could be exposed at the surface and, therefore, easily seen or partially covered by a thin bridge of snow and hidden from view until it broke under the weight of someone walking on it. Either way, they were very deep and potentially lethal.

The sun was climbing higher in the sky, and the rays of light were becoming intense. Sweetner peeled off layers of clothing until he was barechested. Although slightly uncomfortable, Eagen chose to keep his heavy wool shirt on. They were at fifteen thousand feet on a moving river of ice that had taken decades to inch its way across the barren landscape. At this altitude there was less atmosphere to filter out the harmful ultraviolet rays from the sun. The opportunities for becoming badly sunburned increased with altitude as they plodded on. As if that weren't bad enough, the snow and ice were six times as reflective as water. Not only was the radiation raining down from above, but it was being reflected back up at them from the surface and

THIS DAY'S BUSINESS

from the sides. The effect was similar to being in a microwave oven.

In the early hours of the day the walking was easy; it was reassuring to hear the crunching of the hard snow beneath one's boots. The pair navigated by compass and maps, which they found to be surprisingly accurate. With the sun higher in the autumn sky, the warming rays reached down beneath the glacier's surface and transformed the top several inches into slush. Occasionally, they would encounter a patch of soft snow and sink up to their knees, making the trail a real slog.

At four thirty that afternoon they both agreed and shook hands. They had arrived. Concordia was so named by Sir Martin Conway as the Place de la Concorde. It was situated at the confluence of the Godwin-Austen Glacier and the upper Baltoro Glacier. It appeared as a boundless plain of ice with the surrounding peaks soaring to over twenty-eight thousand feet. They were both stunned, in awed silence, at the grandeur. Eagen and Sweetner dropped their packs and sat on them, with their backs to one another. They just stared with open mouths. Once in a while they would shift their positions to gain a new perspective.

"Where is it?" asked Eagen

"Aaah, right over there, in front of us," was his partner's reply as he consulted the map. Sweetner stood up and put his goggles back on. "Godamighty," was all he could say as his eyes kept sweeping upward. Eagen had the binoculars trained on the near vertical southeast face of Gasherbrum IV. The climber in him succumbed to the natural urge to search out a route. "I feel something beginning to pucker," said Sweetner as he concentrated on the immense wall of ice before them. Eagen could only nod in silent agreement. For an hour they sat in rapt silence, entertained by the sound of ice crystals being blown across the surface of the ice, and by the occasional avalanche sloughing off some unnamed, unclimbed wall in the distance.

The chill finally snapped the pair from their trance. It was decided to site the camp about one hundred yards east of where they were. This was intended to put them out of reach of all but the most massive avalanches that might thunder down upon then.

The first of the porters, with Lloyd at their head, were arriving. As more of the weary, heavily laden Baltis trooped into camp, it became apparent to Sweetner that the porters were not using any of the clothing that had been issued to them. He asked Lloyd about this.

The major and Shastri came huffing and puffing along, and they were asked about the new gear. Shastri had the answer.

"Sahib," he said, "Sahib, they say that the warm clothes are part of their pay. They are bringing them back to sell or give to their wives, but they won't wear them for themselves."

Shaking his head, Sweetner just walked away. Thinking to himself, he knew that it wouldn't be his ass that froze that night.

With a well practiced movement, the camp was set up before nightfall. In the center, a pit thirty feet long and twenty feet wide by three feet deep was dug into the ice. In it were placed all the boxes, barrels, and crates holding the expedition's stores. The snow removed from the pit was fashioned into a wall surrounding the supplies. Then, tarps were laid over everything and then tethered to the ice. The tents went up next, first the Sahib's main tent and then the three Base Camp tents, which were intended for the shortwave radio, the kitchen, and the soldiers. The spotting scope and pedestal were erected facing the mountain, and the flags of the two nations were flown from the radio mast. This was town hall for the newest, remotest small city on the planet.

CHAPTER 11

Onward, Encryption Holders

It was one hell of a sunset that entertained them on that first day. Long after the brilliance of the star faded beyond the mountain ridges to the west, the higher peaks surrounding the camp were resplendently swathed in their alpine-glow pink. They jutted so high into the atmosphere that their summits were catching rays long after the source dipped well below the horizon.

Each of the climbing team stood in awe around the only campfire they would see until the expedition was concluded. Whether seated together in their aluminum folding camp chairs or standing around during an idle moment, they were mostly silent. If they spoke at all it was in the hushed whisper reserved for the back of the church. Indeed, they were supplicants in the sanctuary of the grandest cathedral on earth.

The porters made the first night at Base Camp a memorable one. The celebration began shortly after the first stars became visible in the eastern sky. The goats and sheep that had been brought along were slaughtered, and their meat was roasted over the coals. Firewood that had been scavenged from the forests down lower was piled ten feet high and lighted off. This brought on a night of singing, chanting, and dancing. Many an exploit of ancestors long dead was recounted in the stories and song of these happy people. The feast continued long into the night, until the roar of the crackling wood fire was reduced to a whimpering pile of glowing embers.

The following morning, just after breakfast, the porters were lining up, eager to be paid off and on their way. They were straining to hear the Sahibs give the orders to set out the pay table, just as they had in Skardu. Sweetner and the major were seated there with two of his armed soldiers guarding the money pouch. One by one they approached the table, presented their pay card to the major, who in turn handed it to Sweetner, who verified the man's thumb print. Each one was the same. He would receive his wad of rupee notes and rush off to join his comrades for the long journey home. Earlier, the team had picked ten of the more capable and eager porters to stay on as high-altitude porters or Haps. They were to receive double wages and to be outfitted with clothing and climbing gear similar to the Sahibs. They would be the supply chain that kept the upper camps stocked with the necessities of life while the team did the lead climbing and consolidating of the route farther up the mountain. This was the great prize for the Haps. It was their ticket out. On future expeditions they could command more pay, for they would now be more skilled, with a proven track record. If they were resourceful enough, they might even graduate into the lucrative field of guiding tourists. They had a real motive to perform.

By nine o'clock that morning, all of the porters had been paid off, and the camp at Concordia was beginning to empty of its residents. In a speech to the village elders before they left, Shastri reminded them that half would be expected back in three weeks to disassemble the camp and bring as much down with them as possible. The Haps were going about their business, with the Sahibs sorting the gear into piles for Base Camp and higher up. The work progressed until the Haps were issued their gear. From then on they spent their time strutting around like peacocks showing off their new treasures. In the fading purple shadows of a very long day, the expedition settled down to their first meal in solitude.

The dining was alfresco as they sat in a semicircle in the folding chairs outside the cook tent. There was only silence in the air, save for the hissing of the propane stove and the clinking of celebratory whiskey bottles. There was no wind, not even a breeze. The air was deathly still. Occasionally, one of the cooks would turn the roasting meat; the sizzling would break the spell for a few moments. Time for another silent toast. Clink. The next day would bring with it a firestorm of activity, but for the time being, there were many hues of purple, orange, and pink to stare at. A short time later, the six Americans, ten Haps, Shastri the Sirdar, the major, his orderlies, and the radio operator all scurried for the warmth of their sleeping bags. Whatever heat was in the air was quickly lost before the first twinkle of the stars.

"Sahib, Sahib," said the cook. The zippered flap of the tent was pulled open, and the soft morning light flooded in. Buried deep within the down bag he began to stir. "Tea, Sahib. Must get up now."

Eagen propped himself up on one elbow and scratched the itchy stubble of his beard as a scalding mug of sweet tea was handed to him. *Damn*, he thought to himself. *It's freezing cold*. He gulped the liquid until he drained the mug and slid back into the warmth and comfort of his feathered womb.

Moments later he was awakened again. "Sahib, Sahib. Sahib Lloyd says to get ass in gear." With that, he reluctantly pulled at the zipper and rolled out to greet the new day.

Around the breakfast table the team held the first strategy session. Eagen had planned to take Lloyd out to scout the route through the icefall and to search for a place to site camp I while the others held a climbing school for the ten Haps. The Sahibs felt responsible for the safety and wellbeing of these men. Everyone had to depend on everyone else and training was the only way to assure success. Nothing would sink their chances quicker than bad moral caused by an accident.

After breakfast, Sweetner busied himself by laying out the climbing gear into neat piles, while Alan and Eagen glassed the mountain for a potential route, any line of weakness, in the network of defenses that nature provided tall mountains. At nine fifteen that morning, just as the sun was rising above the southeast ridge of Gasherbrum IV, Alan Lloyd and David Eagen set off across the Baltoro Glacier on the last leg of a perilous journey. They were garbed in full climbing gear, a task that took nearly an hour to complete at fifteen thousand feet.

Earlier, as Eagen had struggled with the simple act of dressing himself, his mind had flashed back to a steamy Washington afternoon. It was a dress rehearsal of sorts. Everyone had tried on all their climbing clothing to verify the fit. Dachstein wool made up the large portion of the dress kit. This heavy, oily wool from Switzerland was renowned for its warmth and wear. First on was the wool one-piece long johns with the trap door. Next, the Dachstein knicker stockings, which came up over the knee. The wool pants that stopped just below the knee and overlapped the stockings came in sequence. On top was the heavy wool shirt with a wool sweater over that. As a barrier to the wind, the outer layer was a parka shell of the new cotton/nylon blend in international orange. This allowed the under layers to trap and retain the body's own heat. There was one final suit of armor. It would be saved for when conditions were at their worst. These suits were scheduled for use above Camp III. The two-piece down suit was bulky but very light in weight considering that it made Eagen look like the Michelin Man. The bottoms came up to just below his armpits, held up by suspenders. The great coat, made from the same nylon, had a fully insulated hood with wolf fur around the edges.

When he had tried the climbing suit on, he quickly started to overheat and became concerned that they might be too warm. With a chuckle, he now wondered if they might be warm enough. The crampons, the metal spikes attached to their boots, bit into the firm ice with a reassuring crunch as they made each step. They were roped up for safety, even down on the flats of the glacier. The whole ice scape might possibly be riddled with hidden crevasses, some of which were greater than one hundred and fifty feet deep. Only a detailed survey would tell; even then one could never be sure. In places one could run a tank over the surface with no effect. In others, the weight of a climber would break the thin crust hiding an abyss. Without a rope to arrest the fall, the unfortunate soul would plunge downward only to be lodged firmly against the fluted walls on either side. If the victim were not extracted quickly, death by suffocation or hypothermia was a slow certainty.

With them they carried bamboo wands, the type used in a home

THIS DAY'S BUSINESS

garden. To these they had attached strips of red cloth. These wands would mark the route for others to follow. In the beginning, the way would be discovered by trial and error and resemble the tracks of a drunken cockroach. But with time, it would follow the most efficient and safest way. The narrow track, which had to be constantly maintained, would eventually become a boulevard, widened and worn by the Haps on their supply runs.

Eagen and Lloyd walked a quarter of a mile to the start of the confused and disorganized icefall. It was only several hundred yards long in a straight line but could prove to be the most exacting and certainly one of the more hazardous sections of the climb. When the mountain crumbles and sloughs off the ice and snow, as all mountains do, it all lands at the base to reform into a glacier, a flowing river of ice. It is this river, usually pinched between the walls of adjoining mountains and ridges, that is the quintessential definition of chaos. As it bends and turns, finding the line of least resistance, it distorts and breaks up into chunks much like a child's pile of wooden blocks. The median size is that of a railroad car, with the larger ones exceeding the size of a house. But the challenge would not stop there. It's all moving downhill under the influence of gravity. It might flow steadily at centimeters a month or lurch several feet in the twinkle of an eye. Climbers could safely pass through an area repeatedly for days on end and do it in relative safety, until suddenly, without any warning, a catastrophe would occur. Hundreds or thousands of tons of ice would collapse on the unsuspecting, squashing them like a bug. It was the high altitude equivalent of Russian roulette. Someone on the team started calling it "The Valley of the Shadow," and the name stuck.

The pucker factor was very high for both Eagen and Lloyd as they methodically searched for a route amid the frozen debris. It would be bad enough for the Sahibs who might have to pass that way probably a dozen times in the course of the expedition, but the real concern was for the Haps, most of whom would have to make the trip on a daily basis performing their duties of supplying the higher camps.

The sun was burning off the high morning clouds, and the two climbers found themselves in a large reflector oven. They were hot, very hot, but they dared not peel down much beyond their woolen long-john shirts because the sun's ultraviolet rays would cook any exposed flesh. Already, Lloyd was feeling the insides of his nostrils being burned as the radiation was being reflected upward off the ice beneath them. Although the air temperature was eighteen degrees Fahrenheit, Eagen was sweating from the exertion at a higher altitude, and his dark goggles kept fogging up and obscuring his vision.

Lloyd was in the lead, with Eagen paying out the rope that would hold him in the event of a fall. From time to time Lloyd would come to a serac. Like the one before them, it was a large block of ice that was too dangerous to circumvent. To keep the route as straight as possible, he began to climb over it. Lloyd was out of sight from Eagen, having rounded a corner, but was still in contact with his partner. The rope would continue to slip through Eagen's mittened hands inch by inch. He could also hear the solid *thwack-thwack* of Lloyd's ice axe being solidly driven into the ice, and the *ka-chunk* of his front pointed crampons as they found purchase. Lloyd was literally walking his way up a wall of ice, held only by the thin points of his tools. Every ten or fifteen feet he would stop. From his perch of safety, Eagen could hear the ring of metal on metal as Lloyd tapped on and then threaded in an ice screw. This was a device, a hollow tube of chrome molly steel roughly nine inches long with very coarse threads spiraling around it. It was tapped into the ice until the threads bit and then literally screwed into the ice up to the hilt. At the hammered end was a rounded eye. The whole thing weighed about four ounces and resembled the letter q. When Lloyd moved, Eagen could hear his rack of screws, which hung from a bandoleer across his chest, klank and clink like dull wind chimes resonating in the breeze.

With six hours of hot, thirsty work completed, the pair opened up the route only a third of the way through the icefall. By two o'clock, the first wisps of cloud were beginning to form overhead, a pattern that was to repeat itself with clocklike regularity. It was time to head back to the comforts of Base Camp. Retracing their steps, the two climbers ascended from the bottom of a shallow crevasse to find one of the Haps approaching from the direction of the camp. He was carrying a large thermos of hot lemonade for the thirsty pair. Lloyd and Eagen each took turns chugging the liquid down their parched throats. When Eagen returned to camp, the first thing he did was to chew on Sweetner's ass for letting a man wander beyond the general

THIS DAY'S BUSINESS

confines of the area without being roped up for safety. Although the glacier surrounding the camp appeared safe, it could still be riddled with hidden crevasses capable of swallowing a man whole.

With daylight fading and the temperature dropping, there was a meeting for the whole expedition, Sahibs and Haps alike. Everyone congregated in and around the main tent, the "Big Top" as it was christened. The Big Top was a square tent, ten feet on a side. If one looked closely, he would notice that it was actually a double-walled shelter. The outer layer was of a waterproofed canvas and the inner fabric was a dense weave of nylon to ward off wind. The peak in the center conveniently allowed lines to be strung like clothesline. Two Coleman lanterns and a hanging stove were being put to use as each dangled from the newly strung rafters. It was here that they reviewed the day's progress, made plans for the next day, and listened to the shortwave radio for the weather forecast. Everyone ate the same food, which was a new experience for the Haps who were used to their simple fare. But they drew the line at the Wild Turkey. Being devout Moslems, they did not imbibe.

Eagen expressed his desire that he and Alan be out in front once again pushing the route through the icefall while Curly and Larry devoted their energies to consolidating the route as it existed then. In other words, they would attempt to make sense of what seemed to be aimless scrambling among the chaos of ice. Everyone else would secure a small perimeter around the camp. They would probe the ice with their ice axes, looking for hidden crevasses. This would extend fifty feet out in all directions, and then if none were found, wands would demark the boundary. No one was permitted outside the wands without being roped up for safety.

If any of the Sahibs spoke, Shastri was quick to translate for the benefit of the Haps. Under the white glow of the hanging lamps, the spirits were running high. With their bellies full of food and their snoots full of Turkey, the Sahibs filed out to their three-man tents, leaving the cook and his helpers to deal with the cleanup. Larry started what was to become a ritual of handing out aspirin. This was not so much to ease the pain of a strenuous day but more to combat the headaches that almost everyone was experiencing resulting from the altitude. This was something that effected everyone in one form or another. The only cure was to wait for the body to acclimate to the new altitude.

"Sahib, Sahib, get ass in gear."

Eagen awoke with a start as the cook's helper shoved mugs of piping hot tea through the unzipped door of the tent. Eagen had a bad headache and felt as if he had hardly slept at all the previous night and then it was up and at 'em time. As he sat up and partly unzipped his sleeping bag, he began accepting the tea from the door.

"Christ, it's cold," he said to no one in particular. He kicked at the pile of down and nylon at the back of the tent where Moe and Sweetner were snoring a duet. "Hey, you two. You want to drink this or wear it?"

As the two moles surfaced from their bags and accepted the hot tea, Eagen poked his nose around the tent flap and saw that three inches of new snow had fallen during the night. The Haps were busy banging the tent walls to clear away any accumulation. It was then that he reacted with a laugh to the cook's goofy, toothless grin.

The still air was frigid as Eagen clumsily staggered from the tent with his eyes squinting at the glare off the ice. It was the fog from his breath that reminded him to return and take his goggles and parka.

The steak and powdered eggs with hash browns went down very slowly. The chews were long and the swallows were longer still. He was sick, sick to his stomach, but he had to force himself to eat. It was the altitude again. From somewhere behind the Big Top he could hear the noise. Going outside slowly to investigate, he found Lloyd on all fours straining heroically, but with futility, against a bad case of the dry heaves. It would take time to get used to the thin air up there. Unfortunately, time was in short supply. Everyone would just have to soldier on.

Shortly after nine a.m., Lloyd and Eagen departed Base Camp. They were to pick up where they had left off the day before and, hopefully, make their way to the head of the icefall. Larry and Curly were getting dressed, and would be ready to leave within the hour. Their job was to consolidate the route, making it safer for the Haps who would eventually be passing that way unsupervised. Meanwhile, the Haps, with Sweetner and Shastri, were ferreting out any potential crevasses in the immediate vicinity of the camp. There was no Moe at the breakfast table. He was sick as a dog with a splitting headache and the heaves. He would spend most of the day

THIS DAY'S BUSINESS

lying right where he was. His place was taken by Major Gujral, who was anxious to explore as much as possible. This was as high as he had ever been, and he was feeling fit and eager.

What had taken them six hours to achieve the day before then only required three. They were at their farthest point as the sun reached its zenith. Occasionally, Eagen and Lloyd would stop in a protected spot atop a block of ice. Each would burrow deep into their packs for water or something sweet to munch on. They had stopped for lunch on one such plateau. The air was crisp, the scenery was panoramic, and life was good.

"Listen," Lloyd hushed Eagen. "Avalanche," he continued. Both pairs of eyes were rotating around, hoping it wasn't anywhere close.

"There," said Eagen. "See it? It's coming down off one of the Masherbrum Group."

They were both on their feet and pointing to the massive plunge of ice and snow falling from across the far side of Concordia. It was huge and there was nothing to stop it. From two miles away, it was plain to see that one hell of a lot of debris had broken loose and was rolling like a runaway freight train as it bore down on the Baltoro Glacier. They watched in awe as the frozen tidal wave finally halted, it's energy spent, just a hundred and twenty yards from the camp. From where they were standing they could not see the tents, but they knew there must be more than a few puckered assholes down there. At half past three that afternoon Eagen and Lloyd, both very tired, reached the top of the icefall. They should have turned back sooner but were so close to meeting their objective that they chose to press on. Now it would be dark when they arrived back in camp. They would have to use their headlamps for the last two hours. Being experienced mountaineers, this did not bother the pair, but there was considerable worry when they did not appear by dark.

The going was slow and the footwork was delicate; however, as the temperature was dropping, the snow was firming up rather nicely underfoot. The yellow-white beams from their lamps pulled back the veil of blackness ever so slightly. It was the mind that remembered the way. In the daylight, when passing through a section of the route, as one deliberately placed his boots, the mind was storing every nuance, every subtlety of the ice. It was being stored for possible use later. This was what familiarity with the route was all about. When one's whole world was illuminated in a three-foot circle, instinct would kick in and the way would be found.

Shortly after seven that evening they arrived in camp cold, wet with their own perspiration, and very thirsty. They were immediately ushered to the Big Top where they were plied with copious amounts of hot liquids and questions. Yes, they had made it to the top of the icefall. Yes, they had spotted a possible location for Camp I, and no, they hadn't seen any signs of Larry's and the major's route fixing on their return trip. The major asked them whether they had gotten lost.

Between all the excitement of their accomplishment and after more than a few pulls on the Turkey jug, Alan stood up a little unsteadily and said, "To paraphrase Jim Bridger, who was a famous mountain man of the early 1800's, when asked whether he had ever been lost, he was quoted as saying, 'No. But I admit to being damned confused for a couple of months.'" Amid all the laughter he collapsed into his chair as the strain of the day and the sipping whiskey let their effects be felt.

The next two days were spent consolidating the tortuous and serpentine route. The single biggest help were the twelve-foot sections of aluminum ladders that were a last-minute purchase in Skardu. When lashed together they became a bridge across some of the wider and more treacherous crevasses. Where Lloyd and Eagen had to circumvent them, thus adding distance and time to the route, the ladders allowed a more direct line. What originally took them twelve hours of steady, hard climbing to reach the top of the icefall could now be accomplished in half that time.

On the morning of September eighteenth under leaden skies and light flurries, Eagen and Lloyd set off to establish the route to Camp I. They would depart with heavy packs loaded with several tents, sleeping bags, stoves, and fuel. They were to dump their load at the proposed site and then return to Base Camp for a well earned rest. Others would follow in the days ahead with additional supplies to set up and establish the camp.

The pair made their way from the head of the icefall, wading through waist-deep powder snow.

Whoever was in the lead at the time had the most difficult go of it, because he had to break trail. It was a hard, exhausting plod, and the

THIS DAY'S BUSINESS

altitude was working against them all the way. In all, it took three hours to reach the proposed site of Camp I. From below, at the head of the icefall, the site appeared relatively flat and reasonably protected from rockfall. However, upon further inspection, it revealed itself to be anything but. The area, about the size of a gymnasium floor, was canted at a thirty-degree angle and littered with pumpkin-sized rocks. This last clue was evidence that the two were in a very unstable area. They named it the "shooting gallery," and the proposed site was the target. Their ears strained for the telltale sounds of rockfall: first the whistling and then the twang of rock ricocheting off rock. To a climber, this was a danger every bit as deadly as an avalanche. Both Eagen and Lloyd were on edge because they could hear stones coming down from somewhere but were not able to see them until very nearly the last moment.

The clouds, which had been obscuring the upper part of the mountain for the last few days, had been gradually descending with the resulting frozen precipitation in the form of light snow. This ever-lowering ceiling masked the limestone detritus as it plunged downward from some invisible height. The pair quickly shed their packs in the most protected place they could find next to a large boulder and then, with haste, retraced their steps for the relative safety of the icefall.

Several hours later they came upon Curly, Sweetner, and three of the Haps who had just finished securing a ladder bridge across one crevasse that appeared to be bottomless. In the dwindling light, they all turned on their headlamps and headed down. Eagen and Lloyd were due for a few days of rest.

The Big Top was packed that night as all ears were tuned to the shortwave radio. The eight p.m. weather forecast for the region from All India Radio reported that a large pool of high pressure was sweeping into the region and was expected to dominate the region for the next several days. Cheers went up.

As climbing leader, Eagen took over the meeting and went through his list of expectations for the days ahead. "Okay, okay," he exhorted, "let's settle down to business so that we can get down to some serious drinking." Another cheer. "We've got a three-day window of clear, stable weather in which to establish and occupy Camp I and, hopefully, scout the way to Camp II. Sweets, you and

145

Curly will take three of the Haps who were with Moe that day and hump loads up to Camp I and move in. Be aware that there is grave danger from stonefall so, if you can find a safer place, do it. Moe, you and Shastri will need to take three of the Haps and work on securing the route through the icefall. We've got to make it as safe as possible. Larry, you'll take the remaining Haps, with as much gear as you can carry, up to the top of the icefall. Dump it there and then come back down here for the night. Curly, when Camp I is set up, send your Haps down to retrieve everything that Larry drops off. That's about it. Questions? Yes, Moe?"

"How about radios and oxygen?"

Eagen continued, "Half of Larry's load will be oxygen, and there will be at least one radio with each group. We'll all be on the same frequency, and everyone will tune in at six a.m., noon, six p.m., and at nine p.m."

With that, the meeting broke up, and everyone but Lloyd drifted away for the warmth of their own tents. Sitting before the radio transmitter, he dialed in the agreed upon frequency for the U.S. Consulate in Islamabad and began to make his report.

Sweetner and his crew were off by headlamp just before three a.m. the next morning. The glow from the lamps revealed that it had been snowing for several hours. The icefall was always considered unstable, but it was a bit more so with the sun beating down on it and warming the surface. Curly told Eagen that he was constantly fixing portions of the route because this block or that chunk had collapsed sometime during the day. At night when the temperatures dropped the snow and ice would firm up, and the route would become more stable but not necessarily more safe. Curly and his gang had been doing a good job of maintenance and bridge building when Sweetner's Haps reached the first aluminum ladders. There was hardly a balk from anyone. Sweetner went first, belayed by Moe. Fixed ropes were in place and anchored across each bridge for security. The challenge was to place one's cramponed boots on the rungs without tripping or developing vertigo. The temptation was easy for the eye to focus on the depth of the fissure and not where the climber was placing his feet.To further intensify the delicate situation, the feeble beam of light from the headlamp would only illuminate the gaping jaws of doom for a few feet. What lay beneath

THIS DAY'S BUSINESS

was left to the imagination. That was one case where it paid not to be overly bright. Also, the ladder sections were flexible, and it didn't take much movement to induce an oscillation that only a trampoline could duplicate. The first and last climber across had the more difficult time of it because he would be belayed or secured only from behind or in front. Those in the middle had the assurance of two ropes to save them. One foot delicately placed in front of the other was the mantra.

They cleared the top of the icefall by nine that morning and were en route to Camp I. At noontime, Base Camp opened up on the frequency with Lloyd at the microphone. They were listening for Sweetner to begin transmitting, but there was a lot of interference. Finally, they were heard. The voice was faint and the reception was somewhat garbled because the radio link was largely dependent on a line of sight transmission, but there was no mistaking Sweetner's southern drawl.

Sweetner: Base Camp, Base Camp, this is Camp I, over. Base Camp, this is Camp I, over.

Lloyd: Camp I, this is Base. Reading you, weak but clear, over.

Sweetner: Base, this is Camp I; we just reached the site and are beginning to set up the tents, over.

Lloyd: Sweets, how's the rockfall situation up there? Is there any chance of finding a more protected area? Over.

Sweetner: Christ, you guys named this place correctly. It's bloody dangerous up here. We've already had a few close calls. We're starting to go into the shadows from the southeast ridge so the light is beginning to fade up here right now, but, I think I can see a better location about half a mile further up into the amphitheater. I'll want to check it out at first light in the morning. Over.

Eagen: Sweets, this is Eagen. Don't screw around up there. If you don't feel comfortable with the site, then move back down to the top of the icefall for the night. I'll be coming up in the morning. I'll be bringing three or four of the Haps with me. Is there anything you need? Over.

Sweetner: Other than what you've got scheduled to come up, I can't think of anything special. What time should I be expecting you? Over.

Eagen: We're going to try to be off by midnight so as to reach you before sunrise while the rocks are still plastered in solid. Over.

Sweetner: Very good. We can look over that area I spotted and…oh yeah, bring up some of that rum cake if you have the room. Over.

Eagen: Rum cake, okay. We'll try to leave you some. It's awfully good, you know. We'll talk to you again at six p.m. Over.

Eagen and Lloyd immediately set out to make a list of what they would be bringing up with them in the morning. With the master list in hand, they were hunting through the numbered crates when their attention was diverted by the sound of a muffled explosion in the distance. Rounding the corner from their tents, they could see several of the Haps pointing uphill in the direction of the icefall. They were quite agitated and jabbering unintelligibly among themselves. The major began to question them as he scanned the area with his binoculars.

Hearing Eagen and Lloyd approach, he said matter of factly, "There's been a collapse up in the icefall." Handing the glasses to Lloyd, he continued, "It must've been up where all the snow and ice crystals are still flying all about."

Immediately, their thoughts went to Moe, Shastri, and the Haps. "Has anyone seen signs of them?" asked Lloyd.

"By now, they should've been through that part of it," Eagen said.

THIS DAY'S BUSINESS

"We're not expecting them back much before six p.m. We'll just have to sit tight and wait it out til then."

It was a tense several hours that played out at Base Camp with everyone taking turns at the spotting scope. All were eager to spot any sign of movement from the icefall climbers. At five thirty, the major saw them. All five were just emerging from the shadows of the ice towers where they opened out onto the broad, open glacier. A half hour later they were in camp, very tired, but safe. Moe was the first to reach the tents and report in.

"Yeah, a big sucker collapsed just behind us. Another two or three minutes either way and we'd have been porked. We must've lost a ladder in there, but the whole area will be more stable now; we might even be able to go up and over the debris. I need a drink." With that, they dumped their packs as everyone headed into the Big Top for the evening meal. At six p.m., the Base Camp radio crackled to life, and the call went out to Camp I. Nothing.

At nine o'clock that night Lloyd was once again at the shortwave transceiver trying to establish communication.

> **Lloyd**: Camp I, Camp I, this is Base. Over. Camp I, this is Base; how do you read? Over.

> **Sweetner**: Base Camp, Base Camp, this is I. Over. We've had an accident up here. We lost one of the Haps. Over.

> **Lloyd**: How bad is it? When did this happen? Over.

> **Sweetner**: "We had, what I felt was, a slight earth tremor, and then we saw a large serac collapse in the icefall. The Haps were on their way down from here to the top of the icefall with Curly to retrieve the gear that was dropped off. Apparently, that triggered a rock slide, and Yousef Amahd was struck and killed instantly. No one else was injured. Over.

There was silence on the frequency while those at Base Camp absorbed the terrible news. Moments later, Lloyd came back on the air.

Lloyd: Sweets, what's the status of the camp? Do any of your people want to come down? Over.

Sweetner: Base, we're going to move everything nearer to the head of the icefall and sort it out in the morning. Are you still planning to come up? Over.

Eagen: Sweets, this is Eagen. Larry and I are coming up in the morning with three Haps. We'll be leaving at midnight and should be up to you by first light. How are the Haps taking this? Over.

Sweetner: Eag, they're pretty much stoic about this. I'm sure that they're hurting inside, but they're not letting on if they are. Over.

Eagen: Roger that, Camp I. I'm going to want to see that possible site for Camp II that you spotted. We may have to bypass the Shooting Gallery altogether. Incidentally, we've still got two more days of good weather, so we'll have to make the most of it. Have Curly ready to take a crew of Haps down tomorrow. Over.

Sweetner: Okay, will do. See you in the morning. Over.

With that last transmission, the silence of the mountains returned except for the occasional sounds of invisible rock missiles raining down from the dark and turbulent heights above. They were no sooner off the radio when new plans were formulated under the Big Top. Lloyd started the ball rolling by having Shastri assemble the Haps together. A brief prayer ceremony was conducted for the unfortunate porter and then the work of gathering the loads for the next carry began.

Eagen, Larry, and four of the Haps were away shortly after midnight under an overcast sky. It was beginning to snow. Lloyd stood in the doorway of the Big Top with the light of the gas lanterns flooding out before him onto the tracked-up surface of the glacier. He did not move a muscle until the glow of the headlamps from the relief

THIS DAY'S BUSINESS

crew faded away. This was the first fatality for him in his many years of climbing, a sport that was notorious for its fatalities. He was visibly moved by the events of the past day, yet resolute in seeing the project through to completion.

The snow was quite firm, which made the going much easier. Once the temperatures dropped with the coming of sunset, any loose, unconsolidated powder became firm snowpack. On a bright, sunny day the icefall took on a different air. One with a touch of otherworldliness about it. It was as beautiful and claustrophobic as it was dangerous. However, at night it took on a dreamlike quality. The groans and cracks of the ice as it expanded and contracted were noticeably constant. The devils that dwell in the bile of fear failed to manifest themselves in the usual manner.

Eagen's team was making excellent time through the tricky parts of the white maze. Stopping only infrequently for water breaks to ward off dehydration, they had little difficulty with the ladder bridges.

It is a psychological thing, he thought to himself. *What you can't see or hear can't hurt you.* The collapsed section held them up briefly, but a reconnaissance of the debris yielded a quick detour. It was shortly before six that morning that they emerged from the icefall. They were greeted by the headlamps of Sweetner's team coming down from the Shooting Gallery to meet them. They dropped their packs and began brewing up tea while the situation was discussed.

With Eagen using his binoculars to scan the way ahead, Sweetner began his assessment of the previous night's tragedy. "Come on, I'll show you where it happened."

The two friends walked together in the ethereal light of dawn. They took a track that was already stamped out by the passage of many boots. "We were coming down to retrieve the supplies when I could feel the ice shift a bit; then we heard the collapse in the icefall. In all the excitement I forgot to ask about Moe's crew. I assume they're all right."

"Yeah," said Eagen. "Just barely. It collapsed right behind them."

As the two walked further on Sweetner did not need to tell Eagen where the accident had occurred. The fresh snow was stained a deep crimson for several yards around. Next to the trail lay the murder weapon. It was a rock slightly smaller than a basketball.

Sweetner continued, "We heard a bunch of stones come down from higher up, somewhere over to our left. This one came down from out of nowhere and decapitated him. There was other debris coming down afterwards so we didn't stand on ceremony. We wrapped him in a sleeping bag and lowered the body into a crevasse so that we could retrieve it on the way out. Anyway, it was a sleepless night. One of the Haps later got up to take a leak, and he no sooner left his tent when a five pounder nailed it. He would've bought the farm too!"

"All right," said Eagen. "Let's get out of the area and check out that new site you mentioned." Without the packs, the two climbers were able to travel unfettered up the slight incline to a spot about a half mile away.

An hour of wading through thigh-deep snow brought them to the approximate site that Sweetner had spotted earlier. They were breathless and nauseated from the altitude, but that could not subdue their elation. The site was damned near perfect. It was far enough at a distance from the rotting limestone walls, and it was flat and large enough to hold the little Big Top that they brought up with them. They were, however, vulnerable to large avalanches coming down from the adjoining face of Gasherbrum III.

"Turn around and look up," said Sweetner.

"God O'Mighty," was all Eagen could say as he gazed upward at the headwall. He was awestruck at the enormity, the sheerness. There, before him, was a wall of ice and snow that went up, and up, and up, and up. For eight thousand feet, it went up at a sustained angle of seventy-five degrees. "This will make a great Camp II," continued Eagan as he stood transfixed and mesmerized by the vastness of the southeast wall of snow and ice. "Wait until they see this down at Base." Turning to Sweetner, he said through his Cheshire grin, "Let's sign the lease and move in right away!"

Everyone who was at Base Camp was glued to the shortwave radio for the noontime call.

Eagen: Base Camp, Base Camp, this is Camp II. Over.

Lloyd: Hello, Camp II, we read you loud and clear. Over.

THIS DAY'S BUSINESS

Eagen: Alan, we've established a great site for Camp II, right near the bottom of the face. Listen, I've got a plan that I want to run past you. First, Camp I is a death trap and should be bypassed altogether. The site we have for Camp II is nearly perfect and only an hour further. Second, I suggest that we travel between Base and Camp II only at night when the ice firms up. We had no problems going through last night. Third, we'll be sending down Curly with three of the Haps just after dark so they'll be getting in late. Keep the kitchen open. Four, I'd like to see as many supplies stockpiled up here as possible, using this as Advanced Base Camp. Next, I'd bring you up to run it while leaving the major in charge at Base. Think it over and let me know at the nine p.m. call. Over.

Lloyd: It sounds like a good plan to me. We'll begin to work on the logistics down here. We'll let you know later. What altitude are you at? Over.

Eagen: We're at eighteen thousand feet along the left hand edge of the route where it takes a dogleg to the right. It has an unobstructed view of the face. Over.

Lloyd: Sounds real good to me. We'll consult the photos and talk to you at nine. Over.

On the twenty first of September, a record eleven loads were carried up from Base all the way to Camp II. Even the major, one of his soldiers, and Shastri volunteered for carrying duty. They left Base at five thirty that evening and made the round trip in just over twelve hours. That phenomenal show of team spirit enabled Camp II to resemble a smaller scale version of Base Camp three thousand feet lower at Concordia. The timing could not have worked out better because the weather gods were becoming fickle. The ridge of high pressure that had controlled the weather for the past several days was beginning to break down with worsening conditions expected.

They started as flurries at first, but, as the hour approached for the evening radio call, the flurries gave way to a storm that was dropping snow at the rate of several inches per hour. Eagen turned on the handheld walkie-talkie and opened up the transmission.

Eagen: Base Camp, Base Camp, this is Camp II. Over. Come in, Base. This is II. Over.

When his finger released the transmit button there was only the crackling of interference. Over and over he gave the call. Nothing. After ten minutes of trying, the radio came to life. It was Lloyd calling.

Lloyd: ...amp II, Camp II...Camp. Over.

Eagen: Base Camp, you're breaking up but readable. Try boosting the output. Over.

Lloyd: Camp II, we're reading you weak. Over.

Eagen: Alan, what's the latest on the weather? Over.

Lloyd: Doesn't look good, guys. All India Radio is calling for an extended period of heavy snow followed by high winds for the next seventy-two hours at least. We may already have had our period of stable weather before the winter sets in. Over.

Eagen: Alan, we're already getting snowfall of two inches per hour up here, and I don't see any let-up. Over.

Lloyd: I know, I know. We're starting to get whipped around by the winds too. Will you be able to move upward tomorrow? Over.

Eagen:...amned if I know. We'll have to see what it looks like in the morn...It's...ime to get C...mp II fully o...rational. I'd like you and Curly to bring the box up here and plan to stay. We can then...wait a minute, Alan. Stay on the freq. I'll be right back.

THIS DAY'S BUSINESS

Sweetner had left the comforts of the little Big Top to investigate the noises coming from the storm outside. Ten minutes later he poked his head through the partly unzipped tent flap. Spindrift was finding its way in and around the opening. His face was plastered with wet snow.

"One of the Haps' tents collapsed from the weight of the snow," he said. "I'm helping them dig out. Be back in a few minutes."

> **Eagen**: Alan, we've just had a tent collapse on us. It's okay. After you guys bring up the box, we can send down all the Haps for a rest, then we can consolidate the camp and start scouting the way up to Camp III. Over.

> **Lloyd**: Roger that, David. We'll try to get up tomorrow, weather permitting. Goodnight. Over.

The morning radio call at six a.m. was not optimistic. The deep snow had yet to consolidate, and, for that reason, Lloyd was unable to leave camp with the box or the supplies. The storm had dropped over two feet of snow with the winds gusting to fifty miles per hour. The men at Base Camp were kept occupied by digging out their tents every few hours. They finally resorted to packing snow into walls around each one in a vain and utterly futile attempt to block the wind. Each tent had a structure surrounding it that resembled an igloo without a roof. The force of the wind was causing snowdrifts to form that even reached all the way up the side wall of the little Big Top, a tent that was large enough to allow a man to stand erect and stretch.

Higher up, the situation was worse. The Camp II people had given up on digging out the smaller three-man tents. They removed the aluminum stays that gave structure and form to the quarters and then unclipped the guy lines that held the tents up. The fragile nylon structures were emptied of sleeping bags, down jackets, boots, and other survival gear and were allowed to collapse and be buried under the weight of the rapidly accumulating snow. They could always be dug out and set up later. All eight of them, the Sahibs and Haps alike, were crammed sardine-like into the heavier, and hopefully sturdier, little Big Top. At the noon radio call, the only change in conditions was the depth of the snow. At six p.m., Lloyd reported that the snow depth had now reached six feet, and the winds were gusting upwards of ninety miles per hour. The camp was literally buried.

The besieged team at Base had to dig a ramp upwards from the front door to the surface. With only the roof poking up into the maelstrom, there was no longer a need to dig a trench around the perimeter. With food and fuel aplenty inside, the only reason to breach the surface would be to answer the call of nature, and one had to be very desperate to do that.

With both camps buried, the storm raged unabated, but in their artificial caverns, Meteora's wrath failed to penetrate. All was eerily silent. The nine p.m. radio call broke the monotony of the beleaguered camps.

Lloyd: Camp II, Camp II, this is Base. Over.

Eagen: Base Camp, this is II, reading you loud and clear. Go ahead. Over.

Lloyd: Hello, II. The weather report calls for clearing tonight followed by intense cold and high winds for the next several days. Over.

Eagen: Good news indeed. All's well up here. Immediately after the snow compacts we'll start digging out. When can you start up? Over.

Lloyd: Not tomorrow for sure. We got creamed down here. We'll have to dig down eight feet, because of the drifting, just to reach the tents. We'll try for the day after tomorrow, but frankly, in all probability, we'll need to fix the route through the icefall. It might be the day after tomorrow. Over.

Eagen: Understood, Alan. Right now we can hear a lot of thunder coming from up on the surface. We'll attempt to beat down a trail to the top of the icefall for you. Over.

Lloyd: Roger that. Let's see how things look at six a.m. Over.

Eagen: Right. Until six, then. Out.

THIS DAY'S BUSINESS

At six o'clock the next morning, it was evident that the weather situation had remained static. Clearing conditions with high winds and low temperatures were called for. The team at Camp II was still listening to the strains of rolling thunder dancing overhead.

"Damn," said Larry. "The air is getting pretty foul in here." Sitting up in his sleeping bag, he turned on his flashlight and surveyed the pile of bodies and equipment entwined in a chaos of nylon and down. "It's your socks. They stink. I can smell you from over here." It was Sweetner, musing from somewhere in the corner buried under a pile of sleeping Haps.

"Yo ho ho" came the anonymous chant from the black recesses at the back of the tent.

"Eight dead men in a six-man tent." Larry continued, "We've got to get some fresh air in here. I can't even get the candle to light." On all fours, he made his way over the human pig pile to the chorus of cursing in several languages. Once at the door, he unzipped it only to be met with a wall of snow. "Someone hand me a shovel, will ya? I think we're buried."

"Can't," came the reply from someone. "I'm using it for a pillow."

"You'll be using it for a suppository if you don't hand it over. We gotta dig out," said Larry rather testily.

After much rearranging of the pile, the broad, bladed aluminum shovel was produced and handed over to the front of the tent. Larry began attacking the white wall. After fifteen minutes of probing and shoveling outward, he started digging upward and quickly broke through to the surface; cold fresh air flooded in to replace the warm, stale air. He was able to clamber through the newly dug excavation and stood up with his head and shoulders sticking out.

"Hey, Eag, that ain't thunder we've been hearing. Those are frigging avalanches coming down all around us!"

"Thank God," said Sweetner. "I thought it was the Chicoms and the Paks having an artillery duel."

The loose and unconsolidated powder snow that had fallen in the last seventy-two hours was collapsing under its own weight and was following the line of least resistance down the face of the mountain. Fortunately, Camp II was situated on a slight promontory that allowed most of the tidal waves of snow to flow around the isolated climbers.

It took two days for the Base Camp crew to clean up and make safe the way through the icefall. Fixed lines had been snapped and had to be replaced. Several ladders had disappeared, buried actually, under many feet of snow, and a number of shallow crevasses had filled in. The look and feel, the shape and contour of the whole place had changed. It was as if they were seeing it again for the first time.

At three a.m. on the morning of September twenty-fifth, the crew from Camp II broke trail downward to the top of the icefall to aid their fellow climbers coming up. For the present, there was more danger from avalanches than from rockfall. Ice had plastered the rock faces temporarily sealing in most of what was loose and unstable. Moe, Larry, Sweetner, and Eagen went down into the icefall to retrieve the boxes from Lloyd and Curly. The Haps, still spooked from the accident, remained at the top just short of the shooting gallery.

As anticipated, the team climbing up was having a hard go of it from the deep powder. At sixty-five pounds apiece, the boxes were awkward and unwieldy to carry on the back. Lloyd and Curly were understandably exhausted when they were met. In the steel grey of a silent dawn, the boxes were hoisted upon somewhat fresher shoulders. The whole entourage took just under two hours to return to the questionable safety of Camp II. That morning and most of the afternoon were spent sorting all the equipment that was just brought up.

The Haps were very tired and still faced a six-hour down climb back to Base Camp and a rest. The good news was that they had brought up two of the four cooks from Base. The cooks, who had had no training before this one trip, were expectedly scared but eager to prove themselves. At six p.m., with a hot meal in their bellies, all the Haps turned downhill for the icefall and rest. The six Sahibs and the two cooks were alone at Camp II. At nine p.m. the evening radio call was made.

Lloyd: Base Camp, Base Camp, this is II. Over

Major Gujral: Camp II, this is Base Camp, reading you very weak but readable. Over.

THIS DAY'S BUSINESS

Lloyd: Major, we sent the Haps down at six and they should arrive around midnight. Be sure to leave a light on in the window for them. What is the latest development with the weather? Over.

Major Gujral: They're still calling for clear but very cold temperatures for the next few days. You can expect high wind conditions to be with us for the next several days. Over.

Lloyd: Very good, Major. Tomorrow will be a rest day up here for us and then we'll start pushing the route out and scout for Camp III. We're going to start sleeping on oxygen so make sure there are at least twelve bottles on every carry when they begin. Over.

Major Gujral: Yes, I will, Alan. Good luck. Over.

About three quarters of an hour had passed with the full team united for the first time in several days. They talked of the long anticipated push upward to Camp III and of the logistics. All six of the Sahibs were in their sleeping bags, which was the only place one could be assured of warmth. Moe matter-of-factly pulled himself partway free from his confines and consulted his chronograph and opened a small notebook, which he kept in his woolen shirt pocket.

"It's almost time, Alan," he said. Lloyd, looking at Sweetner, gave a nod in the direction of the zippered tent flap. On cue, Sweetner looked around for his mukluks and grunted as he pulled them on over his feet, all the while straining and gasping in the thin air. With a heave that had everyone adjusting their positions, he crouched in the doorway, then bolted out into the night. Eagen, who was lightly dozing in his bag, felt the rush of cold air on his face. His companions fell silent. Sensing a change of mood in the tent, he propped himself up on one elbow and looked around. Seeing a question on Eagen's face, Larry headed him off.

"He just went to check on the cooks."

Sweetner arrived back a few minutes later. His footsteps crunched in the firm snow as he approached the tent. The zipper came down with one sharp motion, and he wasted no time rolling into the tent.

Sweetner was careful not to bring his snow-encrusted legs in with him. Rather, he elected to sit in the doorway struggling to undo his footwear. It was considered bad form to track in any snow. Once melted, the water would invade someone's bag, leaving it soggy and unable to retain any warmth. The night air flooded in all around him.

"Damn, it's cold," he gasped between breaths. "It's about twenty below zero out there. You should see all the stars out tonight, though." He struggled to catch his breath and went on. "We seem to be above the clouds. I'll bet that it's snowing like hell down below," he said with a note of exhaustion.

"How are they?" asked Lloyd.

"Out cold, snoring up a storm," returned Sweetner between breaths.

Once again, Moe consulted his watch and his notebook. "The bird should be just about coming over the horizon," he said.

Lloyd unzipped his bag and sat up cross legged and reached for his down parka, which he draped around his shoulders. "Okay, everyone, let's get set up," he said. With the exception of Eagen, everyone did the same in unison. They sat in a circle with their backs to the tent wall. Eagen did not have a clue as to what was happening.

Moe reached into his pack, which doubled as his pillow, and extracted a nylon sack. With Eagen looking on, everyone cleared a small circle in the center of the tent. Reaching into the sack, he pulled a dark green box roughly the size of a loaf of bread and another object that resembled a folded umbrella. The umbrella-like object was unfolded and allowed to take form. It was set down on the tent floor and steadied by three folding spider legs. Next, the lid on the box was unlatched and flipped open to reveal a radio device with an attached keypad.

Larry assisted by plugging in the headphones and handing them to Moe. A toggle switch was thrown and the set came to life. Eagen was dumbfounded and watched in silence. Larry consulted his compass, which he orientated to north and then rotated the umbrella antenna until it, too, faced north. Slowly, he slewed the device slightly west and then east of north until Moe signaled him to stop. The contraption was then elevated slowly until, again, Moe told him to stop.

THIS DAY'S BUSINESS

"Gentlemen, I believe that it is time to authenticate." Lloyd's voice was firm and even. With that command, the five men reached into their shirts and each produced a thin slab of plastic, roughly the size of a playing card, which hung around their necks by a chain. Lloyd took his slab in his hands and snapped it in two, which revealed a piece of orange paper. The other four did likewise. Unfolding the paper, each in turn read off the contents, first Lloyd, then Sweetner, Larry, Curly, and finally, Moe.

"Alpha alpha, juliet bravo, zero eight, seven seven, two nine," went the litany.

Moe repeated the cryptic ciphers as he punched them into the keypad. "AAJB087729." He waited for the signal in his headset. At the appropriate moment, he peeled back a cover on the device and revealed a thimble-like button, which he depressed. It happened in only the briefest of moments. A buzzing sound caught Eagen's astonished ears. The code, which had been written in red, light emitting diodes on the panel face, disappeared.

It was Moe who spoke first. "It's on its way."

Less than one minute later the buzzing returned. This time there were three lines of different code displayed on the panel. He spoke directly to Lloyd.

"Authenticate Gamma, Rho, Epsilon, Epsilon."

Lloyd produced a notebook similar to Moe's. Flipping several pages, he stopped at one and ran his right index finger across the text. It was only a moment, but it was a moment that hung heavily in the air. He looked up at everyone in turn and said, "The message is as follows: Prosecute Aurora." All except Eagen nodded their heads.

CHAPTER 12

The Winter Jets

"Okay, okay," said Lloyd. "Just relax and I'll fill you in...completely. Larry, hand me that bottle, will you?" Larry rummaged through the various packs and sacks that occupied every nook and cranny of the tent. Finally, he produced the Wild Turkey and handed it over to Lloyd, who was busy examining his plastic mug for its cleanliness. "I think its time that we all had a snort or two while we work this one out." Pouring about three fingers of the dark amber liquid into his mug, he continued. "David, how much do you know about the history of the region?"

"Not much," was the reply. "I know, for example, that Pakistan broke from India just after the Second World War and that there's been bad blood between them ever since."

"Very good," said Lloyd. "This whole region is one whose history is steeped in misery. It has been invaded and conquered by armies going back as far as Alexander the Great. Ghengis Khan swooped down from Central Asia through these high passes. For a thousand years the great armies of history have used the region as their

THIS DAY'S BUSINESS

invasion route. It is a gateway to the riches of other places. This place, where we're at right now, isn't worth a jug of stale piss, but to get to the places that are worth something, one must go through here. The great tyrants of history knew this and so, too, do the great tyrants of today. The Communist Chinese have eight million men under arms right now and are looking to expand southward into India to exploit its riches and minerals. Skirmishes have broken out all along their common border going all the way back to 1947. The Russians aren't about to let their mortal enemy gain an advantage. They desperately want to establish a foothold in India. That's why they're pouring billions of rubles into arming and training India. They would like nothing better than to drive a wedge between the U.S. and its old ally. They're almost pathologic in their search for a warm water port, especially one that gives their navy access to the Indian Ocean. Right now, if their ships aren't at sea during the winter, they're locked in ice somewhere up in the Bering Sea. You can't fight a war that way. The Politburo sees Uncle Samuel as being mired in Vietnam while we're pledged to defend Western Europe. Mao sees that too. Although the two Communist powers despise each other, they are willing to cooperate on keeping the shitpot stirred. Also, as we withdraw from Southeast Asia, they see our resolve to defend these nations as withering from antiwar angst. If Russia is to invade, it'll be through this region. Hell, on the other side of this mountain range, the Chinese are actually building the Karakoram Highway. They call it the 'Friendship Highway.' Friendship. Yeah, right. If our intelligence is correct, it's costing them in the neighborhood of five hundred to a thousand Chinese lives for every mile of road laid…and this road is designed to handle tanks, heavy tanks. Friendship, my ass. I haven't even begun to mention the visceral hatred that the Pakistani and Indian governments have for each other."

Eagen began to ask a question but Lloyd cut him off. "But wait. It gets better," he continued. "China has already exploded a nuclear device in a place called Lop Nor just northwest of here, on the other side of these mountains; India is suspected of having at least one device, and Pakistan is desperately trying to develop one. This whole region is one incredible powder keg, and all it would take would be for a cockroach to fart and the whole place would go up in one gigantic mushroom cloud . The reality of it is this: everybody hates everybody else and nobody knows what the other fellow is up to." Lloyd's throat was parched from delivering his history lesson and from the thin, arid air of Camp II. He took a long pull on his mug.

"All right, I understand all that, but how does that affect all of us?" said Eagen.

Lloyd continued, "Everybody is suspicious of everyone else. If country A thought that country B was about to get the jump, well, that would precipitate a free-for-all that would make the California Gold Rush pale in comparison. Consider that the Seventh Fleet was coming into port, and the mayor advertised free beer and loose women for the first one hundred sailors who showed up! Now do you see? Those seismometers that we've hauled up here are not just for the benefit of the Pakistani people. Oh sure, that's the bullshit story we sold 'em. They're highly sophisticated motion detectors, better than the ones we seeded up in the DMZ between North and South Vietnam. In this case, if a mechanized army is on the move, they're going to raise one hell of a racket that we'll be able to detect. Don't misunderstand me; we fully intend that any data received as a result of actual earthquakes will be treated and examined in a scholarly and humane manner."

Eagen thought this one over and agreed to the basic premise. "Just one question," he asked. "Why wasn't I briefed on this; why was I kept in the dark?"

Sweetner fielded that question. "That was the Judge's decision. Actually, he wanted to be candid with you from the beginning, but when Emile Chazzi entered the equation, that changed everything."

Eagen was puzzled. "Chazzi? What does he have to do with this?" Lloyd handed the bottle to Eagen, who took it and downed a big gulp.

"Emile Chazzi," said Lloyd, "is a rat bastard of the highest order, who would sell out his own mother's soul to the Devil. He apparently got wind of your upcoming trip and was willing to give you up to his North Vietnamese contacts. It also appears that he was dealing from the bottom of the deck with the Russians as well. It seems that he fancies himself an amateur James Bond."

"Well, you've convinced me, but what I can't understand is why all this surveillance can't be done by a satellite? I mean, if we can photograph a license plate in Red Square from two hundred and fifty miles up, then why not here? Why all the spook stuff?"

THIS DAY'S BUSINESS

Again Sweetner fielded the question. "Do you realize how much time and money it takes to task a satellite? It takes two or three days of computer time just to calculate the change of orbit and then everything must be recalibrated. A proper alignment of the spacecraft depends on landmarks whose precise coordinates are known. The satellite compares the landmarks it sees with the coordinates stored in memory on board. When there's a match it knows where it is and then we can tell it what to photograph. When there's an earthquake, landmarks change. A building collapses here, a boulder topples there. In extreme cases, the course of a river can be changed. By the time a satellite gets its shit together, a week to a week and a half can pass. In that time, any one of half a dozen armies could conceivably be on the march. Tanks and trucks have distinctive seismic signatures, as you are no doubt aware. Hell, those little beauties we brought can detect footsteps if there are enough of them. Once we've been alerted that something is on the move, then we can order up an SR 71 Blackbird and take their pictures from well over eighty thousand feet. We've been sucker punched before by poor or nonexistent intelligence. For example, I refer you to the Battle of the Bulge and Pearl Harbor, just to name two."

Eagen cleared the whiskey from his throat and said, "Well, I'll buy into that, but do you think our Pakistani friends are wise to us?"

"Nah," said Lloyd. "The feedback we're getting is that they're clueless. If they did, it would be 'Good Night, Irene' for us all. Here's something for everyone to chew on while you've got visions of sugarplums dancing in your heads tonight: That plane crash was no accident. If fate hadn't intervened and sent us back to the gate, we'd all be smoking a turd in hell right now. The other night I used the shortwave radio to report in with the embassy. Their investigation showed that the navigational beacon was sabotaged. We were supposed to fly into that embankment."

The exclamations from all added a chill to the already cold night air. Everyone realized just how close they had come to oblivion. "Well, this has been a long evening, and I'm getting pretty cold; besides, we've got to set up the oxygen before we turn in."

Each pair of climbers lay in their down sleeping bags, each with a bottle of oxygen to share between them. The T fitting branched off to the soft, flexible masks that they wore at night. The life-sustaining gas

W.J. O'BRIEN

would allow them to sleep warmer and hopefully remain more fit. It was an uneasy Eagen that turned out his flashlight and snuggled into the depths of his bag, his mind replaying the horror of the flaming wreckage. He eventually fell asleep to the sounds of the tent flapping sporadically in the sparse air and the steady flow of oxygen in his sleeping mask. *Sssssssssssss*.

Lloyd spent a sleepless night tossing and turning as much as his mask would allow. At the six a.m. radio call, he was the only one awake.

Lloyd: Base Camp, this is II. Over.

Major Gujral: II, this is Base, reading you loud and clear. Over.

Lloyd: What's the weather report, Major? It's starting to blow like hell up here. Over.

Gujral: They're calling for a dip in the jet stream over us for the next week at least, with little relief in sight. It appears that winter has arrived earlier than expected. Over.

Lloyd: Just great. It's gusting to seventy miles per hour and we're looking at minus twenty-two degrees. I guess that we'll be staying put for today. Over.

Gujral: Understood. I'm planning for six Haps going up to you first thing tomorrow morning. Over and out.

The day was spent eating, sleeping, and nursing what had become known as the Camp II headaches.

Sometime in the night the oxygen gave out. Although he was in a troubled sleep, Eagen was aware of himself gasping for air. As he slowly awakened he was feeling the cold invading his sleeping bag and the tent vibrating like a castanet from the wind gusts. He joined the others in dozing in the warmest place for the moment.

At five o'clock on the morning of September twenty-seventh, Curly and Larry broke trail again down to the top of the icefall to

THIS DAY'S BUSINESS

assist the Haps, who were making their first carry without the Sahibs in the lead. Eagen and Sweetner began their preparations to go up the huddle to scout a route for Camp III. It took them almost an hour to get dressed and put on their climbing gear. As they sat in the doorway of the little Big Top they struggled with their bulky clothes. Every few minutes they would have to stop and force themselves from gagging on the dry heaves. They resorted to taking a few whiffs of oxygen from their masks.

Lloyd was laid up with a bad headache and was showing signs of a nasty dry cough that would not go away. The two lead climbers set off a few minutes after seven a.m. just as the Haps and Sahibs reached the camp. The first thing that Eagen pointed out to Moe was the angel-hair wisps of cloud streaming off the summit. This was a harbinger of very high winds and brutally cold temperatures.

The two climbers broke trail through crotch-deep powder snow over rolling and undulating terrain for the better part of two hours. The slope was a steady fifteen to twenty degrees until they reached the middle, then it shot up directly to sixty degrees of angle and then eventually to around a sustained seventy-five degrees all the way to a point about a thousand feet below the summit.

Before they started up Sweetner, who was bent over his ice axe fending off an attack of the dry heaves, stopped Eagen in his tracks and asked, "Are you sure you know what you're doing?"

Eagen replied, "If I knew what I was doing, I wouldn't be here! I'm not as bright as I look, you know." Sweetner acknowledged with what appeared to be the faint outline of his raised middle finger showing through his heavy woolen mitts. Eagen then sank the first blow of his ice axe into the frozen rampart.

The rhythm was established. Every fifteen steps would see the two men hunched over their axes gasping for something that wasn't there. Between breaths there was the gagging and the involuntary spasms; then, it was upward for another fifteen steps. The angle was not yet steep enough that they placed snow pickets for protection but that time was nearing. Instead, they relied on their skill. Besides their safety equipment they each carried a five-hundred foot spool of climbing rope and one fully charged bottle of oxygen, which they were to drop at their high point. They would go as high as they could go, then descend for the night. It was an old climber's wisdom that directed them to climb high and sleep as low as possible. What they were bringing up that day would be that much less that someone would have to carry the next day.

There was no warmth in the sun's rays. Even without the wind it was getting colder with every step they took. During a break, they sank the shafts of their axes into the firm snow as far as they would go, tied a figure-of-eight knot in the rope, and clipped it to the axes. They were now protected should a slide occur. Wearily, both just plopped themselves down and panted. Separated by the full one hundred and fifty feet of rope, they were too spent to talk.

At this juncture, their thirst was a real concern. Before they left camp, the cooks had given each a large thermos of scalding hot soup to see them through the day and now, at 22,100 feet, it was time to replenish their energy. In the few hours they had been gone, their soup had cooled considerably until it was now merely warm, but it felt so good going down. The tepid soup was the only way to warm the body's core quickly. Each sat quietly in his own misery facing outward, their backs to the mountain, too tired to appreciate the beauty that was unfolding around them. Both knew instinctively that they must head down soon; they had done their bit for the day.

Reluctantly, Sweetner overcame the deadly lethargy and forced himself up to where Eagen sat. Pulling off his pack, he extracted first the cylinder and then the spool of rope. Eagen did likewise. With no words spoken between them, they turned downward for the warmth and safety of their sleeping bags. They could both see but not care that the clouds were again forming in the lower valleys. The next day it would be someone else's turn to push the route higher.

The climbers returned to Camp II to find Moe and Curly sorting out the gear that the Haps had carried up earlier. At the same time, the Haps were resting up for their descent just after dark. Larry was dividing his time between caring for Lloyd, who remained in his sleeping bag all day with a bad headache, and sharpening his ice tools in anticipation of climbing the next day. Everyone was wasted. *It might take another twenty-four hours to fully acclimatize*, thought Eagen.

The six p.m. weather report was not very encouraging. The major reported that another storm was approaching, and conditions would be brutal for several days. For the first time Eagen was beginning to doubt the outcome of the venture. He remembered counseling the

THIS DAY'S BUSINESS

Judge about winter setting in and the probability of success if it did. *Well*, he thought, *I've seen worse conditions so we'll just play this thing out to the end.*

During the night, the wind picked up to a steady forty miles per hour with higher gusts; this was causing the sharp staccato flapping of the tent and making sleep very difficult. At nine thirty in the morning, when Curly and Larry set out, the wind had yet to abate. Visibility was reduced to less than fifty yards by the loose granules of snow being blown across the steep surface. As they bent themselves into the wind, their goggles would alternately freeze up from the caked-on snow and fog up from the heat loss from around the eyes. It took them six hours to achieve what had taken Sweetner and Eagen only four hours the day before.

The track was obliterated by the blowing snow, and Curly and Larry were forced to break trail all over again. After dumping their loads of rope and oxygen at the high point, they too turned around to go back, only to find the tracks they had just made were already filled in.

That evening in the little Big Top, the Sahibs planned their strategy for the establishment of Camp III. Lloyd announced that he was feeling much better and would be available to make a carry if it proved necessary. Sweetner, who had adapted well to the altitude lower down, was now starting to feel the effects of mountain sickness. His headache was getting worse, and his appetite was dropping off.

The plan was for Sweetner to remain in camp and assist Lloyd with the Haps while the stooges with Eagen would try to go higher. He and Moe would dump their supplies at the high point while Larry and Curly went ahead. Before Eagen descended, he advised Curly that they should start sinking anchors into the snow and ice because the angle was such that if a slip were to occur there would be no way of arresting it, and they would be the first ones to the bottom of the hill.

The lead climbers loaded their packs with two spools of rope and one bottle of oxygen each and set off. With every fifty feet of line payed out, they would stop, anchor themselves with their ice axes and hammer in a snow stake, which was about three feet long with a T cross section and a stainless steel cable through the eye. With that in place the rope was tied to the cable, making it a fixed rope. They were

169

using ascenders on the rope for the first time. That was a mechanical device that was clipped on to the lifeline and worked on the ratchet principle. It would allow the ascender to slide up the rope freely but would bite into and firmly hold the rope when a downward force was applied. Thus, the alpinist would pull himself along in the manner of someone using the handrail on steep stairs.

The wind had yet to subside as Larry finished hammering in the stake. At this altitude it was exhausting and gut-wrenching work. The blizzard of snow particles made it very difficult to see, even with the goggles. The wind chill at that hour was dropping the temperature down to forty below zero. Both men had long since replaced their wind shells for the warmth of their bulky down parkas.

Curly's eyes were tearing so badly from spindrift working its way into his goggles that he had trouble seeing where he was placing his boots. The moisture that was escaping the mouth and nose resulting from their heaving breaths was reforming on their bushy beards that had grown in the past few weeks. Runny noses added to the clots and knots of ice that clung like beads, giving each a yeti-like appearance.

One gust knocked Curly off his feet as he held the rope protecting Larry. They would move up ten steps and then have to stop. Both men were starting to suffer from the dry heaves, and Larry could not hear Curly shouting at him over the wind. Without headlamps it was beginning to become difficult to see the next few feet. Realizing that they had reached their high point for the day, both men attached the loads to the anchor. Turning away they descended the fixed line for Camp II. At the end of the rope, they had great difficulty locating the way beyond. The wind-driven snow had long since erased their tracks.

After consulting their compasses and altimeter, they determined the way back to Camp II and the safety of the tents. They returned three and a half hours after they had set out, completely spent, but buoyed by their progress. They had pushed the route upward another thirteen hundred vertical feet.

At the nine p.m. radio call, the major was not optimistic about the weather. The meteorologists were calling for an extended period of high wind and prolonged intervals of heavy snow. The long-term weather picture was shaping into a typical winter pattern. It was beginning to look like the expedition had enjoyed the interlude that

THIS DAY'S BUSINESS

sometimes exists before the onset of winter. A council meeting that night was held under the little Big Top, for it was realized that Camp III must be established in the next two days or the whole project would grind to a halt.

At first light the following morning, Eagen, Larry, and Curly set off for another try. In the beginning the wind was light and the near still air was crisp. There was little hint of warmth in the sun and even less in the dry air that they were attempting to suck into their lungs. At the point where the fixed rope began, the wind velocity increased steadily until it was pulling at their nylon shell clothing. It was also lifting the top layer of crystalline powder and launching it horizontally.

There was a method to their sweet madness; it was one to be repeated countless times before they slept again. The lead climber would move upward and, every ten or fifteen feet, stop and catch his breath. He would be hanging monkey-like from his two ice axes and crampons, hanging the weight of his body by his bones instead of his muscles. This let him open the wrist loop of one axe big enough to slip an arm through up to the elbow. The object was always to maintain at least three points of contact with the ice. His free hand would then reach for the rack of ice screws. The hand that went through the loop held the screw while the free hand tapped it in until the threads caught. The same tactics used in the icefall would be employed against the southwest face of Gasherbrum IV.

With the threading of the screw completed, a carabiner was clipped to the eye then the rope through it. If the lead climber were to fall now the carabiner would become the fulcrum and he would drop only a foot or two. However, once above the last protection, the climber would fall at least twice the length of rope payed out. Before the end of the rope was reached, the lead man would anchor himself into the ice using at least two screws and his axe for protection. The next man would start up higher still in the hanging belay his partner would take up the slack in the rope as the climber advanced. As the second man climbed past the first, he became the lead climber. In this way they would swap off the demanding and exacting job of placing protection.

With a new spool of rope tied to the outside of his pack, Eagen stepped up into the unexplored, all the while paying out new line for the next section of fixed rope. Upward he went, pausing only to place protection and to rest. At one point he sunk the pick of his axe deeply into the ice bulge, testing it to be sure it would hold his weight. Clipping his harness into the wrist loop on the axe, he was able to hang on the wall, much like a telephone lineman might rest on a pole. Even as he steadied himself the wind was rocking him in place, threatening to work his one piece of protection loose.

Down at Camp II, Lloyd was having a rough time. He was unable to shake the deep, dry, hacking cough that had developed over several days. Each spasm sent bolts of searing pain deep into his chest. Moe was very concerned about him and continued to monitor his lungs for a buildup of fluids. Before his departure for the face, he prescribed Codeine to relieve the pain. If he did not show signs of improvement by the next day, he was prepared to have him sent down to Base Camp with the Haps when they arrived on their next supply run. Hopefully, with a few day's rest at lower altitude he would be strong enough to rejoin the climbers at Camp II.

If ten minutes felt like a long time then Eagen was taking an eternity, or so it seemed to his two fellow climbers who had to endure inactivity. At least while they were moving they could stay warmer. With his ice hammer he tapped the screw into the boilerplate ice, splintering the outer layer. The ice was so brittle that it shattered on impact. He was forced to blast his way through ten or eleven inches of the mountain's frozen armour to find ice that was stable enough to hold the screw when it was threaded in. All twelve inches of the coarsely threaded device were sunk up to the eye. At one point Eagen was forced to take his heavy woolen mitten off to get a firmer grip on the hammer. The tool was so cold that his hand stuck to it. Gritting his teeth he pulled free, leaving skin adhering to the steel shaft. It hurt like hell! Another wave of nausea was beginning to break over him. Was it the pain? Might it be the greasy eggs and ham he had had for breakfast? His best guess was the altitude. He was already breathing less than one half the oxygen he would at sea level, and it was decreasing with each step upward.

The face they were on was rapidly being overrun by the shadows racing toward them. The sense of isolation merely served to heighten his fears. There was only a swirling curtain greyness about him. Looking up, then out to his left and right, there was only the black

THIS DAY'S BUSINESS

void. His one sense of attachment to this life was the small spot of yellowed light directly before him and the dim glare from the headlamps of his companions some one hundred and fifty feet below him. He could not conceive of a worse place for the batteries to wear down. In the snow-obscured light of his headlamp Larry checked his altimeter and yelled up to Eagen that they were at a little over twenty-two thousand feet. Eagen clipped his descender ring to the rope and slid back down to his comrades.

"Well," he declared, "this is as good a place as any for Camp III. Let's get down before we freeze to death."

"Where?" said Curly. "I can't see a thing up there but blank wall that's damned near vertical."

Eagen's only reply was, "Save your breath; we'll tie off the packs with the oxygen and gear here to the fixed rope and then get them when we come up here next." There was no argument from his teammates. They would not be able to survive much longer in the high winds.

When the climbers failed to return around two o'clock that afternoon Sweetner became concerned. Standing outside the little Big Top, he scanned the higher slopes for signs of them but the snow-laden clouds blocked any view up there. Three very cold climbers returned an hour later to large mugs of hot soup prepared by the cooks.

That evening, while huddled in the Big Top, they realized that their tactics would constantly have to evolve if they were to be successful. What worked on one part of the mountain might not necessarily work elsewhere. The wind, it appeared, seemed to abate during the night and then intensify after sunrise. Typically, an alpine start would begin several hours before sunrise to take advantage of firm snow conditions and end sometime during the day when conditions were less favorable. But there, the winds were starting to beat up on them; already there were head colds manifesting themselves. The obvious choice, unnerving as it was dangerous, was to climb during the night. So, a plan for the establishment of Camp III was formed.

Moe brought up Lloyd's condition with Eagen. He had been on oxygen all day while lying in his bag as still as the wracking cough would permit, and now he was starting to spit up slight amounts of blood. Moe checked his lungs again with his stethoscope and determined that the lungs were beginning to fill with fluid; further, he must have ruptured a few capillaries, which explained the blood. At nine o'clock that night, Eagen radioed to Base Camp.

Eagen: Base, this is II. How do you read? Over. Base, this is II. Over.

Gujral: Hello, Camp II, you are very weak. Over.

Eagen: Major, we've reached the site of Camp III but have yet to set it up. The wind appears to let up at dark so we'll be digging it out then. Mark the spot on your map. It's at 22,100 feet in the central gully, along the right side of the face. You should be able to see us with the spotting scope when we get back up there. Also, Alan's not doing too good, and Moe feels that he should go down for a rest. We suspect that he has pulmonary edema and two or three cracked ribs from all the coughing. He'll be coming down with the Haps when they resupply us. Over.

Gujral: Understood, David. We're going to have a problem with your resupply. Almost everyone here is sick with diarrhea. It seems that the two cooks have been somewhat lax in their sanitary habits. I've had to watch them carefully. Right now I've got only two Haps that are fit enough to carry and even they are starting to show signs of becoming ill. We'll have to postpone the carry for twenty-four hours. Is there anything in particular that you're going to need? Over.

Eagen: Sorry about the Haps. Yeah, we're going to need more fuel for the stoves so that we can melt snow for water. We'll need more oxygen, at least twelve bottles; we'll be climbing on it above III as well as sleeping with it from now on. Seems like we're going through it a little faster than we predicted. Over.

Gujral: Understood. The weather report is calling for another storm for the day after tomorrow. In the meantime, high winds and cold temperatures are expected. Over.

Eagen: Roger that. Goodnight. Over.

With some recalculating of their oxygen use, the Sahibs determined that they would have enough to complete the mission and possibly enough to go on to the summit if there were no great delays. The next evening, they would ascend the fixed rope using headlamps and establish Camp III. Since the terrain was far too steep to pitch a tent, they would construct a snow cave. Working together they would burrow right into the mountain itself. There, they would be cramped for space but would be out of the elements.

The following night Eagen, Sweetner, and Larry set off for the fixed rope. They were each carrying packs of around forty pounds. When they reached the foot of the rope, each one turned on his oxygen supply and set the flow for four liters per minute. They had been sleeping on two per minute. The ascenders, with long slings for the feet, were attached to the rope. This permitted the climber to walk up the rope. Up went the footsteps, one by one. The soft synthetic mask protected their faces from the cold. In the fourteen-degrees-below-zero night air, their world existed only in the glow of the headlamps. All else was ink black.

The end of the rope came abruptly. Larry, being in the lead at the time, began looking for a suitable location to start digging. It was Sweetner who noticed the shallow indentation in the snow among the flows of ice. Eagen came up the rope to join him in the concave depression. While Larry anchored himself, the other two set about the digging. The snow was compacted after many years of melting and refreezing. Several hours of excavating in shifts produced a hollow only big enough for the three to sit side by side. More anchors were drilled in the ice on either side so that the three could dig together without fear of tumbling into oblivion. Sometimes they struck veins of light blue ribbon ice, and at others, there were pockets of compacted snow. At two fifteen in the morning, a chamber big enough for the three men and their gear was finished. They climbed in and set their packs at the entrance to seal out the night as best they could.

For the first time in many hours, they were not under the threat of being blown off the mountain. Much to their distress, there was room for only one to move at a time. They would have to enlarge the hole later, but for the present, they unrolled their sleeping bags, broke out the stove, and melted snow for some hot soup. The propane gas cartridges would last only an hour and then would be discarded. This gave them just enough time to get the soup hot. Once away from the flame, the precious liquid chilled rapidly. Compounding the problem, the water at that altitude began to boil at one hundred and thirty-one degrees rather than the two hundred and twelve at sea level. That was barely hot enough to melt the bullion cubes in the pot. After several mugs in their bellies, the urge to sleep became too alluring.

To save weight, their sleeping masks were left down at Camp II. It was either leaving them or the radio; they could not take it all. Each had their own bottle, which they lay between them outside their bags. There, the aluminum cylinders would not freeze as long as their bodies produced heat. The airflow in the climbing mask was set to a flow of two liters per minute. Hopefully, their meager supply would last long enough for a few hours of warm sleep.

Later, during the night, Sweetner's supply gave out, and he woke as if he were escaping from a nightmare. Larry and Eagen swapped off their supply, buddy breathing like a scuba diver until the first radio call of the day. At six a.m. they transmitted the good news.

Eagen: Camp II, this is Camp III. Over.

Moe (at II): Camp III, I read you loud and clear. Your signal is booming in. Over.

Gujral: Camp III, this is Base. Same here. A very strong signal. Congratulations. Over.

Moe: Eag, where are you located on the face? Over.

Eagen: We're at 22,100 feet in a cave. We're desperately cramped, but there's no place like home. Over.

THIS DAY'S BUSINESS

Gujral: David, the Haps made a carry this morning up to II with oxygen and fuel. Are you expecting them to go up to III? Over.

Eagen: Negative on coming up to III. It's too dangerous. We'll do the carries above II. Over.

Moe: Eag, this is Moe at II. The Haps haven't arrived yet. Must be tough going in the icefall. What's the game plan for today? Over.

Eagen: We're going to drop down to the bottom of the fixed rope where we stashed five bottles of oxygen and several gas cylinders. We've got enough for one more day without a resupply, but I don't want to push it beyond that. Over.

Gujral: Bad news here, Camp III. Three of the six Haps turned back; they're still too sick. Over.

Moe: III, this is II, confirming that. I've got three Haps exiting the icefall. They should be here in an hour. Alan is holding his own, but I don't want him going higher. Over.

Eagen: Okay, this is what I'd like to see done. Larry and I are going to drop down to the bottom of the rope. In the meantime, Moe, I need you and Curly to bring up food and fuel. Curly is to come up to III and Larry will go down to II with Moe for a rest. Moe, I feel that you should stay with Alan until he gets better. Sweets will stay up here and work on the cave. Over.

Gujral: Don't waste any time up there. The storm will be upon us by late this afternoon. Again, high winds and heavy snow. Over.

Eagen: Roger that, Major. When I stick my head out of the hole I can see storm clouds forming lower down. III out.

Larry and Eagen descended the rope in time to join Moe and Curly coming up the slope. They were both carrying nearly sixty pounds each and were thoroughly trashed when they set their loads down. The winds were picking up right on cue as the sun broke the ridgeline just above them. Gusts of wind were now rolling over them like surf, with each new wave moving at seventy miles per hour. Like an undertow, the wind eroded the packed snow beneath Curly's cramponed boots and swept him off his feet. He went tumbling end over end across and down the slope until he was pulled up short by the rope. Gathering his wits, he waved that all was okay and slowly picked his way back to the bottom of the fixed rope. It was a narrow escape. If he had not stayed roped up when he had reached his companions, he would have disappeared into the swirling clouds of spindrift. Before the two groups departed, Moe handed a housewarming present of Wild Turkey to Eagen. He said it was for "medicinal purposes only, of course."

Several hundred feet up the rope it was Eagen's turn to be swept off his feet; only this time he was held in place by his ascender on the rope. Up they went, up into the clouds. Every hundred feet both were forced to stop and clear the ice blockages that formed in and around their masks. By crushing the flexible rubber mask, they could break up that which formed inside from the condensation of their breathing. Harder still was the reservoir, the inflatable bladder. To clear the ice they had to stop and hang in their harnesses and take the reservoir in both hands and squeeze the frozen plug up into the mask until the blockage was cleared. Then, they had to remove the mask partway until the chunks dropped free; all the while, they were unable to breathe. With the mask lifted partway, the icy blast would pepper their raw, exposed flesh.

With heavy packs, they struggled against the elements and their own need for self preservation. It took over six hours to reach the lip of Camp III. It was nowhere to be found. The slope was bare. Had an avalanche occurred while they had been gone? Had it swept Sweetner away with it? Moving to the right of the last anchor they saw a hole open in the snow. Sweetner had been busy in their absence. He had dug the back wall of the cave deeper into the mountain and made it wider to accommodate more gear. Unlike the lower camps that could stash the supplies outside and around the

THIS DAY'S BUSINESS

tents, there up at III the angle of the slope would not permit it. Everything had to go inside.

With the excavated snow from the back, he sculpted a wall at the entrance, leaving only a hole big enough for one man to enter at a time. This allowed them to use a pack to seal the entrance like a cork in a bottle. Also, he carved shelves from the ice to get some of the gear off the floor to make more room. However, the greatest improvement was the ceiling. Not only was it raised to allow sitting up, but more importantly, it was domed. With the climbers inside and two candles burning, the temperature would quickly rise to above freezing. Since snow is an excellent insulator, the ceiling would begin to melt and the dome shape allowed the meltwater to run off down the sides where it could be mopped up instead of dripping down onto their bags, thus rendering them useless. The full force of the tempest descended upon the high camp just as they retreated inside.

The conditions at Base were deteriorating faster than the weather. Almost all the Haps were sick with an intestinal virus. Some were becoming dehydrated from the constant vomiting and diarrhea. Of those still functioning, only three were fit enough to make carries up to Camp II. The men under Major Gujral's command and Shastri were the only ones who seemed unaffected .

Early on in the epidemic, they became responsible for their own cooking and sanitary conditions. Being military men they were more disciplined and knowledgeable about such matters. Shastri was quick to follow their lead. Their reward for such diligence was to remain free from any ailments save the altitude to which, by now, they were fully acclimatized.

Although they were aware of the impending storm, they were still surprised by its ferocity. With half of them unable to contribute to the defense of the camp, they rapidly felt the vise grip in which nature had them. Once again, the buildup of snow began. It set down on the consolidated foundation of the last storm and accumulated from that point. There was little time for sleep, only for the constant digging out and the shoring up of the Big Top. At the outset, everyone retreated to the large group tent. It was easier to defend one structure with their limited manpower than it was five or six smaller ones. In these conditions a small tent could quickly become inundated, its occupant suffocated.

Higher up at Camp II the problem was every bit as desperate but for different reasons. In contrast to Base, Camp II had only moderate snow but the winds were extremely high. Larry and Moe were forced into the white rage in a futile attempt at building an ice wall on the unprotected side to deflect the stronger gusts. In one of their trips outside, Moe brought the handheld anemometer, or wind speed indicator, and recorded a gust of one hundred and twenty-four miles per hour. Fortunately, he had clipped in his harness to his ice axe and sunk the shaft deep into the ice before it struck. As he held the instrument over his head, he was taken completely off his feet and held suspended in midair. He was being flown as a kite by the weather gods. Only the ten feet of rope he allowed himself saved him. The wind was so fierce that, paradoxically, in the face of so much rushing air, he was in danger of suffocation.

Higher still at Camp III, the conditions were evil and beyond all human endurance. However, in the "Bat Cave," the three uppermost climbers were comfortably sitting up in their shirtsleeves playing poker with matchsticks for chips. The thick walls of snow insulated them from the torment a short distance outside. With a pack stuffed in the doorway, they had only to contend with the occasional blast of spindrift that managed to leak in from the edges. Their only contact with the world was the radio.

The major's analysis was correct, or so it appeared. Winter had set in, and the expedition was reeling under the brunt. Nature was wringing every last drop of moisture out of the atmosphere and dumping it throughout the region. The storms that were forming elsewhere were arriving serially, like trains, and the whole of the Karakoram was the switch yard through which they passed.

The jet stream, that invisible river of moving air, known to all high altitude aviators and mountaineers alike, had dipped into the southernmost of its latitudes and was intent on jackhammering the whole of the region. It was not uncommon for the winds to exceed a hundred and fifty miles per hour as they circled the globe. Relentless and without mercy, the winter jet stream was the taker of lives. For three days and nights the invisible grim reaper played his best hand.

Inevitably, the relative comforts at Camp III began their predictable slide into degradation. The Bat Cave was never intended to be in use constantly without some form of repair. The meltwater

THIS DAY'S BUSINESS

from the elevated temperature was ponding up faster than it could be sponged or collected for drinking. As a result, everything was becoming damp. The down garments, the sleeping bags, and parkas were the first to fall victim to the soggy state. When the wet feathers clumped together they would lose their ability to loft or retain body heat. The three were beginning to lie in their misery, constantly chilled. The will to survive and the will to stay were waging war with one another.

Communications during the storm were impossible until its passage. When contact was reestablished, Base and Camp II could not talk with each other. The antenna mast had been snapped in half, and what remained was no longer able to penetrate the icefall. However, due to their position with respect to one another, there was still a link between Base and Camp III. Fortunately, there was also a radio link between II and III., so everything had to be relayed from Base to the Bat Cave and then down to Camp II. At six p.m. on the night of September thirtieth, radio contact was reestablished.

Gujral: Hello, Camp II, this is Base. Do you read? Over.

Eagen: Base, this is III, reading you loud and clear. II, this is III, are you on the frequency? Over.

Larry (at II): We're here, Eag. We've been worried about you. Over.

Eagen: Major, what are the conditions like with you? Over.

Gujral: They're desperate, David. But, we're holding our own. Over.

Eagen: Moe, how's Alan? Over."

Moe (at II): He's not doing too well. I'm sending him down as soon as possible. Over.

Eagen: Can you and Larry make a carry to III before he goes down? Over.

Moe: No, Eag. He's got to go down with the Haps ASAP. Over.

Eagen: Major, how many Haps can you send up next time? Over.

Gujral: I can send up four plus Shastri, myself, and two of my men. What do you need? Over.

Eagen: Excellent, great news. We really appreciate the effort. We need just about everything, especially dry sleeping bags, the summit tent, oxygen, and fuel. Over.

Gujral: We'll adjust the loads and start up in about three hours. Over.

Eagen: Moe, get Alan ready to go down with the Haps, then plan to come up to III. Larry, plan to carry up to III today. We'll drop down to II when the Haps come up. We'll have to take the boxes up to III with us. Over and out.

They pulled the cork on the Bat Cave and descended into the frigid night, one by one. Their only lights were the headlamps and the stars. At three o'clock in the morning of October first, they met up with Larry who deposited his load at the foot of the ropes and then all four descended further to Camp II. The first thing they did was to check on Alan's condition. He was in some pain from the cracked ribs. But what had Moe most concerned was the fluid buildup in his lungs. If they did not get him to a lower altitude and fast, he would drown in his own juices.

Lloyd did not want to go down but realized that he would never survive another forty-eight hours at eighteen thousand feet. Between spasms of pain, he showed Eagen and Sweetner the reconnaissance photos he used to mark the camps. Handing Eagen a magnifying glass, he instructed him to scan the Chinese side of the peak for a place to set up the boxes.

"If you place Camp IV here at around 24,000 feet, look straight across to here," he said. Pointing to a shadowed spot on the glossy

THIS DAY'S BUSINESS

photo, he continued, "This is where it should go. There appears to be a large crack there. Hopefully, it will be large enough to place them both. Where do you anticipate placing Camp IV?"

Eagen studied the glossy with the magnifying glass and then said, "Right on the ridge, straight across from the crack. It looks possible. What do you think?"

Lloyd, between bouts of hacking, replied, "Anywhere along there is fine. Just don't endanger yourselves any more than you have to." Everyone nodded in agreement.

Moe came back into the tent saying that the Haps were going to try to go down before the icefall became too unstable. Moe opened his medical kit and produced a bottle of pills.

"Alan, I'm going to give you some amphetamines. This will get you up and running and, it is hoped, get you through the icefall. Take two now and two more later when you feel these wear off. They might even help dry you out in the meantime."

They hoisted Lloyd to his unsteady feet and helped him to the door of the little Big Top. Moe put one of Lloyd's arms around his neck and helped him walk to the top of the icefall. It was obvious that Lloyd was unable to assist in his own evacuation. Under Moe's direction, two of the Haps set about boiling water while he bundled Lloyd into his sleeping bag. Next, he laid out a climbing rope in the snow so that it resembled a cargo net. As he finished, the Haps were directed to pour the boiling water onto the rope. Within minutes the rope was frozen solid. They now had a litter with which to carry their stricken friend to lower altitudes. Everyone waved as they watched a good man leave his part of the expedition. Moe would return the next day, after he had Alan stabilized at Base. For the others, they picked up their heavy loads, including the boxes, and headed back up the rope.

The boxes were damned heavy and, at sixty-five pounds each, were a lung buster. Sweetner and Larry drew the short straws for the honor. Aside from the boxes, each was carrying an oxygen bottle to aid them. The valves were opened to six liters per minute and then increased to its full flow of eight. It was worth the expenditure to assure their safe delivery. At a spot about eight hundred feet short of the Bat Cave, Larry's supply was exhausted, and Sweetner's was nearly the same. It took an additional hour to secure themselves and hook up a fresh bottle for both. Sweetner and Larry finally made it back up to Camp III where they dropped their loads and themselves. They were utterly spent.

Meanwhile, Eagen and Curly chopped out a small platform to house the boxes. As the sun came around the southwest ridge, the winds returned with all their debilitating effects. It took just under seven and a half grueling hours to see all five men safe in the cave built for three. Once more the cork was set in the entrance. The team up at Camp III slept through the six p.m. radio call, but Eagen caught the nine p.m. transmission.

Eagen: Base, this is III. How's Alan doing, Major? Over.

Gujral: Not so good, Eagen. He has a high fever and is sometimes delirious. Is there anything we can do for him? Over.

Eagen: We'll have to get back to you on that one. Camp III to Camp II, Shastri, can you hear us? Over.

Shastri: Yes, Eagen. We are well here. What do you want us to do? Over.

Eagen: Okay, everyone. We're going to talk over the situation and be back in one hour, at seven p.m. Over.

It was decided that Alan must be evacuated entirely off the mountain and down to a hospital. At the same time the route to Camp IV must be pushed through. It must be established by the day after next. As seven o'clock arrived, the radios crackled to life.

Eagen: All right, everyone, listen up. This is going to be complicated with a lot of people moving about. The chances of an accident will go way up if we're not careful. First, Moe will go down to Base to assist Alan. Major, you will need to send up three Haps to meet him at the top of the icefall and then they are to descend with him. Two. Major, can you call for a helicopter evacuation for Alan? Over.

THIS DAY'S BUSINESS

Gujral: I'm sorry, Eagen. We anticipated this and made a call several hours ago before we lost the antenna. There were no helicopters in the region capable of coming up this high, I'm afraid. If we are to evacuate him, we will have to carry him down to Bardumal. Over.

Eagen: Shastri, we're sending Moe down the ropes by himself at three o'clock. If need be, don't wait for the Haps to come up through the icefall. Go down with him until you meet up with the Haps, then come back up to Camp II. Understand? Over.

Shastri: Yes, Eagen. Will do.

Eagen: All right then, Larry and Curly will drop down later and retrieve the supplies that Shastri drops off when he comes up to meet Moe. Sweetner and I will go up to site Camp IV. Over.

Everyone acknowledged their part in the high-altitude ballet.

CHAPTER 13

Entombed

It took Moe nearly an hour to get dressed, even with the oxygen. He was still spent from the carry up to Camp III. In the tiny Bat Cave, every move had to be thought out in advance. The hard part came when his bulky climbing suit prevented him from putting on his crampons. Larry had to assist. At two forty-five in the morning, he pulled the cork on the narrow door, turned his headlamp on, and grimaced. The frigid night air had already invaded the hole. He reached out and hauled in a bight of the fixed rope, which he attached to his climbing harness. The wind was blowing spindrift through the opening; before long, he and everyone else had a thin coating on their sleeping bags. Moe stuck his booted legs through the entrance and wormed his way out. With one look around at his companions, he smiled and then slid down the rope. In moments the glow from his headlamp was lost in the night. In a few hours, with any luck, he would be at the bottom.

The noon radio call confirmed that Lloyd's condition was getting worse and that the major was preparing to evacuate him. With Shastri

THIS DAY'S BUSINESS

escorting Moe down into the icefall, that would leave just the two cooks at Camp II, neither of whom spoke much English. In their hypoxia it did not occur to anyone that when the major evacuated Lloyd it would leave the Haps with little or no leadership at Base Camp. If an accident happened higher up, someone would be well and truly screwed.

At first light Larry and Curly went down the rope to retrieve the load that Shastri had dumped while waiting for Moe. Meanwhile, Eagen and Sweetner wiggled free from the hole and bit their axes into the ice, paying out rope behind them. They were committed to the establishment of Camp IV. The snow again had turned to ice a few hundred feet above the Bat Cave.

At this altitude, the wind lashed at the slope continuously and had polished the ice until it was diamond hard. Where it normally took two or three whacks of the ice axe to produce solid protection, it now took five or six. The extra expended energy was lost, never to be regained. The ice would shatter into dinner plate sized pieces and then fall, rarely bouncing on its way down. Sweetner, who was belaying Eagen, had to be constantly alert for flying missiles heading his way. Chop, chop, chop. Eagen's arms were burning from the exertion. No sooner had he jackhammered down through brittle ice, he would clear away the debris only to find another layer just as hard and every bit as brittle. Finally, solid ice was reached. He sank an ice screw in and torqued it down flush with the eye. Eagen exhaled for the first time in what felt like minutes. His lungs were burning, his arms were burning, and his legs were beginning to shake like a sewing machine from standing so rigid.

Sweetner was freezing. Having pulled the hood on his wolf-fur-trimmed parka as tight as possible, he could not block out the wind or shards of ice that were raining down on him from Eagen's hammer work above. It was his turn to start climbing the fixed rope that Eagen had tied off. At least the strenuous climbing would help keep him a little warmer.

Eagen's next attempt at sinking an anchor went badly. With one plunge of the hammer a chunk of ice the size of a turkey platter pulled out and landed in his lap. The unexpected force kicked his cramponed boots out of their hold in the ice. Suddenly, Eagen found himself hanging solely by his axe. As he dangled, flailing desperately, trying to swing the hammer in his other hand, he felt his right arm being pulled from its socket. With forty pounds in his pack, pulling earthward, every muscle, every tendon was being stretched. For a brief instant he looked down and focused on the infinity beyond his boots to the icefall nearly seven thousand feet below. He was scared. He was shit-yourself-empty kind of scared. In an odd, detached sort of way, he wondered just where he would bounce first if his ice hammer should pop out. Would he bounce at all or would he just take the big ride all the way to the bottom, bringing an unsuspecting and startled Sweetner with him? If he had not slipped his hand through the wrist loop and cinched it down, he would now be well on his way to eternity.

Twisting himself around, he was able to catch his crampons on the ice and take the weight off his wrist and stabilize himself. Gasping and gagging in his mask, he was afraid of vomiting, for he would surely drown in a place many miles from the nearest water.

He saw it coming down at him. To Sweetner it appeared as big as a house and was growing larger as it bounced its way toward him. From his training, he knew that he could not move. He had to wait until the very last moment and then, almost reflexively, dodge the icy bullet. There was no way to predict the trajectory of the frozen missile until it was practically on top of him. He just hugged the ice wall and tried to make himself as small as possible. It grazed the top of his pack and very nearly spun him head over heels outward into space. Like his companion a hundred feet above, he too gasped in his mask while he struggled to gain his equilibrium. Against the roar of the wind, they yelled up and down to each other. Their words were lost to the elements immediately after they were spoken.

Quickly, the angle began to ease up. It was not as steep as it had seemed only a few feet lower. He was so focused on the vertical that he was barely aware that he had climbed to the skyline. Eagen had reached the ridge and the best possible site for Camp IV. Looking upward and to his left was the summit just fourteen hundred feet higher. Eagen threw a leg over the other side and stared into the vastness of China.

The two men sunk deep anchors into the wind-compacted snow and dropped their empty cylinders over the far side. They left only two spools of rope and their boot prints at the high point before they

THIS DAY'S BUSINESS

rappelled or slid down the rope for the Bat Cave.

Upon their arrival, they found Larry in the doorway tending to the six p.m. radio call. There was a worried look in his eyes.

Eagen was excited and yelled as loudly through his mask as his parched throat would allow. "Larry, we reached Camp IV!"

Larry weakly smiled as he pulled his mask away from his bearded and sunburnt face. "Moe hasn't made it down to Base Camp yet," he croaked. The two climbers stood outside the hole and tried to make sense of what they had just heard.

"Let us in!" Sweetner gasped. The pair wasted no time in escaping the torment outside.

Eagen: Major, what can you tell me? Over.

Gujral: Eagen, three of the Haps with Moe and Shastri haven't made it back yet, and I fear the worst. We heard something very large collapse in the icefall. There must've been a tremor. Over.

Eagen: Well, did you investigate? Over.

Gujral: Our remaining Haps are either too ill or too spooked to go up into it. Over.

Eagen: Major, you just can't leave them. You must send someone. Offer them anything, just get someone up in there, now. Over.

Gujral: I will do that, even if I have to go up there alone. We're evacuating Lloyd at first light. We must get him down to ten thousand feet for the helicopter. If we're not there the day after tomorrow, they won't wait. Over.

Eagen: Understood, Major. Do your best. We're going up tomorrow to establish Camp IV, and, if the weather holds, we'll have the seismometers in place the day after that. Over and out.

They were stunned. Moe could not be missing. They must have strayed off route in the icefall and were spending the night somewhere, waiting for dawn. Eagen could not afford to send anyone down for a search and rescue. Larry and Curly were needed at Camp III to be in support of him and Sweetner. The boxes had to be in place damned quick before the winter claimed them all. The plan was for all four of them to go up to and dig a platform from the snow, and then Sweetner and Eagen would occupy the top camp. Larry and Curly would drop their supplies of food, fuel, and oxygen, then descend back to Camp III. If time and soul permitted they would bring up the boxes, making a second carry for the day.

Four hours of climbing the fixed line saw Eagen and Sweetner back on the ridge while Larry and Curly waited fifty feet lower, anchored to the icy wall. Until the platform could be dug out and leveled, there would not be enough room for them all. On either side of the five-foot-wide ridge, the world dropped away almost ten thousand feet. The exposure was beyond description!

When they shoveled the snow it was unnecessary to throw it. The wind clawed at it, blowing it away in a puff. They had only to loosen it and break it into clumps before the winds snatched them away. Both men were intent on their work as best as the buffeting would allow; for if they were to avert their attention, vertigo and the wind would claim them. Two hours of strenuous chopping saw the platform dug. They stopped only long enough to change bottles and to ditch the spent ones down into the abyss.

Larry and Curly were beginning to shiver uncontrollably by the time the tent was set up, and there was enough room to come up with their deposit. When that was complete, Sweetner motioned with his mittened hand for them to go down to the Bat Cave immediately. Curly waved and they descended, as the sun was well beyond its zenith, and the shadows they cast grew long.

With nightfall approaching, Eagen took one look around and quickly crawled into the tiny, nylon summit tent. Sweetner wasted no time in joining him. Sorting their gear, Sweetner asked Eagen if he wanted to sleep in China or Pakistan. Eagen's reply was "the middle." At six p.m., the two highest earthbound men in the world opened the radio call.

THIS DAY'S BUSINESS

Eagen: Base Camp, Base Camp, this is IV. Over.

Nothing. No contact.

Eagen: Camp II, do you read Camp IV? Over.

Only static and the carrier frequency sounded from the tiny speaker.

> **Curly**: Eag, this is Camp III reading you loud and clear. We won't be able to bring up the boxes tonight. Larry and I are at the end of our tether. We'll be up first thing in the morning. Are you all settled in up there? Over.
>
> **Eagen**: Yeah, we're all set, but we're on the ragged edge, literally. If one of us farts, it'll be all over but the shouting. Over.
>
> **Curly**: I can't see any lights or movement from the lower camps. I hope that they all didn't go down. Over.
>
> **Eagen**: Save your breath for the morning haul. Goodnight. Over.

The two were completely spent from the exertion that day but not so spent that they failed to notice the clouds gathering around the lower flanks of the peak. They were privileged to watch the sun set into a sea of purple and orange clouds with the adjoining mountains slowly transforming into islands. Without any contact from Base Camp they were uncertain that anyone was there at all. The same could be said for the status of Camp II. In a situation such as theirs it was easy for the imagination to conjure up the idea of abandonment. It was an idea that had to be ruthlessly squelched before it brought on panic. The major would not strike Base Camp and take off. Yet, he did have to evacuate Lloyd. He would be sure to return, wouldn't he? He had given no indication of his plans after the successful evacuation.

At last count there had only been eighteen cylinders of oxygen remaining above Camp II. Whatever was left to be done would have to be completed soon because three bottles per man were not going to go very far. Larry and Curly were going to need one each just to haul the boxes up to Camp IV; two a night would be used for sleeping. Eagen and Sweetner would require two to fix a route out onto the Chinese face and another two to actually hump the heavy loads into place. This left a reserve of only six cylinders. If the weather were to close in again as it was currently doing there would be nothing left for the descent.

The storm did come up and envelope Camp III, but higher, at Camp IV, there was only wind, and such a wind it was. During the night, Sweetner held the portable anemometer out the downwind entrance of the tent. The tiny sensing instrument broke when a gust registering one hundred and twenty-seven miles per hour flattened the tent. The full reality of their situation, the gravity of it, was beginning to unfold.

Through the night, their nylon shelter crackled and rippled from the ceaseless flow of air rushing past it. Neither could communicate with the other without shouting, although they were less than two feet apart. Even this was becoming increasingly more difficult because the oxygen was drying out their mouths and throats. Eagen pulled his mask away to say something. As he did he saw that Sweetner's eyes went wide. He looked down into the mask and saw blood. Everywhere that was covered by the mask was caked with dried blood. Eagen had had a nosebleed for some time and had not noticed it in his exhausted state. The tiny capillaries in the lining of his nasal passages had more than likely ruptured from the prolonged exposure to the low atmospheric pressure and the arid air. There was no sleep for them that night. Sweetner commented that the wind sounded as though they were perched directly beneath a jet engine running at full throttle. They lay in their misery and awaited the dawn.

The silence was deafening, or so it seemed. Exposure to the constant roar had left them both with a continuous ringing in their ears. The only clue that the wind had died down sometime during the night was that the tent was not shaking so violently. Carefully, Sweetner unzipped the tent on the down-ridge side facing away from the summit and listened, but only heard his own eardrums still buzzing. The thermometer registered minus seventeen degrees,

THIS DAY'S BUSINESS

practically a day at the beach. That day was the day. They were either installing the boxes, or they were going to die trying.

The radio link was established with Camp III on schedule. The plan was for Eagen and Sweetner to secure a route out along this large crack that they were to call "the Chimney Route" and then return for the boxes. Meanwhile, Curly and Larry would be fully suited up and ready to lend support should it become necessary. It took them both almost two hours, because of the cramped quarters in the tent, to get fully dressed.

Since he was the more experienced of the two, Eagen went first while Sweetner held his safety line. Stepping through the low doorway of the tent, he threw a leg over the edge and straddled the ridgeline much like a child who has climbed a tall tree might straddle a limb.

His eyes were drawn upward along the dorsal fin that was the southeast ridge of Gasherbrum IV. Here and there the knife edge was blunted with gargoyles of ice and snow; their drooping gaze protected the flanks of the mountain's defenses. Off to his left lay the frozen wastes of snow and ice of countless peaks and glaciers. As he looked toward his right, toward Sinkiang Province, there were only wisps of clouds billowing up from the brown, barren plains below. While waiting for Sweetner to set up the ropes, Eagen stole one more glance up the ridge toward the summit. The sky above was a deep, flawless cobalt blue pierced only by the stark white of the summit cone. There, it accentuated the deep violet of the atmosphere above. The sky had a brilliance to it.

There it was, off to his right along the face. It was a slight joint, a line of stress or weakness in the rock. The crack, barely a quarter of an inch wide, ran horizontally outward for several hundred feet and then gave the appearance of angling upward until it faded among the veil of clouds. If this crack system did not take him near where he wanted to go, he would be forced to drill holes in the granite for expansion bolts. He shuddered at the thought of having to expend that much energy. It had nearly worn him out just getting dressed.

Eagen selected a flat-bladed piton that hung from his harness. With a single swift motion he leaned as far forward as he was able. Straining to maintain his balance, his left gloved hand inserted the piton into the crack. With his right he searched for and found his hammer. After three hearty whacks, the iron blade rang like a church bell. It was in solid. Through the eye of the piton he clipped in a carabiner and then through that he clipped in one of his etriers. This was a flexible ladder made of tubular webbing with five webbing steps. Once the etrier was in place Eagen would gently, ever so gently, ease his weight onto the rungs. He knew that if it held, he could expect to bounce up and down on it with impunity. On the other hand, if it didn't hold his weight, if a part failed...It all came down to a question of commitment.

He turned in his frozen saddle toward Sweetner, lifted his goggles, and winked. His companion nodded briefly. Eagen took a deep drag of oxygen and swung his leg over the side as if he were dismounting a horse. With the adrenalin pump set to high, he stepped out into China. It held.

On that side, unlike the one they had just ascended, there was little snow. It was just wind-blasted rock and small patches of ice with handholds that sloped down and outward like slates on a cathedral roof. Crab like, he moved, horizontally, gingerly, all the while searching for the next piton placement. Again and again, every four or five feet, the process would repeat itself. By leapfrogging his etriers he was traversing across the face. He had to struggle with himself to focus on the immediate task at hand. With more than ten thousand feet of nothing beneath his boots, the exposure was intimidating. A slip now would entail one hell of a pendulum where he would roll over and over, end over end, until the stretch in the rope pulled him up short. In all probability, a spill there would injure them both.

Meanwhile, Sweetner was sitting in the cramped doorway of the tent tending Eagen's lifeline. Shivering from inactivity, cursing from boredom, he could only pay out the rope, inches at a time, for his partner who had long since disappeared from view in the gathering clouds. The demand for more rope sliding steadily through his thick mitts was the only clue to Eagen's whereabouts.

Larry had the radio on in the Bat Cave in the event they were needed. He had the cork out from the doorway and was anxiously awaiting some word from his friends higher up. If a call for help did come, it would be from Sweetner because Eagen would be on the other side of the mountain in another country. It might as well be another world.

THIS DAY'S BUSINESS

He was gone for what seemed like years to Sweetner. The Chinese Face had long since cloaked itself in shadows, and the thermometer had been dropping for hours. Adding to it all, the spindrift being blown up from the Pakistani side was now beginning to accumulate inside the tent. If it melted from their body heat, everything would become sodden and then frozen. Tugging once more at his parka in a vain and futile effort to keep the frozen powder from running down his neck, he cursed. He cursed again as it melted and gravitated along the pathway of his spine. After enduring several hours of this, his ass was very cold and quite damp. Sweetner heard the clinking and clanking of the rock tools just before he saw his partner.

Eagen clawed his way back to Sweetner on the same rope he had just installed. He was approaching the limits of his endurance. With great difficulty, Eagen tried to get his leg up out of the webbed stirrup and back over onto the ridge. After two unsuccessful attempts, Sweetner hobbled out of the tent to a struggling Eagen just three feet away. Grabbing Eagen's harness, he dragged his companion back into the raggedy shelter. Munching the last of the hard candy that he had taken with him, he lay prostrate in the tent door.

Eagen was thoroughly spent from the day's effort. Even with three hours of daylight remaining, there would be no coaxing him much beyond where he lay. Between Eagen's bouts of gasping and fits of coughing a deep, dry hack, Sweetner pressed his friend for information.

"How far'd you get? What's it like out there? Did'ja see the chimney?" Eagen could only nod and clutch his chest as another wave of uncontrollable coughing struck him.

Several minutes later Sweetner had his friend zipped into his soggy sleeping bag, climbing suit and all. The codeine lozenges from the medical kit were snuffing out the searing pain in his upper chest, and his breathing was returning to a somewhat even state thanks to a fresh bottle of oxygen that lay between them.

"Well…just how far did you get? Or were you just over the lip out of sight whacking the bishop for hours?"

Eagen grew a Cheshire grin and calmly responded, "All the way up the chimney. This main crack runs pretty much horizontally for three hundred feet or so and then arcs upward, leading to the base. I had only twenty feet of rope remaining after I placed an anchor there.

Then, on the way back, I ran a fixed line from the spool I carried in my rucksack, so we'll have double the safety rope."

Both the climbers passed the night drifting in and out of sleep, munching on the last of the hard candy, and taking whiffs of oxygen. Each question or statement was carefully thought out and composed with an economy of words. The response was usually a grunt to the affirmative or negative. There was precious little energy left to speak.

At some point well after midnight, Sweetner spoke from the Chinese side of the tent. "You got any jokes?"

Minutes later came the response, "No. You?"

"Nah, but I got a limerick, if I can remember it." In the pitch black Sweetner sat up from his bed shivering, cross legged. He pulled his mask up to his face for a few quick hits and slowly rubbed his hollow eyes. Slowly, he shook his weary head and said, "It's gone. The thought just vanished in the wind." Reseating the mask, he lay back into his bag and tried to sleep. Eagen did not force the issue for he knew how spent Sweetner felt. He himself had little energy left as he fumbled for a match and lighted the small candle lantern that hung suspended from the crown of the tent.

The morning arrived without fanfare and neither climber had gotten more than four hours' sleep. While Sweetner busied himself fitting fresh oxygen cylinders to their masks, Eagen went out the back door of the tent and dug out the boxes. From his lethargy he pondered the mornings task. His only consolation was that the wind was probably nonexistent out there. All hell was on the Pakistani side.

One at a time, they hoisted the heavy fiberglass containers by the straps onto their pack frames. With the aluminum bottles their load was very nearly eighty pounds. The gas flow was turned up to the maximum of eight liters per hour and then both men set out onto the face. In their down-filled climbing suits, they were both sweating profusely, losing the precious water they had labored so hard to produce. The simple act of melting snow for water had cost them almost all the fuel that they had carried up to the top camp. Currently, they were expending it through their pores and exhaling it into the ultra-dry atmosphere. With an enormous weight hanging from their shoulders, the straps biting into their necks, the two uppermost climbers traversed the rock face on the safety line.

Time became a pointless concept. It could have taken them

THIS DAY'S BUSINESS

minutes or days to scale upward and across to the chimney. The large crack he had estimated averaged about four feet across and narrowed as it went upward. But, at the bottom of it, where he was about to stand, it was bell shaped, big enough to dance in, and partly flooded with compacted snow.

Sweetner was the first to reach the confines of the natural formation. He quickly moved to the back, allowing room for his struggling companion. Upon reaching sanctuary, Eagen squatted with his back to the rock. He was shivering as much from his quickly freezing sweat as from the strain of existing on the edge for so long. Pulling his mask away, he took notice of the congealing blood that was flowing once more from his nose. Pulling off his goggles and then the mask, he reached for a handful of snow in an attempt to scour the inside of his mask clean. Squeezing it between his mittened hands, he broke up a plug of red ice that was forming in the regulator valve. *What a disgusting sight*, he thought as the crimson slush splattered on the snow at his feet.

Sweetner helped him remove the fiberglass millstone from his pack and yelled into his right ear, "Come on, help me set this thing up." Reaching into his parka, Sweetner produced an L-shaped wrench that was hexagonal in cross section and clumsily undid the flush, mounted bolt from the first case and then the second, which exposed the latches to the locking mechanism. He attempted to open the lid to the first case but it held fast. The second failed to yield as well. He lifted his goggles and rubbed his weary eyes that were, by now, quite sunken in their sockets. With his ungloved hand he wiped it across his mouth and noted the bloody traces caked onto his beard as well.

Returning to the problem at their feet, Eagen tapped his friend on the shoulder to gain his attention and pointed to his mask. Sweetner scowled at the unsavory mask and replaced it. "Right. Thanks." He had been becoming slightly hypoxic in the few moments he had it off. "They're vacuum sealed to guard against tampering. I forgot." Even at the low pressure, at those altitudes the outside air pressure was greater than that inside the boxes, thereby hermetically sealing them both. A further twist of the bolt hole broke the tamper-proof seal on the first box and then the second. Both produced an audible sucking noise. Eagen attempted to intervene but was stopped by his friend.

"Let me do that, will you? That's pretty sensitive equipment."

Sweetner responded with, "I know it is, but I've got a handle on it. You can assist."

There was puzzlement in Eagen's eyes as he started to feel the effects of the altitude. He fumbled for his still damp, bloody mask and attempted to make an airtight seal over his nose and mouth, but his beard, which was caked with his dried and congealing blood, was not seating correctly. Using his left hand to hold it in place he mumbled, "What do you want me to do?"

The answer was as alarming as it was calm. "For now, just watch."

The lid of the first instrument, as well as the second, was pulled back. Eagen's stare narrowed and fixated on the contents. "Hey, those aren't the seismometers! What the hell's going on?"

His partner was too busy to look up at Eagen, but responded, "Not now, Eag, for the love of God, not now. I'll explain it all back at the tent."

Sweetner attached a black cable to a port on the end of one of the casks. Handing the other end to Eagen, he pointed to the connector on the outside of the one that Eagen carried over. He attached it and locked it down in the manner that Sweetner did. His partner flipped open a panel revealing a small screen and keypad. This was very similar to the one he had seen on Moe's spook radio. From around his neck he produced a key and inserted it into the locking mechanism. Pointing to Eagen's box, Sweetner told his friend to lift out the flat, dull-grey, honeycombed, mirror-like square and to open up the panels until they locked in place.

"Pull away the padding, there. See your seismometer?" Eagen nodded in the affirmative. "Now activate it, just the way they showed you." The row of three amber lights blinked on twice and then changed to a steady green. "Good," said Sweetner, "now the seismometer is activated. All right, that's the antenna," he said, pointing to the honeycombed panels. "Point it up as far as it will go. Be careful not to bend anything."

Eagen noticed that an amber light flashed on then went to steady green, only this time it was on the cask in Sweetner's box. Eagen observed in silence as his fellow climber tapped in a ten-digit alphanumeric code on the keypad. It was the same code, Eagen noticed, that had been used earlier down at Camp III in the little Big

THIS DAY'S BUSINESS

Top. The screen flashed a simple message five times. It read, "AUTHENTICATED."

Sweetner handed the hexagonal wrench to a mystified Eagen and pointed to his box. "Seal it carefully and then lock it down with this." Eagen complied. With that completed, Sweetner slid both connected boxes about ten inches further into the back of the chimney so that they would be more secure from the elements. Before he sealed the lid on his box, Sweetner rotated the key counter clockwise once. The screen now read, DEVICE ARMED.

"ARMED? What do you mean, ARMED?" Eagen croaked through his mask. "What in God's name do you have there?"

"Not now, Eag, not now," said Sweetner with some impatience.

Eagen blurted out between gulps of air, "Yes, now. What have you just done?" Sweetner gook-squatted on his haunches as he pulled his mask partway off his face. Turning away to the right, he stared for a few moments out onto the brown hills of China off in the distance. Taking two deep hits of oxygen from the mask he held in his right hand, he turned his gaze back to Eagen.

Calmly and with a deliberate voice he said, "We have just activated two man-portable atomic bombs! Now, get your ass clipped into the rope, and let's get back to the tent. It'll be getting dark soon!" The afternoon sun was dimmed by the high, thin alto cirrus clouds that only teased of warmth. The rainbow-colored ring around the sun bespoke not of water vapor but of ice crystals in the thin wisps. They were the harbinger of bad weather; they were the avenging angels.

It took them little more than an hour and a half to make their way back to the ridge. Eagen was livid all the way. The anger had summoned up within him the reserves, the will, to make it back just so he could hear Sweetner's explanation. This was the second time he had been lied to, and he was ready for answers. As he pulled himself up near the ridgeline, he felt the blast. He had almost forgotten about the constant wind while they had been in its shadow. Sensing that he was coming to the end of his oxygen supply, he selected one of the few remaining full bottles and dragged it inside the tent with him. Sweetner followed in the wake of the aluminum cylinder and zipped the door tightly shut.

There was silence as they both prepared for the night. "I'm waiting," he said.

Sweetner was dreading this moment but there was no avoiding it; there was no way of escaping it. "Okay, here it is. Everything Alan told you was the truth; I swear. It just wasn't the whole truth. As in most things in this life, there's more to the story. The seismometer will detect any troop movement and alert us, but if the Chinese decide to move on India or Pakistan, they must come through these passes, more than likely over the Karakoram Highway. Before we can react to it, they can have a million men plus tanks and trucks running through here, and there isn't a thing we can do about it. There's only one way we can deny an army that large, and that's to nuke them."

"How big is the yield?" asked Eagen.

"They're not very big...fifty kilo tons each, but it isn't the size of each one that counts. When they both go off at the same time, the shock wave is compressed so much and then rebounded, the effect has a theoretical equivalent of up to five times that of each individual one. But again, it isn't the size of the blast that counts. It's the heat and radiation; you know, 'it ain't the meat, it's the motion.' Think of where we placed them. Even up there, the place is a natural amphitheater on a grand scale. The blast would be directed to the north, northwest, effectively sealing off the highway. Not only that, remember Alan asking you about Lop Nor, the Chinese underground nuclear test facility? Well, they need large amounts of water to cool their reactors, so it's built on a river, a river that just happens to have its origin up in these mountains. It is expected that the heat from such a blast would melt damned near every glacier for miles around. The meltwater that wasn't vaporized would put that whole valley under several hundred feet of water." He stopped long enough to take a few deep gulps of oxygen from his mask. "Now, if that didn't do the trick, there are enough unstable faults in the region that would rupture to the point of producing large earthquakes that would collapse the whole complex. In short, we would use a manmade event to trigger a natural event. Diabolical, huh?"

Eagen thought a moment and asked, "Yeah, but what about the Russians?"

Sweetner's response was quick. "Screw the Russians. They fear China's nuclear potential more than they do us. Hell, if they knew what we were up to, they'd probably give us a medal. Consider this: If we're bright enough to think of it, don't you think they've thought

THIS DAY'S BUSINESS

of it?"

Eagen could see most of Sweetner's argument but was too spent to care. He rummaged through the last of the food and found some cookies and fruitcake. "How much fuel do we have left?" he asked.

Sweetner hefted the last fuel bottle and shook it to gauge its contents. "About a little over a pint. Just enough to heat up some soup and melt some snow for water," was the reply.

Eagen was rubbing his temples to ease the pain of a splitting headache when he said, "Sweets, we've got to go down tomorrow, before sunrise. I want all of us at Camp II by nightfall so we can mount a search for Moe. It's time to get the hell out of Dodge."

It was getting too difficult to talk. As close as they were in the cramped little tent, the wind outside was increasing in its intensity. There was nothing left to do but try and shut out the fury.

The six p.m. radio call went unanswered, but at nine o'clock that night Camp IV was in touch with Camp III.

"We must've slept through it," said Larry. He confirmed that there were not enough supplies for a summit bid and might as well go down. There was no mention of either box. Eagen thought it best to say nothing about this over the radio. Larry and Curly were, by now, living in squalor in the Bat Cave. Their sleeping bags were never able to dry out, leaving the occupants cold and miserable. There was enough food but not enough fuel to cook it properly.

Up on the ridge, Eagen lay in his damp bag and suffered in silence while Sweetner tossed and turned, unable to find a comfortable position in which to sleep. Even the sleeping tablets they took weren't enough. Their own body warmth had melted the snow beneath the tent until it conformed to the contours of their bodies. This could be tolerated only so long as they did not stir.

They were both in that dream state where they were neither awake nor asleep, but merely existing. The jet engine had begun its roar again, and the guy lines supporting the frame of the tent were vibrating so wildly that they were humming. Both men knew that daybreak, if it were to come at all, was a long way off.

The sun was so warm and Sweetner was so comfortable, just perfect for a snooze on the beach, listening to the surf and the gulls. He could spend the rest of eternity there. He did not want to move a muscle. There was no wind to stir the warm sand. It was so peaceful and so far away from the cares of the world. The day would be perfect if only he could...breathe. Sweetner sat bolt upright, scared nearly out of his wits; he was being asphyxiated!

Ripping off his mask, he inhaled sharply several times, but there was barely anything to breathe in. Panic started to well up from within him. He reached out to awaken Eagen, to alert him that he was in trouble.

Eagen was shaken from his own dream state. Sweetner was hyperventilating and was making moves toward the tent door. Eagen realized what was happening as he switched on his headlamp just in time to stop his friend from plowing through the fragile nylon door.

Reaching into the back of the tent, he pulled at the parka that substituted for his pillow and threw it over Sweetner's head and croaked as loudly as his parched throat would allow. He woke Sweetner from his nightmare. Eagen was now feeling the effects of hypoxia, the lack of oxygen, only he was conscious and better able to deal with it. He thought he was hallucinating when he finally managed, with great difficulty, to light the tiny candle lantern that hung from a hook at the peak of the tent. He watched in amazement as the little light source started doing the Irish jig in response to the buffeting of the tent.

They apparently had run out of oxygen. It appeared that the valve had been threaded incorrectly, and an inadequate seal had allowed some of the precious gas to escape. Now they would be fighting for every breath until they were down to at least Camp II.

The jet-engine roar of the wind had kicked into afterburner and was attempting to destroy them. The up-ridge end of the tent, the one facing the summit, was taking the brunt of the tempest and was beginning to shred. After a close inspection, the dancing candlelight revealed the stitching in the seams was being pulled asunder. As the pressure of the wind was building, the little shelter began to collapse inward on the pair. Although they had secured the tent loops by sinking ice screws and two foot long pickets into the snow, the constant buffeting was working them out, loosening them from the ice. The slight wall of snow that they had packed around the edges of the tent to deflect the wind had been eroded, leaving it exposed and vulnerable. With the stakes being pulled up, the onrushing madness was now working its way underneath them. Inch by inevitable inch,

THIS DAY'S BUSINESS

the climbers were surrendering room to the inwardly collapsing walls. The floor was pulsating up and down in concert with the in and out of the sides. Eagen could hear the clanging of the ice screws as they attempted to work themselves free. Sweetner crawled over Eagen to the downwind side and unzipped the door only enough shine his flashlight out. Quickly, he secured the zipper.

Eagen asked, "What's it like out there?"

All Sweetner could say was that there were rocks the size of golf balls flying horizontally. Now they were both scared. If one of those rocks, like a load of buckshot, were to pierce the tent, the inwardly rushing air would inflate it like a parachute, and they would be airborne. They would learn what it would be like to be in Auntie Em's house with Dorothy and Toto.

There they squatted with their backs to the collapsing nylon wall, interlocking their arms, hoping to stem the relentless onslaught. All the while they were riding the whoopee cushion of air tunneling its way beneath the floor. The storm was trying to peel them from the face of the earth. Eagen had only one more card left to play. Afraid to move for fear of letting the tent collapse further, he used his right foot to search for his axe. Dragging it up within his grasp, he raised it as high as the low ceiling would allow and drove it downward through the floor. Sweetner was sitting on his in the semi darkness and had little trouble finding it. He did the same as Eagen. At least if the tent ripped free from its moorings they would still have one last hope of remaining in contact with the mountain. Eagen tried not to envision what it would be like with the tent flailing about in the wind, its occupants trapped inside, knowing they were doomed, just waiting for the end and never seeing it coming. Unable to keep his eyes open any longer, he rested his forehead on his knees and dozed off to await the morning or the end.

At approximately the same time, they both became aware of the deathly silence. Sweetner nudged his partner awake. It took Eagen a few startled moments to realize that he was still among the living. The wind had died down to the point that they were no longer in danger of the tent coming loose.

Sweetner said it first. "I think it's time to go down. It should be sunrise in a few minutes anyway." He unzipped what was left of the tent door and stepped outside. While Eagen was gathering a few items to take with him, his friend called jubilantly back into the tent, "Hey, there isn't a cloud in the sky."

Eagen was about to answer when they both heard it. It was the sound of a sheet being ripped, only many times louder. From inside the doorway he watched as his partner prepare to descend the fixed rope for Camp II. Then he felt the platform slump. It could only mean that their perch was collapsing. The Pakistani side of the mountain was beginning to divest itself of the snow that had adhered to its steep flanks. Throwing all sense of caution to the wind, the pair abandoned the tent and descended, leaving the remains of Camp IV intact, taking nothing with them but their lives. They rappelled far faster than prudence would dictate, for the mountain was threatening to collapse on top of them; it was their only chance for survival.

Down and down they descended on the fixed lines, stopping only long enough to switch ropes. Sweetner went first, followed several hundred feet later by Eagen. This was to minimize the load on any one section of rope. Even at such relatively short distances, they were often out of sight and hearing of one another. Although nearly vertical, the route dropped into narrow gullies and over sagging ice bulges. If either climber were to encounter trouble, the other would probably never be aware of it until it was far and away too late to do anything about it.

As they came to the end of one rope where it was attached to an anchor, they each had to execute the delicate task of unclipping from it and attaching the next lower section to their safety harnesses. Each time they put the initial load of their weight on the line, they were taking the ultimate gamble with their lives.

With their emotions stretched thin for days, their sleep-deprived and oxygen-starved brains wrestled to stay focused. Each delicate task, whether it was placing a footstep or correctly threading the safety line through, the descenders required a herculean effort of will and concentration. Would the anchors hold the weight of their descent? Would the ropes, which were showing signs of fraying, suddenly part? There was no way to know for sure.

In a little under an hour they had dropped down the two thousand five hundred feet to the sight of the Bat Cave. But it was nowhere to be seen. The complexion of the entire face had changed. When last there, they had known it to be an Anastasi village affair dug into the

THIS DAY'S BUSINESS

bosom of the mountain. But now, a bowl had been scooped out of it big enough to play a game of half court basketball. Where the face had once risen to damned near vertical, there was now an edge they could peer over. Signs of fresh avalanche activity were everywhere. Dangling from the last few feet of the fixed rope, they surveyed the destruction and pondered the fate of their two close friends.

Beneath Sweetner the rope had snapped and was frayed like a cauliflower showing evidence of being pulled apart. The rope, designed to hold the weight of a jeep, had been subjected to a force far greater than it could handle. Sweetner released his grip on the rope, letting it slip through the descender ring on his harness. Gritting his teeth, he slid off the end and dropped freely the last twenty feet into freshly churned powder snow. He landed on his back with a plop.

Eagen, some fifty feet above his partner, watched until he was assured that Sweetner was all right. There was nothing else he could do. There was nowhere to go but down the last few feet and drop beside his friend. His main concern then was not to trigger any new avalanches.

They were able to move around without the umbilical of a rope connecting them. Using the shaft of their ice axes they probed the powder, hoping to find their missing companions or any artifacts from the Bat Cave that could lead them to its resting place. After twenty minutes of searching, Eagen came upon the shredded remains of a tent, and a human hand sticking through the compacted snow.

They both dug until they were exhausted. Their efforts yielded an orange sleeping bag with Curly, its suffocated occupant. Further digging revealed odd bits and pieces of equipment from the Bat Cave, but nothing more. There was no sign of Larry. Apparently, the avalanche that the two had heard from up on the ridge had collapsed the cave, trapping and crushing its occupants. Mercifully, Sweetner thought, they had never known what hit them. Camp III had been thoroughly scoured from the face of the earth. There was nothing they could do for their friends except rebury that which they disinterred. Their tears were freezing to their beards as they finished the job.

Would they get down, or would they too succumb to the mountain? Which way should they go? The familiar route down to

Camp II, which still remained four thousand feet below them, no longer existed. Just over the lip, just fifteen feet away, remained the vertical drop. Could they survive a night outside with no tent, no food nor water? If they did manage to survive the night, which way would they go down? Would there be a rescue party coming up to look for them? If the major succeeded in evacuating Alan, would he come back to Base Camp? What if he witnessed the massive avalanche and assumed that there were no survivors? Dammit, there were survivors...for the time being.

The helicopter had just lifted off the rocky field next to the goat herder's stone hut. The major had his doubts about Lloyd surviving the flight back to Islamabad. When he secured the door on the two-man observation helicopter, he could see that the American's lips and the flesh under his fingernails were already turning blue from the lack of oxygen. They had done their best to bring him down as quickly as possible and at a terrible price. The evacuation had cost his sergeant his life in the river crossing, and the remaining Haps had deserted him. The poor buggers were probably half crazed from the urgency to evacuate Lloyd. It was during the night that he saw them and the Sirdar sneak away. He was positive that they had gotten themselves turned around in the dark, having never been up that way before. He could swear by Allah that they had taken the path back to Base Camp. But, he thought, the mind plays cruel tricks when one is under great stress.

Gujral and his two remaining soldiers set their course for Base Camp. Everybody there must be worried about their friend, he felt. As the sun was ready to crest the southeast ridge of Gasherbrum IV, the major, only a half mile away from Base, heard it. It was a sharp crack, similar to the report of a high-powered rifle as the bullet goes supersonic. He was still too far away to make out any camps, but he could see the millions of tons of ice and snow spilling, boiling downward. Nothing in its path could divert the onrush, not even the icefall. The path of the frozen rage veered at a distance from Base Camp, but the wind blast, the wall of air being pushed ahead of the monster, soon swept over him, knocking him off his feet and covering

THIS DAY'S BUSINESS

him with a thin blanket of pulverized ice crystals.

Taking stock of his situation, thanking his God in Heaven for his good fortune, he saw that he was still among the living. He was, however, convinced that the Americans were not. He wept for them, he wept for his sergeant, and then he turned his back on their granite monument. It was time to go down into the world of the green and lush, the world of the living.

<><><>

Sweetner caught the movement out of the corner of his eye. It was not a rock or piece of ice tumbling down, but whatever it could be was moving slowly upward. A climber? Perhaps it was the major with a rescue party. He was wearing the bright orange clothing that was issued to the Haps. His features were indistinguishable with the hood of his parka pulled up and the goggles in place. The figure bent over his ice axe with every few steps. By now Eagen saw him too. The man was alone; there was no rescue party. At least someone from down there had made it up. There was a way down after all.

The lone figure gingerly climbed off the ridge where it joined the lip and clumsily approached to within fifteen feet of the two survivors.

"Major?" Eagen called out. "Is there anyone else down there?" The climber pulled back the wolf-fur-trimmed hood and lifted his goggles for a better look. "Shastri! You're alive, thank God." Eagen and Sweetner started toward their rescuer but were abruptly stopped by Shastri's raised left hand.

"Where are the others?" he asked.

"There are no others," said Sweetner.

"How did you make it up here then? Where's everyone else?" They started toward him again.

"Stay where you are, both of you."

The two Americans were puzzled by his commands.

"Shastri, what's going on? Lets get down from here," said Sweetner.

"If either one of you moves, I'll kill you both!" Shastri was no longer the peasant leader who spoke broken English. He was fluent with a slight British accent. In removing his right hand from within his parka, the Americans saw that they were both staring into the barrel of Shastri's nine-millimeter Browning Hi Power automatic pistol.

"Shastri, what the hell's wrong with you? You could kill somebody with that. Put it away. Now!

"What have you people been up to up here?" said the Sirdar. "What was your mission, and what exactly was in those two boxes that you so carefully brought with you?"

"Seismometers, you asshole. What do you think?" said Eagen.

"Do you take me for an imbecile? You Americans have always been so damned arrogant. You come into a country and take it over as if you own it and then you treat people like dirt. I've seen your kind before. I lost my whole family to jackals such as you, and I vowed that if I ever got the chance I'd pay you back."

Sweetner, realizing the gravity of the situation and seeing how unstable Shastri had become, was trying to distract him.

"Shastri, is it more money you want? Tells us. Who are you working for?"

The Sirdar spat back, "Who? Money? Right now, I'm going to kill you both if you don't tell me what you're doing up here. As for whom and how much, I am employed by your friends the Russians to keep an eye on things around here. They're heavy-handed pigs, but they pay well, in American dollars I might add. But, I'm going to kill you for me, now tell me," he demanded.

Eagen lunged at their tormentor as Sweetner reached for his ice axe. Shastri, now confronted with two simultaneous threats chose the closer of the two and fired once. The 115 grain copper-jacketed bullet struck Eagen in the right side just below the nipple. There was an explosion of feathers in front and behind him from the down in his parka. The impact spun him around and corkscrewed him to the snow.

At the same instant, Sweetner had his axe in his hand and closed the distance. He put his full weight into the swing and drove the sharp pick of his ice tool into Shastri's face just below his eyebrow. The Browning went off again as the Sirdar reflexively threw up his hands. He was dead where he stood. The force of the blow knocked him backwards to begin his four-thousand-foot descent. Sweetner's momentum carried him to the edge where he barely managed to stop

THIS DAY'S BUSINESS

his slide by digging in his crampons. He was able to see the orange-clad figure vanish into the white void below.

Reversing his slide on his belly, he crawled through some of Shastri's brain matter or Eagen's blood, he wasn't sure which. Upon reaching his moaning friend, he dragged him upslope some thirty feet from the abyss. He unzipped Eagen's blood-soaked parka and pulled away at the layers of clothing until he got down to flesh.

Rolling him over on his left slightly, he told Eagen, "Don't worry, man, it looks like an in-and-out wound. It appears to have gone clean through."

Remembering the remains of the tent they had found from the ruins of the Bat Cave, Sweetner staggered back up the slope. His drunken steps were the result of hypoxia brought on by the exertion of dealing with Shastri, his slide right to the edge of the precipice, and finally, the dragging of his injured partner to a safer spot. He pulled at it until it was free from the snow. He brought it to his stricken friend and placed him in it so that he was completely covered, so as to keep him warm. It did not take long for the blood to stain the tent. Eagen was conscious the whole time but was going into shock.

"Hey," said Sweetner, "this is what's left of the Camp IV tent. The whole site must've come down just after we abandoned it! I'll bet that it beat us down here."

The shock waves from the two high-velocity shots echoed off the mountain walls surrounding them. This apparently weakened the snow just enough to begin a cascade of powder on top of them. Sweetner ran back to the blood-spattered site to retrieve his hat. Just as he picked it up, there was a shudder in the ice beneath them as the ledge dropped away. In slow motion, it reminded him of the trapdoor giving way on a gallows. With his eyes as big as saucers, the void opened up and swallowed Sweetner whole, crashing its way down the face. He was gone. Eagen, alone, was not sure if it was the waves of pain or the snow that were washing over him. His world quickly went black as he felt himself being tightly packed in coarse, granular ice.

CHAPTER 14

"That Which Does Not Kill Me..."

When he stopped tumbling, Eagen felt the weight of the overlying snow pressing down on him. The tent had become his burial shroud. No light filtered down to him; no sound invaded his tomb. He could not orient himself; there was no frame of reference, and no way to know where he was. Was he right side up? Upside down? Was he still alive? Did he somehow awake to find himself dead and buried? He did know one thing: This would be his grave if he did not act quickly. He would be there until nature took its course. The accumulating snows, over the years, would compact down, forming glacier ice. The glacier would flow downhill under the influence of gravity like so much melting ice cream, and in about fifteen millennia his frozen and thoroughly desiccated corpse might come out at the bottom many thousands of feet below. He would be an object of nourishment for the goraks, the local crows that dared to fly high in the rarefied atmosphere. Alternatively, he might be the subject of intense scrutiny by future archeologists who would view him as a window back to a long forgotten age. He was totally disorientated.

THIS DAY'S BUSINESS

Wildly, he thought to himself, *God, if you get me out of this, I swear I'll never again...*

There was very little movement allowed in his tomb and even less air. Eagen could feel panic and the bile well up from deep within him. Second only to being eaten alive by some wild creature was the horror of being buried while still alive. If he were able, he would claw at the lid of his nylon casket like a character in an Edgar Allen Poe novel. That, however, was not the raving of an opiated dream. Fighting to stay in control, he could not help thinking that this was how it would end: alone and gone without a trace, maybe never to be found.

Desperately struggling to remain conscious, he thought that his left arm was pinned beneath him at an odd angle. The pain was only now dimly making its presence known. His right hand felt as if it were plastered across his face. Wiggling his "free" hand down to his chin, he attempted to retrieve a knife that he kept in a breast pocket inside his parka. He could feel it. Problem. Major problem. Eagen was left handed. The knife was in his right breast pocket. Summoning the will to survive, he tore at the garment. If he were on the surface, the down feathers would burst free in the wind. In a perverse way he grinned to himself. Those same feathers could be used if he earned his wings this day...the hard way.

With as much squirming as his predicament allowed, he managed to open the blade. It was then that he discovered he could wiggle his feet; in fact, it felt as if the toes of his boots were almost free from the snow. The knife pierced the roof of his nylon coffin. He thrust his right hand up through the slit as much as the searing pain, coming from his armpit, would permit. The weight of the snow was becoming lighter as he moved. He began to thrash as violently as his limited mobility let him. The naked hand felt pain as it broke the surface; it was being stung by countless crystalline needles driven by a ceaseless wind. Repeated stabbings at the surface brought his whole arm up, then his knees could move. Moments later, a gasping head broke free. He was alive.

Eagen soon discovered that he had wound up on his back in a head-down attitude. Looking back up the slope, he tried to determine how far he had slid. To his horror he noticed that he had come to rest only four feet from the very edge that had collapsed beneath

Sweetner. Death had not been cheated yet, merely postponed. He still had to get down off the ledge and to the rib of rock on his left that headed out of sight. Taking stock of his situation, he realized that he was still alive for two reasons. First, the tumbling of the tent had kept him near the surface. Second, a stove and some pots in the tent had landed in such a way that provided an air chamber, giving him just enough air to breathe while he freed himself. Otherwise, he would still be wrapped, mummy-like, in his nylon sarcophagus. If he had been placed in his sleeping bag he would never have escaped.

There was the wind, always the wind. Mountains made only three sounds: avalanches, rockfall, and the wind. Everything else, even the human voice, seemed artificial. Wild thoughts were flying through his head. His survivability was being called into question. Even if he had not been shot, his chances of getting down were near zip. If anyone remained at Camp II, he might make it. Looking about him he tried to pick up clues to pinpoint his location. He needed to know where he was on the mountain. Only then could he descend. Would Shastri's route be the one to explore? Would descending via the headwall, alone, with absolutely no backup, be the way? One misstep would be his last.

Lying in the snow, half out of the tent, he could feel the wind begin to pile up the fine powder snow over him. It was as though the mountain were still trying to claim him. Curiously, he felt the waves of nausea and was beginning to sweat profusely. Eagen knew the symptoms. He was going deeper into shock. If he passed out now, he would freeze to death in short order. With his left hand, he scooped up some of the fine powder and rubbed it over his face and neck to revive himself. He wriggled free from the tent and made a valiant try at standing up but could only get to his knees. He vowed that he would walk if he could or crawl if he must. Shastri's route was his choice. He would stick to the ridge as far as it would take him. If, with an enormous amount of luck, he managed to survive the climb down, the ridge route should eventually bring him to the Baltoro Glacier, roughly two miles northeast of Base Camp. Surely there must be someone down there.

Taking stock of his equipment, he was elated to find his short ice axe still with him. It still remained secure in its holster attached to his harness. This would prove invaluable to him on the descent. He still

THIS DAY'S BUSINESS

had his crampons on, an assessment he made after gaffing himself in the left leg . Sweetner apparently forgot to remove them when he was placed in the tent. There was no rope. That took the big ride with Sweetner. He did, however, have shelter. Realistically, there was no chance of getting down to the glacier before nightfall. That meant plunging temperatures and lots of wind. To get down alive, he must first survive the night.

Eagen sank both of his spiked boots into the snow and pulled at the remains of the tent, which was still partly encased in the compacted avalanche debris. At last, most of it ripped free. With his prize came the remnants of a foam sleeping pad, which would provide some insulation from the cold of the ice; it was just big enough to sit upon. He folded up the piece of tent, arranging it lengthwise, and cut off the two remaining guy lines and tied those to the tent. Slipping his head and left arm through the loop, he wore his house bandoleer style. Fortunately for him, he was still in his climbing suit and heavy parka. Now, if he only had some chocolate to nibble on, he would be set.

Slithering like a crab, he moved his way down and to the right to pick up the ridge. On his ass with his feet moving and guiding him, he left his mark on the powder snow. Upon reaching the ridge, Eagen noted that the clouds were forming once more, lower in the valleys. From experience, that meant high winds and heavy snow.

Down he went. Every twenty feet or so he would have to stop and repeat the ritual of wiping the sweat from his face and breathing as deeply as possible to keep from passing out.

Eagen was dropping in altitude quicker than he realized and came to a small ledge on the rock. The ledge would allow him to bivouac for the night. It was the only reasonably level surface around, and the surrounding boulders would act as a wind break. In the fading yellow light, his watch showed three thirty in the afternoon. The sun would be setting, even from up there, behind the distant mountains, in another half hour. He knew that it would be dark as hell by then. He debated. Should he try to get lower where there was more oxygen and less wind? Should he stay put and ride it out there? *A bird in the hand*, he thought.

Eagen could have elected to lay out on the ledge. It was twice his width, but the edge was right there. Instead, he chose to spend the night sitting up on the pad with his back to the rocks. It seemed like forever before the remnants of his tent were as weather tight as possible. There was no way he was going to roll over in his sleep. That is, if sleep were possible.

His chest was still burning, and he favored his right arm. From his harness, he unhooked a loop of nylon webbing, and with it he made a sling for his injured right side. At least it did not hurt quite as badly with his arm immobilized.

From within the shredded remains of his red cocoon, he hunkered further into the recesses of his parka. It was cinched up as tightly as he could get it. Eagen was thirsty, so very thirsty. Was it from blood loss or just from the ultra-dry air? It was tempting to reach out for some snow to melt in his mouth. Unfortunately, that would lower his body temperature and cause him to be colder. It was time to wait for sunrise.

He was only vaguely aware of the storm when he awoke at two thirty in the morning. The onslaught of trillions of molecules of air flowing around his perch had him wide eyed. It took him a few minutes to realize that he was safe with the rocks at his back. Strangely enough, he was warm. Was this a delusion? He had heard that freezing to death had an almost pleasant quality to it.

It was almost predictable. Shortly after sunrise the storm would abate. The powder that fell from the sky last night would lie still, until it was picked up by the ceaseless wind and deposited elsewhere, sometimes creating ground blizzards. Conditions were sure to worsen come nightfall. He must make good use of all the daylight hours.

There was just enough light to see the tiny thermometer that was pinned to the zipper pull tab on his parka. He blinked several times to clear away the fog of sleep so that he could read it. It registered a bone-chilling ten degrees below zero. *No wonder*, he thought. *No wonder my lungs burn so much when I breathe*. It was time to set off before the uncontrollable shivering began.

Once again, crab-like, he descended, skirting rocks and badly exposed ledges, always looking for the easiest way, the safest way. There were times when his right side burned so badly that he passed out from the pain. Upon regaining consciousness, he would sometimes notice that he had been on the move, driven by his subconscious desire for survival. It was similar to driving a boring

THIS DAY'S BUSINESS

stretch of highway and suddenly realizing that twenty or thirty miles had passed, without a recollection of having driven them.

Sometimes Eagen would crawl, other times he would hobble, until his energy gave out. It was at least twenty hours since he had had any water or food to speak of. His lips were severely cracked and dried from the blood; also, his voice could only croak when the pain resurfaced. He was praying that there was some type of first aid kit remaining at Base Camp—assuming he found the camp.

At twelve thirty in the afternoon, Eagen crested a bulge of ice to his right and set eyes on Base Camp for the first time in two weeks. There was something out of place there. It was deserted; no, it was abandoned. The only occupants were several goraks scavenging the contents of a pilfered supply box. The partially collapsed Big Top was vacant, save for the drifted snow and the ransacked debris of the cook tent. What little food had survived the elements and the birds was inedible, and the bottled water was allowed to freeze and had burst its containers. Someone, he could tell, had gone through the place and stripped it, and then destroyed what he could not carry away.

"Who could do this?" he asked himself. "Who would do this?" Bandits, perhaps? He needed shelter, and more importantly, water and food. As he crawled to the entrance of the Big Top, the waves of pain once again washed over him. Before he went unconscious, the last thing he saw was a camp lantern, smashed flat, slowly being covered by the wind-driven snow.

CHAPTER 15

Resurrection

How dark and strange the world is, he thought, *when everything is black.* He was the undead, for sure—capable of conscious thought, but little else. His body floated through the void effortlessly from one vision to the next. Eagen felt the sensation of warmth and wellbeing coming from somewhere within him.

There were voices too, but they were on the very edge of his hearing. He knew that someone was speaking, but where? Who was doing the talking? It mattered little, for the words were indecipherable; they just hung there on the periphery like fresh wash drying on a clothesline, somewhere out in the distance. Was this the state between Heaven and Hell? Was he trapped, somehow between the living and the dead, his soul condemned to roam throughout eternity? The jet engines returned. Eagen made a mental check of his ethereal body. "I feel whole, yet cannot prove it," he said.

It just hung there so radiant, the crystal spider. Suspended, it was much like Eagen. The light refracted off its many facets as it spun its translucent web. It was beautiful, the way it was illuminated from

THIS DAY'S BUSINESS

within. Against the coal-black backdrop of infinity, the crystalline spider had his rapt attention; he was mesmerized. Vibrations. Had the wind returned? He was being jostled. In his solitude, his spirit floated effortlessly in the void.

Voices again. They were much closer this time. They had come in from the edge. Two. No, three voices. Eagen could distinctly pick out three distant voices, but they were still unintelligible. Closer came the voices. Yes! He could hear her.

"Dr. Eagen? Dr. Eagen? Can you hear me? Do you need something for the pain?"

The veil of obscurity was lifting, and the sea of fog was dissipating. He was beginning to see shapes and light coming closer; he was returning to the surface, to the world of the living.

"Lie still; you're in good hands now," she said.

The female voice was soothing, reassuring. "Don't go away, please don't go away," he cried. Eagen was screaming as loudly as possible but could not be heard. He could see nothing. The spider, like the female voice, was gone.

Voices again, closer. "Dr. Eagen? Can you hear me?"

"Hmm," was all Eagen could get out, and that was with supreme effort.

"Dr. Eagen, I'm Dr. Sanford. You are safe now. You're in a military hospital in West Germany. When you were brought to us, you were in very serious condition."

Eagen felt someone take his hand. He squeezed it for all he was worth.

"Very good, Dr. Eagen," said Sanford, acknowledging the squeeze. "Don't try to talk just yet. At least we can communicate. We need you to listen for now. You were badly sunburned and snow blind. You are suffering from the cumulative effects of exposure, frostbite, and dehydration. In fact, your kidneys almost failed. Then, there's blood loss from the gunshot."

At the mention of the word gunshot, Eagen began squeezing Sanford's hand rapidly.

"Any one of those could've killed you. Anyway, you're in capable hands now. The nurse will be by to give you something for the pain." With that, the doctor's voice disappeared.

Within minutes, or months, Eagen heard the softly approaching

W.J. O'BRIEN

footsteps. "Dr. Eagen, you're going to sleep some more. The doctor has prescribed something for that pain," said the female voice. Again, the spider emerged from the fog.

The footsteps approached, lightly once more. "Dr. Eagen, this must be your lucky day. Some of the bandages come off, and you have visitors. Are you up to it?" asked the female voice.

"Hmm," was Eagen's less-than-eloquent response. There were the footsteps from either side of him, tending to his face. Layer by layer, off came the gauze. The room was dark at first, but Eagen could see the dim outline of drawn blinds and a white uniform standing nearby. Slowly, gradually, form and dimension had meaning.

"We were afraid that the snow blindness might have caused more permanent damage; however, I'm confident that you will eventually recover most of it," said the white-clad figure.

There were four of them, hovering around like seagulls poised in midair. There was the nurse, his "bringer of the spider." To her left were two doctors, and then there was the Judge.

"David, my boy. How are you? No. Don't try to speak." Turning to the others he said, "Would you folks give us a few minutes?"

Dr. Sanford spoke for the others, saying, "Very well, sir, but only for a few minutes." The medical people quietly left the two alone. "David, I'll get right to the point. Did you deliver the box?"

Up to that point, Eagen's face had been the picture of someone who was in pain. There was the occasional grimace from the throbbing of his right foot. However, when the Judge mentioned the box, Eagen's expression changed to anger and perplexity.

"Is it in place?" the Judge asked once again. Eagen responded with a nod. "Very good. Later, you will have to fill in the blanks for us as best as you can, but this is what we know so far. You were found by three goatherders who brought you down to Bardumal. From there, word went out to Skardu, and then we evacuated you to Islamabad, and from there to here. You were very lucky with that gunshot wound. The bullet, apparently, was deflected by a rib front to back and then exited. Aside from blood loss and some infection, there was no damage to any vital organs; however, you will have one very nasty scar under your armpit. The bad news is that you lost two toes from frostbite. They turned gangrenous and had to come off. There might be some slight scarring from the sunburn, but that can be corrected later, I'm told. We are going to need a detailed report concerning what happened up there, but that can wait a few days until you can speak. You have questions, I'm sure," said the Judge.

Eagen could only croak the words as he looked in every direction. The Judge caught his meaning. "Here? You've been here for a week, but it was four or five days before that when you were found. I'm told that you were delirious most of the time. I'm deeply saddened to inform you that we found no traces of anyone else. It would appear that you are the only survivor. They were very good men, and..." He stopped to compose himself. "And, I was particularly fond of Bobby." He continued, "When you feel up to it, there are two police detectives who need the speak with you. Anyway, we'll talk later." The Judge backed away, waved, and then departed.

He walked the twenty feet or so down the hall and turned into the coffee room that was adjacent to the nurses' station. From there he was joined by three other men.

The first one asked about Eagen's condition. The second inquired of the jurist, "Do you think he suspects anything?"

Judge Brooks poured himself a cup of the day-old liquid, turned to face the questioner, and said, "For his sake, I hope not."

They came up to Eagen's bedside. The two of them were on official business. In a well practiced movement, they both produced their identification.

"Dr. Eagen, I'm Detective Sergeant Jeremiah Murphy of the Boston Police Homicide Division, and this is Detective Lieutenant Warrick of the Massachusetts State Police."

Warrick was the next to speak. "Dr. Eagen, I'm assigned the Suffolk County District Attorney's office, and we need to ask questions of you. I'm sorry that we have to interview you while you are recovering, and we've been asked to keep this as brief as possible. But, we have an ongoing investigation that you might be able to help us with. I'm sorry to have to inform you that your former girlfriend, Allison Babbage, was found murdered four days ago. We are satisfied that you are not involved in any way, but we're running down any and all leads."

Eagen's eyes were passive on hearing the news. There had been so much wrung out of him in the last month that there wasn't much left for sentiment. The medication was beginning to take effect as the cop was talking. He felt himself beginning to float again.

The detective continued, "Not only was Miss Babbage from a prominent family, but the other victim, an Emile Chazzi, has a father who is a diplomat with the French Government. The elder Mr. Chazzi has also been reported as missing. This makes for a very thorny situation, Dr. Eagen, one in which we are compelled to investigate."

Eagen looked at both policemen with a question on his face. He was only able to croak her name. "Allison dead? How?"

The cop continued. "Dr. Eagen, there are one or two peculiarities about this case that we need to shed light on." There was a pause as Murphy sifted through some papers that were in the file folder in his hands. "Both victims were found by a boater on the Charles River. They washed up against a support beneath the Mass Avenue Bridge." As he was speaking, Warrick handed Eagen several photos of the scene. "Both bodies appeared to have been in the water for only a day or two, but they were tied together at the neck with a lamp cord. That in itself is not unusual. However, when they were autopsied, the coroner found something quite puzzling. Both victims had a playing card wadded up and stuffed down their throats. Additionally, Mr. Chazzi appeared to have been tortured before he was killed. He had numerous broken bones. The medical examiner believes that they were both asphyxiated and then their bodies dumped in the river. Because of your relationship with Miss Babbage, we were hoping that you could tell us something about either one of the victims and the significance of the playing cards."

Eagen was having a hard time focusing on the fuzzy pictures. They did not even look like anyone he knew. These gruesome photos could've been of nearly anyone. "Cards?" he asked. "What cards were they?"

Warrick referred to his notes and stated, "They were both the ace of spades."

Eagen was getting very tired; his eyelids were already too heavy to keep open. He set the pictures down and made a noise that, to the police, could either have been a groan or a chuckle. Fighting the effects of the drug, Eagen summoned up the will to say, "Ace of spades? Sweetner used them in 'Nam. He'd put one in the mouth of each dead gook. It was a bad luck symbol for them, but he's dead now." He wanted to cry for his friend, but there just weren't any tears

THIS DAY'S BUSINESS

left. Besides, he was floating once more into the void, and the voices were receding.

There it was again, the spider, spinning its gossamer web. Intently watching the creature go about its business, his thoughts drifted back to Sweetner, to Allison and that rat bastard, to all the good times and danger he had shared with the preacher's son, and to the spider. *What a strange cocktail*, he thought, *happiness, sorrow and ... morphine.*

Five Years Later

The man emerged from the Checker Cab just as the heavens added a crescendo to an otherwise dreary, windy, and steady rain. He quickly turned up the collar of his already soaked raincoat, and picked his way among the mid afternoon traffic on the busy street. His destination was the underground parking garage of the nondescript government office building, which was ahead and to his right.

He wasted no time in walking down the ramp to get out of the weather. Staying to the right along the retainer wall, he was ever mindful of his footsteps, careful not to slip on the thin surface of oil and exhaust fumes that coated the pavement. As the angle eased off at the level just below the street, he quietly walked to the far end of the subterranean cavern where the exit sign blinked its short circuited code. It took less than a minute for the elevator to come down. Before entering, he casually scanned behind him to see if anyone had noted his passage. Confident that only two rats, who were playing tag on a trash bin, were witness to his arrival, he stepped in and selected the button to close the door. Upon sensing the stale and dusty air of the confining car, he reached into a side pocket and produced a set of keys. Selecting the appropriate one, he inserted it into the lock on the floor selector panel. This allowed him to ride up one floor past the highest numbered button. It was clearly not intended for the casual passenger.

The armed security guard was waiting for the man as the doors opened onto a floor that few knew about and fewer still ever suspected to exist. After the identification check was completed, the man turned down the hall and entered room 27.

A middle-aged secretary acknowledged his presence by saying, "The deputy director is expecting you. Please go right in." A buzzer released the magnetic lock on a gate and the glass door behind it. The man entered.

"You're sure?" The deputy spoke first as he opened the file cabinet.

"I'm sure," said the man.

"Yeah, but are you really sure?" shot back the deputy as his fingers danced over the manila indexes.

"Look, this case has already been closed by your people upstairs; discussing this with you at all is a courtesy," he added. With a short pause, the man continued. "I was there; I had a hand in it. When he fell, he went at least seven or eight hundred feet before he impacted the first rock outcropping. I watched as one arm and something else, probably his rucksack or his head, came off. His body bounced into the air and disappeared over the edge. Any object falling that distance quickly picks up speed. From there it was over six thousand feet, nonstop, to the glacier below. Yeah, I'm sure."

The deputy, handing the file to the man, approached a three-cushioned, overstuffed sofa and threw himself into it, landing in a sprawl. With his feet toward the window, facing away from the man, he reached to his right and picked up one sheet of typing paper from the top of a one inch pile, crumpled it, and made a hook shot with his right arm over his head into a netted basketball hoop. The wad dropped through and down into a wastebasket. The well rehearsed motion obviously pleased the deputy.

The man took the file, opened it, and with his head still down, walked slowly to the deputy's desk and deliberately sat down, his eyes never leaving the packet. Staring back at him from both the left and right halves of the folder were two black-and-white photographs stapled to the three-quarter-inch thick file. They were the close up front and side views of one Shastri Bhottisavi, now deceased.

After twenty or so minutes, the man looked up from the file. He hadn't noticed that the clouds to the west were trying to break, that the sun was setting, casting darkness where the long afternoon shadows once held court. If it were not for the soft green glow from the banker's lamp at the deputy's desk, the room would be devoid of

THIS DAY'S BUSINESS

color.

He exhaled deeply through his nose, cocking his head to the left, noting the way the rose patina from the partially hidden sun played on the double-paned windows. At once he appreciated the contrasting shade of the lamp to his right. The only sounds occurring within the room were from the occasional turning of a page in the file and from the crumple, swish, plop of the wadded paper, which was now starting to gain some depth on the floor of the office.

The man, hunched with his elbows on the desk and his hands crossed at the wrists, looked up over the lamp. He stared off into the distance with the thousand-yard stare he had seen too many times before on others. This time it was the memory movie he was replaying that was responsible for his eyes locking on infinity, not fatigue and indescribable horror.

As if he were a deer transfixed in the headlights of an onrushing semi, all it took was another hook shot from the deputy on the couch to break the man's concentration. As the deputy director was about to reach for another sheet of paper, he was asked, "Where's Eagen now?"

The deputy stopped, thought for a moment, and replied "As of three days ago, he was somewhere out on the Mid-Atlantic Ridge, I think."

After lighting his third cigarette in twenty minutes, the man asked, "What time is it out there?"

The deputy thought for another moment and said, "Well, it's close to six here. It must be nearly nine or ten out there. Hey, let's grab some dinner and a beer."

"Soon," said the man. "How do you get the marine operator on this phone?" He was about to reach for the receiver when he stopped. Feeling a slight shudder rush up his spine, he bowed his head as a supplicant before the alter and said, "Better yet, I'll meet him as the ship docks."

THE END

Printed in the United States
46205LVS00005B/115-123